Advance Praise

"In this atmospheric coming of age novel, Newton explores how an unexpected death is not just an event, but a change of climate. Or it is a body of water in which family and friends are now floating unmoored, rocked by waves of heartache, guilt, and the many other forms of grief. The Michigan childhood of beaches, bicycles, and babysitting as a backdrop for loss is beautifully, achingly rendered."

— Bonnie Jo Campbell, author of *Q Road, American Salvage*, a National Book Award Finalist, and *Once Upon a River*, now a motion picture

"Set in a moment in American life as fleeting and moving as a perfect June day, *The Remnants of Summer* is a tender story of grief, guilt, and growing up. Dawn Newton's novel exposes the pain in one 1970s lakefront community then digs deeper to show the strength underneath."

— Julia Phillips, author of *Disappearing Earth*, a National Book Award Finalist and *New York Times* Top Ten Book of 2019

D1468433

The Remnants of Summer

The Remnants of Summer

Dawn Newton

Apprentice House Press
Loyola University Maryland

First Edition

Library of Congress Control Number: 2021930145

Hardcover ISBN: 978-1-62720-338-8
Paperback ISBN: 978-1-62720-339-5
Ebook ISBN: 978-1-62720-340-1

Printed in the United States of America

Design: Mackenzie Britt
Promotion plan: Samantha Howath
Managing editor: Kelley Chan
Cover art: Barbara Hranilovich
Author photo: Nathaniel Dalton

Published by Apprentice House Press

Apprentice House Press
Loyola University Maryland
4501 N. Charles Street
Baltimore, MD 21210
410.617.5265
www.ApprenticeHouse.com
info@ApprenticeHouse.com

To Esther and LaVern, Linda and Lori,
Tim, Rachel, Connor, and Nathaniel

For the molds we've cast and broken,
the light and love we've shaped, and
the melodies we'll carry onward

1
Counting
June 29, 1973

Iris woke to the pinpricks of sunburn on her forehead. She raised her hand and touched her cheek, feeling the warmth of her skin and knowing freckles would soon crowd her face. She hadn't intended to fall asleep. Almost three hours had passed, and now it was dinnertime. The beach area below appeared nearly empty, with only one toddler splashing at the edge of the water with her mother. On the catwalk, a fisherman sat with his pole in the water on the quiet Michigan afternoon, day far enough gone that the scent of a charcoal fire from a nearby property wafted through the diamonds of the chain link fence surrounding the beach park. Enclosed by a fence on three sides, the beach area on Williams Lake provided property owners in the neighborhood association with the opportunity to enjoy the water from Memorial Day through Labor Day weekend. On Labor Day, the docks were pulled out of the water to signal the end of summer and herald the coming of fall. The summer beach privileges were available for the small fee of a beach key – and the tacit understanding of a critical warning: "No Lifeguard on Duty."

Iris couldn't see her brother Scott on the swings or on the big dock. She waited a few minutes, expecting his shoulders to emerge from under water. Maybe he'd tried to do five underwater front flips in a row in less than ten seconds, his most recent record. But several minutes went by, and he didn't emerge. The beach key was still pinned to the corner of the towel where she'd put it when they'd arrived, but that didn't mean anything: he could have left the beach with any group of people opening the gate to go home. Iris was frustrated with Scott for making her worry, but guilt about falling asleep made her seek out explanations for his absence.

Maybe he was just trying to let her rest. He knew she'd slept little the night before. She'd told him as much with her yawns. After gathering up her towel and suntan lotion, she surveyed the beach area one more time and let herself out the gate. She trudged slowly around the block to her house, two streets away from the lake.

As Iris reached her house and walked up the long, narrow driveway, her mother, home from her job at the library, called out the kitchen window for her to set the table. Iris went first to the back yard to hang the beach towel on the clothesline; a warm flush spread across her chest when she saw the straight lines strung between the two poles, unadorned with clothespins or sagging cotton. Scott's worn towel with the big green frog and the letters spelling "Your pad or mine?" was missing. And then she realized that when she'd surveyed the beach to look for him, she'd seen a stray towel, not next to hers as it had been in the beginning but thrown over a bench. A worn towel, with a large splotch of green.

She could barely make her legs walk into the back of the house, afraid to face her mother, afraid to confess she'd lost track of her eleven-year-old brother. She went inside and entered the bath-room, lathering her hands with soap to wash off the suntan lotion and the sand. She opened the kitchen cupboard and took down a stack of five plates, which she carried to the dining room and placed on the table. She took a deep breath and went to find her mother.

By the time her father came home from work forty-five min-utes later, dropped off by his ride, the Merchant family's worry had cemented. Iris's mother had called a few of Scott's friends, who hadn't seen him, while Iris had walked back and forth to their small beach on Williams Lake two more times, making herself trudge on the oiled road in bare feet without flip flops to punish herself for sleeping when she should have been watching him. On the last trip, Iris retrieved his towel from the grass, hoping it would be drenched, but it was warm, sun-dry.

She kept waiting for her mother to say, "Iris, how could you?"

With her father, they all walked down again; the fisherman was no longer on the catwalk, but the lady who lived next to the beach gave them the man's address, and they tracked him down. All he'd observed, he said, was a young kid practicing his strokes. He'd swum back and forth in the swim area like he was doing pool laps between the two buoy-anchored ropes. The man didn't remember much more than that.

The first inkling they had of Scott's swimming challenge came when they were back at home in the living room and the phone rang. Iris's father bolted up and snatched it off the wall.

Iris listened as her father's voice rose on the phone call in the way it did sometimes, the teeth-clenched intensity that meant anger or frustration. His voice sounded the way her sunburned face felt,

3

taut and reactive but irrelevant compared to the fear that she knew was building inside all of them. When her dad got off the phone, the intensity increased: the boy had admitted the secret challenge issued the previous afternoon – to see who was brave enough to swim diagonally across the lake to a bigger neighborhood beach, one kitty korner from their own.

Yes, the friend said, they were supposed to meet at the beach that morning, a fact Scott had not shared with Iris. But the boy had eaten too many hot dogs at the county fair the night before. He needed to postpone the swimming challenge until the next day. It had just been the two of them who were determined to go through with it. He called Scott, but no one had answered the phone. Scott and Iris must have already left for the beach by then.

People did it all the time; it wasn't that far, Iris told her mother. People from school who'd done it with friends bragged that it wasn't even tiring. Iris tried to convince herself that he wouldn't be so foolish as to try it, that Scott knew better. He wouldn't attempt such a thing when she was in charge. Especially after their parents had given him the lecture about responsible behavior once their mom took the job at the library to make ends meet. Especially once Iris became Scott's designated "babysitter" for the summer while everyone else was at work. Babysitter. She knew he hated that word, but she had convinced her mom that they didn't need outside help. "At fourteen, I can get a work permit," she reminded her mom. "And I already took that babysitting class at school."

Her father contacted a neighborhood friend who used to work on the State Police dive team; another neighbor placed a call to the local police. Shortly after seven-thirty in the evening, while Iris's sister Liz was still at work, her father set out with his friend at the wheel of a motor boat. He stood at the bow, looking out over the small lake. Iris and her mother waited at the beach. Iris watched her mother light a cigarette, take a puff, and blow the smoke into the summer evening air. Her mother had never been a chain smoker, but with the newer job at the library, she'd had to practice going without a cigarette. Her off-hours smoking had increased.

When Iris couldn't stand the silence anymore, she caught her mother's attention and gestured toward the swing set, where five single bands hung from chains in U-shapes, ready to be formed into seat buckets, next to a sixth pair of chains ending in a toddler-sized plastic seat with a protective bar. As Iris headed toward the equipment, her mother gazed at her blankly, so deep in thought, almost without recognition, before she gave Iris a brave smile that years later Iris would see over and over again in her dreams, plumbing it for its meaning.

Iris began counting the moment she pushed off, telling herself that her dad and his friend would be back with Scott by the hundredth swing. Then it was two hundred, and three hundred. She must have lost count for a while, but every time she roused herself, a number materialized in her head, and that number became the new place from which to continue the counting.

A police car drove up to the beach parking lot, and Iris saw some neighbors let the patrolmen in, and they propped open the larger beach gate, the one for boat trailers.

Iris tried to keep her count while distracting herself. Their father had planned to take them to the county fair the next day. The same fair where Scott's friend had eaten too many hot dogs. Scott had saved fifteen dollars from weeks of chores. Both he and Iris loved the stuffed animal prizes. The year before they'd made their father try for some of the bigger animals and had lucked out with a black gorilla for Scott. Iris had used all her money and was trying to coax more out of their father. Scott gave their father two more dollars and told their father to go for the purple poodle Iris wanted. When their father won the poodle on the fifth pitch, Scott yelped louder than Iris did, proud of their father's success, happy for Iris's prize. They each had two tickets left, and stuffed with cotton candy, hot dogs, and creamsicles, they'd selected the Tilt-A-Whirl. While they rode on it, Liz sauntered back from where she'd been visiting with friends. In their circulating chamber, Iris and Scott turned the wheel in front of them as fast as they could, and soon all the tents and the people became a blur of red, blue, and pink. The sugar from the cotton candy lurched into Iris's throat from her stomach, and she hung on, knowing the ride needed to end. Scott's teeth still flashed white with a smile, yet when they both tumbled off the ride, he dropped his head for a moment.

Liz and their parents stood waiting to take everyone home, and Iris could see a taunt waiting in Liz's eyes as she looked at them. "No way I'm sitting in back," she said, laughing as she squeezed into the front seat between their parents. Iris and Scott pushed the stuffed animals into Liz's arms and fell into the back seat of the station wagon.

Neither Iris nor Scott would give Liz the satisfaction of watching them puke their guts out. On the way home, as the dim, eerie blue lights of the fairway glowed through the back window, they rested their heads on the vinyl upholstery, keeping their chins up, the strands of Iris's dark auburn hair tilted against Scott's chestnut mop, their faces catching the breeze from the open windows. As Iris's fist slowly unclenched, Scott's fingers crawled to hers on the seat.

At the beach now, Iris gripped the chains tightly on either side of her seat, letting the thick metal loops dig into her palms. She was on the 9970th swing when she saw the boat coming in and her mother walking down to the end of the catwalk.

If the boat kept idling and inching forward so slowly, maybe Iris could do the thirty more swings it would take to get to ten thousand, and she could tell him how much energy she'd expended on his behalf. But when she said 9,991 in her head, her mother squawked. Another noise, this time a wail, filled the lake, and a floodlight came on at the house next door. Iris knew she would have to keep swinging forever.

2

The Key to the Beach

May 11, 1974

In the late spring following the long fall and winter after Scott died, Cunningham's Drugstore piled mounds of flipflops on their shelves in teal, coral, and royal blue, replacing Easter merchandise with rows of tanning oils, hair remover lotions, and swimming ear plugs. Perhaps it was then that they all started to feel more acutely the stranglehold of Scott's death. Or maybe it was one of the other innocuous events that launched that second summer in the family: the rehiring call Liz received from the ice cream store asking her to pack cones for the summer after the winter hiatus. Or their mother's boss at the library telling her to turn in her summer vacation time request. Or the annual newsletter from the neighborhood beach association.

One day the pale blue flyer arrived in the mail, announcing the line-up of summer events on Williams Lake and listing the addresses where neighborhood members could purchase their annual key to the beach. Twenty dollars, an increase of five dollars.

The notice may have sat in a pile of mail on the counter for days before Iris perceived its presence. When she finally opened the trifold flyer and recognized the association imprint on the heading, she sat down in the living room chair, stunned and confused to realize the extent to which her family had distanced themselves from the events of the previous summer.

She and Liz had plowed through the school year, Liz at Parsons High, and Iris at the junior high. It was good that they were separate. Liz drove the old Pontiac Catalina her dad had fixed up, and Iris rode the bus, their paths crossing only at home. Single-minded workhorses, they moved forward, often plodding, but still moving.

And yet, here it was again, the beginning of a new beach season. Did they want to pay the money for the key to enter a beach that they walked halfway around the main neighborhood circle to reach?

Iris and Liz were both home from school for the day, with only a few weeks left until summer break. Occupying opposite ends of the house, they did their dutiful daughter routines, Liz running the vacuum cleaner in the family room while Iris chunked through potatoes with a faulty peeler, once scraping her knuckles, needing Bactine and a Band-Aid.

Their mother was due home from the library in the next hour. When Iris finally put the potatoes in the water and set them on the stove, she looked back at the pile of mail on the counter, the blue flyer again buried halfway in the middle, where she had replaced it. The phone rang, followed by the vacuum cleaner's sudden silence and Liz's weary but insistent, "I'll get it."

Would they even buy a key to the beach this year? The thought wrapped around Iris's middle like a too-small inflatable ring compressing her stomach. Iris knew exactly where last year's key could be located in Scott's room. A collection of keys hung in a tangle on a hook in his closet, some on shoelaces, some on braided leather or yarn from the summers Iris had done crafts during a local summer program. Scott liked to collect the keys, save them, even though the association officials changed the lock on the beach gate every summer. "I have bred a family of pack rats," their mother liked to say. The key from the previous summer was on a braid of yellow, red, and orange yarn. The number "43" was imprinted on it, which meant they were the forty-third family to purchase a key that summer. Iris wanted to have it, just to hold on to it awhile, maybe to give her courage to buy the new key, even if the family never used it. Iris probably wouldn't go to the beach with her friend Rosemary anymore, but she felt the Merchant family should at least own the key.

They lived in a small neighborhood that bordered Williams Lake, one of the many neighborhoods that had sprung up in the 1950s as beach communities. People had previously vacationed in small cottages next to the lake. But then a neighborhood of small starter homes emerged. Their father, in purchasing the property years ago from a neighbor, had guaranteed their privilege to use the beach and the water in that small private area that served their neighborhood. The homeowners on Destan Drive whose property rested right on the banks of the lake didn't need beach privileges; they just walked out their doors. They had boats and picnic tables and landscaped gardens next to the water, enjoying their lake property with flair and confidence. But those houses a few streets removed from the lake on perpendicular and circular and parallel streets in the neighborhood needed a key for lake access. Like the Merchant's. The key served as a bargain. Buying one gave you admittance, but you needed to respect the property and keep drifters out. For that reason, the gate locked in both directions; it kept a person out, but it also kept a person in. Without a key, anyone walking the outer circumference of the lake could retreat from it only by trespassing on a homeowner's lake property. If a person tried to exit through the beach property, they would have to wait for a member to let them out.

The homes on the lakefront property on Destan Drive were idyllic, many of them sprawling. Those who didn't have property directly on the lake lived in much smaller, starter homes on dirt roads connecting to the beach on Williams Lake Road in a community called Sunrise Country Club. But Iris, Liz, and Scott didn't care about the size of their house; they loved that they lived in a neighborhood with a beach, loved that their little house earned them "beach privileges." The small beach contained a designated swimming area with buoys and ropes to mark it off and offered "the small dock" to which younger kids could walk and another "big dock" to which adults and teenagers swam, where the water was over everyone's head.

The key that would open the gate to the beach Iris loved – until the new lock was replaced in two weeks' time, the letter said – hung on the closet hook in the room none of them dared enter.

* * *

People had told them not to worry about Scott's room right away. "You don't want to deal with it before you're ready," they said. "Close the door. Or keep it open, whatever feels better. Just don't make yourself sift through those things now." Since he had died the previous June, Iris knew of only one time her mother had been in there – to strip his bed. Iris had seen his sheets and comforter in the basement, waiting for the wash. She imagined what it had been like for her mother, tugging the sheets out from underneath the mattress. Iris wouldn't have been able to resist burying her face in the white percale, searching for his scent. A neighbor had offered to keep the room dusted, just until they were ready, so sometimes during the school year they'd come home to see Mrs. Sherando wandering through the house, a can of Pledge and a dust rag in hand. Iris thought Scott would have loved that – having his own maid.

Iris had been in the room only a few times since he'd died. To put the key away that day after his funeral, when it seemed to glare at her from the dresser where she'd thrown it after they realized what had happened to him. To filch the stuffed gorilla he'd had on his bed since the previous summer, moving it to her own bed so that she, too, could remember the grass-stained, ketchup-dripped smell of him.

As Iris opened the door, a patch of late afternoon sun appeared on the wood floor, materializing like a chalked rectangle on schoolyard cement. She reached her hand over to the right wall and flicked on the light switch, tiptoeing across the floor to the closet, easing the sliding wood door to the right, and reaching up into the corner where the old key on braided yarn dangled. Grabbing it from the hook, she clenched the key in her palm, tightly enough so that she could feel the metal edges digging into the flesh. With her other hand, she yanked the sliding door back to the left to close the closet and turned to leave the room.

Then she stopped. She looked around the room. The bookshelf held the car models Scott had put together with their father, only a few because as much as he loved cars, he found working with small parts tedious. In the corner of the first shelf, a thin box of drawing pastels sat on top of a sketchpad. Iris couldn't remember where he'd gotten the pastels or when he'd used them. On the windowsill, a small clay pot collected dust, the once green shoot emerging from the dirt now shriveled up. Maybe an end of the year science project. Some clipping he'd planted with their mother.

A drawstring bag of marbles still rested on top of Scott's dresser, rounded shapes sticking out from the cotton fabric of the bag. He hadn't used them at all that last summer. How could she remember that detail now and not even notice it back then? Above Scott's bed, a 1973 Detroit Tigers pennant hung, the players in the team picture wearing their navy hats with the white "Old English D," and an orange tiger prancing on the felt cloth above the photo. A photo of him from Easter the previous year sat on the dresser also, and she realized that that his hair was long then, too, always in his face. Yet during the winter before he'd died, he'd agreed to go once to the corner barber with their father.

Iris had intended to stay in the room just long enough to get the key while Liz was on the phone, but the bulging bag of marbles beckoned. She plopped down on the hardwood floor, making her legs into a vee, her thighs sticking to the wood because of her shorts and the heat. Tugging at the drawstring closure on the bag, heavier string than she'd remembered, she opened it and gently spilled the marbles onto the floor in front of her.

He'd had an impressive collection. There were at least fifteen of the bigger marbles, some of them pearlies, bright ambers, and turquoises. Lots of the medium-sized marbles, cat's eyes. Iris picked one up and rolled it between her finger and thumb, watching as the blue leaf-shaped crescent seemed to undulate in slow motion. He even had five steelies, not the little ones, but the big ones, which their dad had probably brought home, a bunch of ball bearings he didn't need at work. Iris organized them by size first, then by color, until she had a pattern in front of her, and she felt powerful again like she did when Scott was younger and made her play soldiers and they arranged their men in rows, knowing that making them advance was the hard part; they could never do it in a phalanx, like in real life; they had to move them one by one, their fingers the propulsion. "Modern warfare," their dad said.

The door opened. Iris had been so quiet, yet still someone had discovered her. Liz stood in the doorway, her face almost white. She placed a palm on either side of the door frame. "Why are you in here?" she asked. "The potatoes were boiling over. I had to turn them down." She'd ignored Iris most of the ten months since Scott had died. Iris had grown accustomed to sullen. Hostile was a surprise.

"Looking for something," Iris murmured.

Liz walked over and stood behind her. "You can't take his marbles," she said flatly. "You can't take anything; we'll divide it fair and square."

"I was just looking," Iris said.

"You may think I'm too old for some of this stuff, but it was his, so I want it," Liz said.

15

Iris nodded.

"So, you need to put that away and get out now," Liz said. Iris figured then that something had set her off. Something at school in the last week, or maybe the sultry heat of the day, a reminder for both of them.

"I'll put them back in a minute," Iris said.

"No," Liz insisted. "Now." She went to stand against the wall, her hands on her hips. "Now," she said again, her voice rising.

"Liz, you're being ridiculous. Just let me stay here for a while. I'll put them back."

"Ridiculous?" Liz asked. She continued her unflinching stare, her honey-blonde hair falling against both of her prominent cheeks, her hazel eyes stony. "And don't even think about taking his money," Liz said. "I know there's some left in that piggy bank." She nodded her head toward the dresser, where a plump pink bank sat with a pig snout facing the window, a large crack, mended years ago creating a gray line from the right ear of the pig to some end point on the underside. "Don't even think about it." Her lips were set, the thick lower one turned out and pouty across the bottom of her face.

"Why would I want money?" Iris didn't understand her sister's anger. "Liz, come on!"

"My brother's things," Liz said with hushed outrage. "My dead brother's things."

For a moment they were both silent. Iris had wanted to explain to Liz that she just needed to look at the key, but she suddenly understood her sister's fury. "He's my dead brother, too."

Liz came over and knelt on the floor next to Iris, reaching down to grab the bag. Then one by one she scooped up the marbles from the floor and dropped them in, hard, making them crack against the others. Iris tried to take the bag away from her, but Liz held it over her head, close enough to Iris's ears that she could make Iris listen to the smack of glass sphere against glass sphere. Iris hated the sound, hated Liz for her capricious fury, springing out of nowhere.

"Liz," their mother said from the doorway. She must have entered the house without their hearing her. In that moment of Liz's distraction, Iris took the opportunity to grab for the bag, now almost full. Something within her was wily enough to hang on for a minute, so that for five seconds or so, the two of them were engaged in a tug of war. When Iris saw the flints of anger in her sister's eyes, her teeth clenched just like their father's, she almost let go. But finally, Iris wrenched the bag free. She stood up, and in one fluid motion hefted it up above her head, the drawstring open, marbles cascading out from between her fingers. It was a half-full bag that hit the wall behind Liz, making a strange, clacking thunk as it slid to the floor.

Liz's body shook, and her face was red with tears. Her shoulders shrunk into a hunch as she struggled past their mother. "You should have taken care of him," she yelled at Iris on her way out of the door. She thundered down the hall, her cries escaping from her throat.

For ten months Iris had been waiting to hear those words from someone, and now that they had come, she felt only relief at the truth. They didn't have to hide it anymore. Their mother looked at the marbles, some still rolling against the baseboard. "It wasn't your fault, Iris," she said. Then she went after Liz.

Iris didn't believe her mother. They all thought it was her fault, every one of them. Yet still, she wanted her mother to stay and offer some words, or even a physical touch, a gesture.

Instead, Iris was left to clean up the marbles, to place them carefully in the bag, ignoring the ones that got chipped from their meeting with the wall. She left them there, damaged spheres, like the corpses of dead bugs, littering the corner. The patch of light had disappeared from the floor, and Scott's room felt clammy, airless. Iris flicked off the light, stepped into the hallway, and closed the door to Scott's room, hearing the wood settle into its frame.

3

The Lake House Palette

June 8, 1974

On the Saturday of the week before school let out for the summer, Iris's father walked her down the street to his friend Sheldon's house after breakfast. Iris had loaded everything she thought she'd need into her bike basket and walked the bike by the handlebars next to her father, who had told her, "Be ready and willing to work," in preparation for the meeting. Sheldon lived on Wertz, his house on the canal that was an offshoot from Williams Lake; the water dipped in at the point where Destan Drive ended in the neighborhood. It narrowed to a twenty-five-foot swath and meandered along next to Wertz and then next to another leg of Cumberland, following a landscape of houses and dirt roads before meeting another stream and opening up to become another lake.

When Iris and her father reached the fork in the road and turned right from Cumberland, their own street, onto Wertz, two loud quacks came from behind the bushes in a nearby yard. Iris directed her bike to the hedge and peered over, knowing the sounds likely came from the pair of ducks that wandered the neighborhood a couple times a day, doing morning and evening strolls as they visited each yard. "Do you think they could be the same ones every year?" she asked.

"I don't know," her father said. "I suppose, for at least a couple of years." He stopped and walked over to the side of the road himself, where Iris stood looking into the yard. "Listen, I just want to say before we get to Sheldon's that this experience will be good for you. Work has always been good for me, helping me get my mind off things." After another set of quacks, Iris watched her father's lips flatten out into his small grin as he nodded a hello to the ducks. "Sheldon can be an oddball, a decent oddball, but still an oddball. Just a heads up."

"I understand," Iris said.

She didn't, really, but she stayed silent and moved her bike back onto the road. They kept walking, until they reached Sheldon's small bungalow, which sat just off the road, the yard behind facing the canal.

They entered the gate near the mailbox, and Iris put down her kickstand after pulling her bike off onto the grass. Then she followed her father onto the paving stone walk that bordered the right side of the house. Sheldon sat on an aluminum lawn chair on a long thin dock behind the house, his fishing pole in the water. Iris's father held his fingers to his lips as he left the soggy grass and approached the edge of the catwalk. "You're living the Life of Riley, Sheldon."

Sheldon lifted his hand, not even turning, pointing at his pole in the water.

Iris's father turned back to Iris and whispered, "The Life of Riley."

"You're just jealous 'cause you never were a very good fisherman," Sheldon said. He turned around then and waved them down the dock.

"Like hell," Iris's father said.

"You scared my fish away." Sheldon placed the pole next to him and rose from his chair, taking a few hollow sounding steps on the slats of the catwalk as he came to greet Iris and her father. He took her father's hand and shook it before turning to Iris and offering his hand to her. Iris raised her own hand slowly, unaccustomed to the adult formality.

Sheldon had moved into the neighborhood a few years earlier, and Liz had told the family at dinner one night that some of the older kids had started to make fun of the new guy in the neighborhood, calling him a loony old man. He painted lots of garage doors in the neighborhood, scenic depictions of forests with deer, rabbits, fallen logs. Their father had never said a word, but a few years later, when he decided to have an old friend paint the garage door, Liz later reported to Iris that the man who'd stood in their driveway for a few days was the very same looney old man her friends had told her about. "An old Navy buddy," her father had said.

"Definitely older," Liz told Iris later.

"This is Iris, the daughter I told you about. She needs something to keep her busy," Iris's dad said. He was right. Iris didn't feel much like babysitting since Scott had died. She'd sat for the Young family next door a few times, but in the middle of the night, once the kids were asleep, she'd start to pace the living room, looking out the front blinds, walking through the house and checking the doors. When she'd see the kids in their beds, ankles still grimy from their days, she recognized their vulnerability, how easily they could be spirited away.

Sheldon looked up, squinted at Iris. He had small eyes, and they were almost buried behind his big glasses and low brow. "I can't pay much. And it's hard work." He gestured his head up the canal. "There's a house on the lake. Empty. Buyers want the whole thing painted. I need the walls washed, some of the trim sanded. Sometimes I'll work right alongside you, but sometimes I'll be on other jobs."

He looked at Iris's dad, shaking his head. "I'm trying to finish this house on the other side of town. A very picky lady. A widow."

Then he winked at Iris. "Wants me to stay for lunch, then dinner. Then 'Can you redo this one wall over here? It seems there's a smudge.'" He had raised his voice to do the imitation, and abruptly, his lower, scruffy voice returned, startling Iris. "What I'm saying is, can I trust you to work on your own?"

Iris nodded.

"Okay," he said. "It's just up the hill and down the street on Destan. I'll take you."

"She's got her bike," Iris's dad said.

"I can just bike over," she said.

"Well, sit tight," Sheldon said. "I'll load my truck and then you can follow me. It's halfway around the block, maybe ten houses."

"I'm going to let you get to it," Iris's dad said. "I'll see you at home later." He nodded at Sheldon and turned around, heading back to the road.

Iris walked around to the road side of the house. She'd packed a peanut butter sandwich and a thermos of grape Kool-Aid for the day, but she didn't want to eat yet. She'd also brought the transistor radio her parents had given her the previous year for her birthday and a paperback by Agatha Christie. She sat on the bicycle seat and balanced herself, holding the book open against the handlebars.

"I'm ready," Sheldon called a few minutes later from the small garage. "If you pull off to the side, you can just follow me."

He backed a small green station wagon out of the garage and punched at something on his dashboard; the garage door slowly went down, revealing the forest scene he must have painted there: pine trees, a stream running through a valley, thatched cottages in the distance, with birds perched on a myriad of branches. Sheldon's house was half way up the hill where Wertz met Destan, and Iris tried to maintain her balance and work the pedals to gain enough momentum to crest the incline, but Sheldon was already several car lengths down Destan before she finally jumped off and walked her bike, keeping his green station wagon in sight, curious about which driveway he would enter. When his left blinker lit up, she realized that the driveway he'd pulled into belonged to a family she hadn't seen in a while. Their kids were younger, so she might not have noticed if they moved away. As she reached a plateau on Destan, she got on her seat and began pedaling the short distance to the house at which Sheldon had stopped.

When she pulled behind his station wagon, he motioned to her to move her bike onto the grass. "I'll be leaving soon, after I explain a few things to you," he said. "Don't want to run over your bike before I even know you well enough to determine your attachment to it," he said.

"Thanks for thinking of that," Iris said.

"I try to be a thinking kind of guy, not that it does me a lot of good," Sheldon said.

He motioned to a few buckets and drop cloths in the back of his wagon; Iris grabbed them and followed him up the sidewalk to the front porch.

"I am trying to remember some stories I could tell you about your Dad that are age-appropriate," he said, as they walked into a living room empty of anything save a few paint cans.

"How long have you known my Dad?" Iris said.

"Since he was twenty. Before he met your mom."

"In the Navy?" Iris said. "I heard you were Navy buddies."

"Actually, I knew him before that. When he was kind of wild."

"I didn't know he was wild."

"We were all wild. Wild and immature."

"The kind of wild that leads to trouble?"

"Oh, Iris," Sheldon sighed. "We've just met, and I'd feel bad telling your dad's secrets."

"I don't need to hear my father's secrets, at least not today. But I wouldn't mind hearing some funny stories," Iris said.

"When we open these cans, we'll see how funny paint is," Sheldon said. "Stay tuned."

* * *

Iris stood in front of the large picture window, which was flanked by smaller windows on each side, looking out at Williams Lake. Sheldon had set her up with a task before he left for the other painting job he'd lined up. The lake edge lay not far from the house, the water itself quiet and calm, scallops of light spackling the surface. Already a few water skiers braved the early-June-cold waters. The year before, Iris would have been down at the association's beach front already, if only to sit on the shore with Rosemary.

In warm weather, Iris could bicycle ten minutes in any direction and run into a substantial body of water, turning a corner and meeting a wide expanse of blue, the color so cold and fresh-looking that her spine prickled with a shiver. In the winter, when her bike was locked away in the shed, she could scarcely tell the lakes from the land, especially after the first big winter storm; both were covered with snow, and though Iris knew the terrain well, she found the blanket of snow disorienting. The shocking white and the stinging scent of cold in her nose twisted her sense of direction, and like most Michiganders, in winter she would only know a lake when a road sign posted next to it conveyed its presence. The entire state of Michigan hosted over 11,000 lakes. Not just Great Lakes, but Big Lakes, Crooked Lakes, Silver Lakes, Bass Lakes, Pontoon Lakes, and Cranberry Lakes.

When you were a kid in Michigan, the best place to spend your summer was in the middle of the lake. By the time Iris was fourteen, she had been in forty-two of those lakes. She could compare them in terms of their rocky or sandy bottoms, their blue or green surfaces, and the absence or presence of troublesome weeds in their deep or shallow waters.

Part of Iris wished she had the nerve to call Rosemary, just to say a polite hello, not to mention anything of significance, not to remember out loud any of the previous summer's events. Just to remember their summer routines and patterns and honor their shared commitment to dwelling within easy reach of the waters they loved. But life had grown more complicated.

A warm breeze fluttered through the screens of the open side windows. Iris put her gloved hands in the water, saturated the sponge, and started on a new wall. It wasn't hard work, but Sheldon had told her to put some elbow grease into it, not like she was giving some fragile baby a bath. The sponge scratched a faint rhythm as she rubbed it against the old paint on the wall; she gazed up at the water outside just as a speedboat passed by.

Seeing the water still made her stomach lurch, yet she felt its pull as well, the ripples dancing under the slant of the sun, sparkling.

That summer before, in the month leading up to Scott's death, Iris and Rosemary had started the beach season in their usual fashion – by heading there the day after school let out. The new beach key had glistened on the yarn around Iris's neck, the light catching it as she met up with Rosemary before they wound their way around the block to the beach gate.

Now it was June again, and the lake appeared just out the window in front of her, though she was at the other end of Destan from the beach. When she looked down in the bucket after scrubbing two walls, she could still see Rosemary's face. Mysterious and smiling, but haunted. On that first day to the beach, there had been a pack of kids from their school congregating by the shore, a few feet down from where the toddlers sat. Iris spotted the boy she knew Rosemary had a crush on, standing next to another girl from their school, Gail, who was more outgoing and boisterous than Rosemary or Iris. Gail sat down abruptly, on one of the green benches under the tree, where people sought shade, or a place to leave their towels. And the boy who'd been standing next to her, Allen, the boy Rosemary liked, bent over just as suddenly and sank his lips onto Gail's. She tilted her head backward against the top green slat of the bench, so that Iris and Rosemary, even lying flat on towels on the downward slope of the hill, had a clear glimpse of Allen's tongue as it navigated into Gail's mouth.

They'd made it through a third of that previous summer, and then Scott had died, and then, during the school year, Gail and Allen had broken up. And Rosemary danced with Allen one night at a school dance. And then they were together.

Iris didn't know how to talk to Rosemary anymore, couldn't tell if she was happy. Rosemary had always had a way of pulling her troubles up inside of her, making everything on the outside smooth and cool, like a turtle shell.

In the bucket, the wall-washing water had grown filthy, a murky gray, no sign of the bubbles or foam indicating that the cleaner still held potency.

4

The New Subdivision House

June 9, 1974

On the next morning, Iris spent a few hours at the Lake House scrubbing down the walls in the room Sheldon had indicated. He had told her he would pay double time for that Sunday if she put in a few hours prepping the walls he wanted to paint Monday. After she locked up, she climbed on her blue hand-me-down bike from her sister with the little basket in front. She'd left it on the side walk-way, kickstand down, pulled off to the side so it wasn't in Sheldon's path, should he stop by. The night before she'd pumped up her bike tires, with the idea of exploring after she finished her work.

But when she reached the part of Wertz just after Sheldon's house, where the hill bottomed at the intersection of Cumberland, she was surprised to see Rosemary further down on the canal part of Cumberland, pushing a baby stroller, its large aqua awning hanging over the baby seated underneath.

Iris wasn't sure she was prepared to talk to her, and she contemplated increasing her pedaling with the hope that she could whiz by before Rosemary saw her. But she felt a pang of guilt and made herself back pedal to brake, pulling off the road into the high grass by the street name signs where there was less dust for a child to inhale.

Rosemary started talking before Iris even said hello. "I shouldn't have taken her for a walk," Rosemary said. "I forgot that they haven't oiled the roads yet, and the wheels on this stroller keep kicking up dust." She steered the stroller to the edge of the road where Iris straddled her bike. "I've been thinking of calling you, but I got a babysitting job today."

Iris leaned over to look under the canopy. "Pretty eyes," she said. "Whose kid?"

"New people further down Cumberland. They have a nice house on the canal." The baby's curled hand came out to the side of the stroller, and a clank and a rattle sounded simultaneously. Iris reached down to grab the yellow plastic rattle from the overgrown grass at the base of the street sign pole, where the black paint coating was peeling away, the rusted metal showing through.

"Wonderful," Rosemary said, shaking her head and pulling the hem of her shirt from her waist to wipe the toy she took from Iris. "Thank God she doesn't put things in her mouth yet." She looked up at Iris, examining her face before glancing down again. "I'm sorry I haven't called. It's just been a busy year. Allen and everything."

"I should have called, too," Iris said. She reached out and ran her finger along the aqua trim topstitched at the seam of the stroller's awning piece. "I'm happy for you." She tilted her head and smiled the slight upturn she had practiced so many times in the mirror, the one that she'd relied on all school year.

"I don't know if this Allen thing will last, but we'll see." A squeal rose from the stroller, and Rosemary lifted the back wheels and maneuvered them closer to the road. "Maybe we could go to the beach next week?"

"Ohhh," Iris said slowly. "I'm...." She paused and exhaled. "Not sure I'm ready. You know. The water. Scott."

Rosemary bent over the stroller, the curtain of blonde hair hiding her face, so Iris didn't have to see it. "Oh my God, I wasn't thinking," she said.

"No, it's okay," Iris said, "Really." She dreaded getting back on the bike and pedaling up another hill. It seemed overwhelming. "Not a big deal. I'll call you next week. Really." She smiled again, trying to convey a confidence she didn't feel.

The baby gurgled a long sound, and Rosemary put the stroller wheels back on the road. "Or I'll call you," she yelled, her back already facing Iris, the words coming around the side, faint, along with the dust from the road.

* * *

Iris looked both ways on the half mile stretch of paved roadway that made up Williams Lake Road, forming a natural boundary for one end of the neighborhood, the lake itself the other major boundary. Once she crossed Williams Lake Road, she headed toward the area she and Rosemary had dubbed the "New Subdivision," another neighborhood of homes not far from their own that had begun development years after their own subdivision. But building had stopped in the last year, not just because of the winter ground freeze. Money troubles, Iris's dad said.

Iris had been thinking a lot about the boundaries of her neighborhood and how long she'd stayed within them. On that Sunday morning, she'd woken up prepared to trespass.

She and Rosemary had ridden their bikes over there frequently the previous summer. Past the string of occupied houses, the smooth, unblemished pavement played out underneath their bike tires. That was the primary beauty of the New Subdivision – the paved roads – providing bump-free bike rides without the dodging maneuvers that their own dirt roads required. Once they'd travelled beyond the occupied houses, the neighborhood became still with just the sounds of a few cardinals and peepers from a marsh that began in the wide-open space behind one of the houses on a cul-de-sac where the development ended. Beyond that area, a golf course had been planned, the golf course to be named "Lake Meadows." The Lake Meadows golf course property was even older than the New Subdivision, but the sign proclaiming its development was sun-bleached, spots of graffiti in the upper corners framing the description of the golf course and its proposed holes and features.

"It was a silly idea," Iris's father had said. "Factory workers and welders don't play golf."

Iris counted off seven unfinished houses before she reached the house she'd had her eye on the previous year. At the end of the cul-de-sac. White with burgundy/maroon shutters, vacant and unfinished. It seemed strange that this house with few windows and doors would have shutters, like somebody wasn't thinking and iced the cake before baking it. Iris rode her bike around the back and parked it by the unfinished porch so no one in the occupied houses down the street could see it from the road. The back door opened easily, and she stepped inside, shivering when she realized how cold it was in the empty hull without the warmth of the sun.

Seeing Rosemary on her way to this house had been unsettling. She'd wanted to call her, almost as much as she'd wanted to get on her bike and visit this house. But she wanted to trespass alone, and she wanted solitude. Even with the freedom she'd recently gained from working with Sheldon in a new environment, she still felt antsy, unable to settle her brain or find a way to relax into a summer rhythm. Working at the Lake House gave her a glimpse of the water and the activities that would be so vivid down at the beach. But she still wanted distance, wanted to move outside her boundaries. The New Subdivision House would give her new terrain.

She walked around as if she were Sheldon preparing to paint, deciding if the owner's color selections would work in each room, depending on the light coming in the open windows. She walked around as if she were Scott, still alive and picking a room at a new house their parents might buy. In the family room, a box of nails sat in the corner, thin white ones, next to a sheet of whitish gray paneling. Upstairs in one of the bedrooms, a piece of molding was propped up against the wall. Construction materials lay poised, in a state of readiness – waiting to be put to use, waiting to come to action.

Iris remembered then that she'd packed some snacks and a transistor radio for working on the Lake House walls. She went out the back door to retrieve them from her bike basket and brought them back into the house.

An open doorway off the kitchen appeared to lead to the basement, yet when she looked down the stairs, expecting darkness, she realized that this basement had light coming in from some source. She clunked down the wooden stairs. The large room she stepped into had a sliding glass door at the end where the light poured in from the marsh that lay beyond the back yard.

Her mother had always wanted a finished basement. Outside, a red-winged blackbird landed on a cattail and throated a trill which Iris heard not through the glass of the doorwall but from the framed window opening to the left of the doorwall. When she stepped into the corner to survey the area, she noticed that there were two interior doorways back near the stairs that led off to other rooms. In one there was a large tub sink and a drain in a cement floor. The laundry room. In the other room, off to the side, the floor that she stepped onto appeared to be composed of an odd mixture of dirt and sand.

She knew from her dad's talk with other neighbors about the various ways that basements were made – usually before the rest of the house, but sometimes after. It seemed so odd that most of the basement would have a cement floor, yet this one would be composed of sand and dirt. She lowered herself to the gritty surface, pulling her knees to her chest. Then she took off her shoes and socks, putting her feet in the cold sand, like she was at the beach. She rolled her jeans up to her knees.

She sat like that for quite a while, pushing her toes into the dirt and sand mixture, submerging them and then wiggling them free, the way she and Scott had done during vacations. When they had beach fires, Scott would always beg for s'mores.

The radio announcer on WRIF introduced Roberta Flack, and Iris almost turned the radio off because that sad song had played in her head nearly all year. But instead, she stood up and pretended she was Rosemary in their school's cafeteria one Friday night when the disc jockey at the school dance picked a slow song. A tall boy appeared from out of a corner where the guys stood in a clump. He tugged on her hand. She reached her arms up, joining her fingers behind his neck, and Roberta Flack sang "Killing Me Softly," about a girl watching a stranger who was strumming his guitar and somehow singing about the girl's heartache. Iris moved her hips slowly, now on the sand-dirt basement floor of a half-built house, the side-to-side sway within the legs of her shorts feeling rhythmic, the faint smell of cut grass in the air. She wondered how it felt to be Rosemary, dancing with Allen, swaying with the trembling notes.

When the song was over, Iris turned the radio off. She pulled her socks and shoes back on, erasing the song and the dance from her thoughts.

She didn't deserve the kind of comfort that came from dance floors and warm bodies. She needed punishment. She needed her parents and her sister to confront her and shame her for what she'd done and what she didn't do to keep her brother safe. She climbed up the basement stairs to the main floor, walked out the back door, and rode her bike home.

5

Pernicious

June 10, 1974

As Iris came into the family room where her mother sat in the big brown chair with wide arms, she experienced a Polaroid flash moment in which she saw her brother in the same chair, baseball cards lined up in neat rows on the upholstery of the arms after he'd recently purchased new packs of gum from the store. But after Iris closed her eyes in a slow blink, she opened them to her mother holding an iced tea, droplets of water already misting the glass from the heat. She glanced up at Iris and offered a smile, but her eyes were worried and serious. "Another boy," she said, "They're going to give details in a minute." Asleep in the easy chair across the room, Iris's father rumbled a faint, after-dinner snore, the kind that would eventually wake him up, ten minutes into the news.

Liz sat closer to the television, perched on an ottoman just a few feet away. When Iris tried to make eye contact, Liz looked down at the floor. "Oh, shit," she said. "Not again. I am so tired of death."

"Liz," her mother said. It was a one-word warning that meant the equivalent of "Don't get started." On whatever. Their mom wiped her hand along the side of her glass, collecting water, then against her red shorts, making a small patch of darker red.

It had been just over a month since Liz had confronted Iris in Scott's room, making a claim on his belongings and augmenting Iris's guilt. Since then, Iris had developed a two-fold strategy: she tried to stay out of her sister's way, but when she was in the same room, she attempted to be cordial and to conceal her anger and hurt at her sister's intense reaction. During that same month, their mother procured a beach key, attached it to a freebie key chain from a local car dealer, and hung it up on a hook in the hall cupboard, emphasizing to both of her daughters that they must notify her before using it. Since Liz put in over thirty hours a week at the dairy store in the summer and spent her off hours with friends, Iris knew her mother was speaking directly to her.

"SSHHH. It's coming back on," their mother said. Iris had been passing through the family room but she lowered herself to the floor and folded her legs to wait for the news story.

After the commercial, the Channel Seven newscaster announced that an eight-year-old boy had disappeared from his neighborhood. According to the report, he was last seen riding his bike around the neighborhood with his friend, but the friend said they had split up shortly before five o'clock so each could head home for dinner. The parents emphasized to the police that it was unlikely that either boy would travel outside their bike riding boundaries. Iris watched the newscaster's face, and soon she couldn't hear words anymore, she could only see the dips in his head, the way he bent his chin down on some words, raised it up on others, his clear blue eyes honest, moist, sad. The screen changed, the boy's face appeared, and Iris's mother inhaled.

"It looks like a younger Scott," Liz said, her voice soft and horrified.

"I don't think so," Iris said quietly, not wanting to contradict Liz openly.

The television screen flashed a picture of the kid's neighborhood, focusing in on a flyer posted at the neighborhood market. "Christ, next they'll be interviewing his teacher at school, or the woman who sold him a candy bar each week," their dad said from his chair. He'd woken up. "They should leave those people alone."

"Even if they don't want to be alone? Even if they need to get the word out?" Their mother shook her head. "What do you know about this kind of situation anyway?"

"If that kid is like the others, he's dead," Liz said.

"Scott was eleven," Iris said, her voice quiet at the edges.

"Ohhhhh," their mother said on a long sigh, "We shouldn't even watch; it's too depressing." She stood up from her chair. "That poor boy. And his family." She shook her head and rose to go to the kitchen.

The killer had taken three victims so far. Each was found seven to ten days after being reported missing, and in each case evidence from the body indicated that he'd kept them alive until the very end, right before he dumped their bodies in parks, wooded areas, out-of-the-way places still accessible enough that the bodies were discovered not too long after he left them. That meant the boy might even be watching himself on television. He might be in a room, lying on a bed, propped up against a pillow, his arms and legs bound at the wrists and ankles. Tape at his mouth, or maybe no tape, because no one would hear his screams anyway. And when the boy's face appeared on the screen, there would be a scrape of a chair leg on the floor as the kidnapper, not yet a killer to the boy, pulled his chair closer to the television, almost more fascinated by the picture of the boy than by the real thing, bound and motionless a few feet away, his own eyes taking in the picture of himself, wanting to put his hands out to touch the newscaster and say that he was alive, still alive, waiting for them to find him.

Looking back, you never knew what occurrences formed the catalysts, the propellers, the causes of catastrophic events. *Pernicious*, Iris thought. She'd learned the word a few days earlier, in a *Reader's Digest* quiz. It was kind of like when you hung the wash out on the line, using a clothespin to connect the sleeve of a T-shirt to the waistband on one side of a pair of underwear, and the next clothespin to connect the other side of the waistband to the shoulder of a nightgown. Everything touched; no one thing stood alone. Iris felt that the missing children were the first bad things that happened that second summer, though sometimes it seemed that all her life there were these harbingers of disaster, pointing to other wicked things to come.

6

Soft Serve

June 11, 1974

When Iris got back from working at the Lake House with Sheldon, the afternoon sun had come out from behind morning clouds, and Liz, on a day off, lay on her stomach, her bikini top undone at the back to allow for even tanning. The sheen on her legs just underneath her turquoise bikini bottoms glistened even from a distance. Liz always used baby oil to moisturize her skin before tanning, believing that it made the pores more receptive to the sun's rays. She had developed a method in the last few years of tanning for brief bits of time early in June. By mid-July, she would be a golden brown, her olive skin tones helping her build an enviable tan over her entire body, particularly her face.

She lifted her head and raised her sunglasses when Iris opened the garage to put her bike away. "I left you a message on the counter," she said, and then dropped her head back down.

Iris felt that she'd been given a clear directive about the message – whatever the subject matter, Liz did not wish to bear it in spoken words or anything that might be characterized as a discussion. Iris sighed loudly and went in the back door. Near the phone, Liz had printed a note in large black marker:

2:30

Iris –

Rosemary called.

Call back, please.

Iris put her transistor radio on the counter and went into the bathroom. When she came out, she looked at the phone mounted on the wall, the circular plastic piece with its alphabet trios located underneath every finger hole created for dialing. She picked up the phone and dialed Rosemary's number, wanting the connection but leery of exposing her emotions.

"Two questions," Rosemary said when she answered. "One. Do you want to go to Cate's Corner Market tonight? They installed a soft serve machine, I heard. We could walk or bike after dinner. Two. I need to ask a favor. My neighbors next door, the Langleys, need a sitter Friday night. But I've already promised to babysit that baby you saw me with, so I wondered if you could sit for the Langley kids? There are two children, mild-mannered. At least for me."

Iris twirled the long cord on the phone like it was a jumping rope, watching it slap against the living room carpet. She didn't want to do it. She still loved being around kids, but the thought of babysitting filled her with dread. Her parents understood that, even if they didn't speak about it, which was why her father had gotten her the job with Sheldon. She didn't want to be responsible for anyone's lives, even in their own homes. But she couldn't find a way to squirm out of it. And Rosemary needed her help. This was Iris's chance to do something for someone else. Iris couldn't explain to Rosemary that she was part of the tight ball of random threads from last summer that Iris hadn't yet untangled. Even seeing Rosemary, hearing her voice for a moment made Iris's tongue dry and awkward in her mouth.

"Okay," Iris said. She surprised herself.

"Great," Rosemary said.

* * *

They'd decided that walking would make it easier for talking and eating ice cream. When Iris told her parents where she was going with Rosemary that evening, Liz said, "A soft serve machine? Huh." Iris didn't stop to ask what her sister meant.

She walked down Cumberland toward Rosemary's house which sat in front of the curve where Cumberland Road veered left and became Rutherford. It formed a back-way route through the neighborhood to Williams Lake Road. As she approached the house, she could see Rosemary in the front yard with a can of Off, spraying her exposed skin. Her thin arms and legs were whitish-pink, not beige-olive, like Liz's. Iris had always admired the way Rosemary seemed so at ease in shorts, not pulling at the leg openings or jerking at the waist like Iris did. Rosemary's clothes just seemed to rest on her body like another layer of skin, like a coating.

Rosemary put the can of repellent on the front porch and joined Iris in the road with a hug. A crow sounded in the trees above them, and Rosemary laughed. They walked in silence at first, up the slight incline, sandals kicking pebbles. Finally, Iris said. "I'm glad you called. I've wanted to connect, but I just haven't." She shrugged her shoulders as if to explain that she didn't understand her reasons herself. "I didn't tell you when I saw you – I got a job helping a guy with his house painting. That guy who paints those garage door murals."

"That sounds interesting," Rosemary said. "Do you like it?"

"I've only been doing it a few days – my arm muscles get sore sometimes, but it's quiet, not as demanding as babysitting."

"You probably didn't even need the job I called you about."

"It's okay – good for me to earn money."

"I talked to my neighbor, and she said seven o'clock would be great. And if you walk there, she or her husband will drive you home," Rosemary said.

"Good. I'll write it on the calendar."

"I really appreciate it. I just started babysitting for these people a few weeks ago. The kids are easy. And right next door. I'd like to be their regular, like you are for the Youngs."

"No problem," Iris said. She knew that she wasn't being entirely truthful. She was aware now of the overwhelming responsibility that babysitters took on, and she felt deeply flawed, like a fake diamond in a mystery novel that no one suspects is fake until the brilliant detective points out the flaws in the gem, and then everyone knows the truth. She wanted to change the subject. "So, I don't want to pry, but since it's been so long – what's happening with Allen?"

They'd reached the end of Rutherford where the road met Williams Lake Road, just after the big curve at the corner where the canal ended at the culvert, next to the marsh. Iris and Rosemary walked single-file next to the guard rail, Rosemary first. Iris saw her shoulders droop for a minute and heard her sigh. They made it past the rail and the boggy water, and Iris caught up with Rosemary, taking the side closest to the lighter evening traffic approaching behind them.

"We ended the year okay," Rosemary said. "But he called to tell me last week that his parents got him a job at Mackinac Island. Whose parents do that?"

Iris thought of her father's act of seeking out Sheldon. "And he doesn't want to leave you?" she asked.

Rosemary's lips quivered, and she pressed them together and bowed her head. "I have no idea. He certainly doesn't seem all broken up about it."

Iris fell quiet for a moment. The evening insects sawed at the air while she tried to understand Rosemary's feelings. She and Rosemary had talked the previous summer about what it would be like to have a boyfriend, someone who loved you and wanted to spend time with you. She hadn't been jealous when Allen asked Rosemary out; Rosemary was prettier than Iris. It made sense that boys would like her more. But she was sad to have her friend drift away and travel in a different group of friends during the school year. And maybe Iris was jealous then. Maybe she just didn't want to admit it. "I don't know what to say, Rosemary," she said finally.

"He said he'll send me his address. And maybe he'll even call me from the island – from a pay phone. I have doubts."

"I don't know him very well," Iris said. "But I knew you liked him, so I was glad."

Rosemary made a face. "I don't know how well I know him. We'll see. Thank God he'll have to write first. I'll just try to forget about him until I hear from him."

As they approached Cate's Corner Market, Iris noticed the line forming at the side of the building. "What's this?" she said.

"The soft serve line."

"Oh," Iris said. She wanted to turn around and go back down the road they'd just travelled. There were too many people.

"It's probably only a half-hour wait with this kind of line," Rosemary said.

"You've been here before," Iris said.

"The weekend it first opened. My parents buy all their meat here," Rosemary said as they joined the end of the line that wound around the back of the store. "It's sort of like having a Dairy Queen without all of the selections. They usually have a couple of flavors, I guess."

"We've always gone to Richland for ice cream," Iris said.

"Yeah," Rosemary said, "with a car. But that's another mile up the road."

Iris and Rosemary took a position leaning against the brick of the building's exterior, which Iris felt through her T-shirt. She thought about Liz, scooping ice cream down the street at Richland's, each cone a product of a muscular fight against the rock-hard ice cream and the easily splintered cone. She felt guilty seeking out another ice cream.

They'd reached the part of the line that straightened out and provided a full view of the front door to the market. The door opened to the inside, and the bell clanged again. Gail Fanlon and her little brother walked out, both carrying chocolate. Iris turned to look at Rosemary's face, but her friend was staring calmly at Gail, watching as she moved toward them.

"They're out of vanilla," Gail said. She seemed to be talking to Rosemary, but then she turned to Iris and said, "How are you guys doing?"

"Great," Rosemary said, her voice high and bright.

"Have a good summer if I don't see you at the beach," Gail said. And she reached out and pulled the back of her brother's shirt to get him on the path back toward their neighborhood. "I'll tell Allen I saw you," Gail added.

When she'd walked far enough away from where they stood, Iris turned to Rosemary. "What does she mean about Allen? Why is she talking to us?"

"We're friends now," Rosemary said in a soft voice.

"Really? For how long?"

"I don't know," Rosemary said. "I can't remember. But she's still friends with Allen."

"She seemed to want to make that pretty clear," Iris said.

"She's not a bad person," Rosemary said. "I mean, she's flirty and everything, and she likes Allen to do things for her. But she's not really mean, like, in an evil way or anything."

"I'm just surprised, that's all," Iris said. "I thought she was the type who got mad about things like..." Iris paused. "...someone dating her ex-boyfriend."

Rosemary shrugged. "I try not to worry about it. Allen likes everyone to be happy."

They reached the door, and more kids came out the other side, chocolate soft serve topping their cones.

"So, it's just the chocolate then," Iris said.

"Oh, I don't know," Rosemary said. "I thought there were three spigots on the machine, but maybe there are just two, and the vanilla isn't working."

"Yeah," Iris said. She let her voice trail off and moved forward in line. "That's too bad."

"Oh, Iris," Rosemary said. "I completely forgot. You're allergic to chocolate," she said.

"It's okay; they might have another flavor," Iris said.

They watched as each customer came out of the store, some with brown bags of groceries or in some cases just a white package, meat from the butcher case. But the people carrying cones all seemed to carry the same flavor – chocolate. "It's okay," Iris repeated. "I'm pretty full after dinner. I don't need any more calories, really."

On the way back to the neighborhood, Iris watched as Rosemary licked her chocolate ice cream cone in a methodical fashion, her tongue first smoothing out the natural ridges the soft serve machine had made with each layer by creating circular furrows in the ice cream and then occasionally making five or six vertical swoops up the triangular mountain piled atop the cone. Rosemary held the cone off to the side and licked around her lips, cleaning off chocolate smudges. Then she pressed her lips together and looked at Iris.

"Before I met Allen, I thought that kissing would be like eating an ice cream cone. I was really excited about it. But it's a lot different. Wetter, like sucking on a popsicle."

A car went by and hit a small pothole in the road, and Iris was glad for the sound and the distraction. She felt like all the people she knew lived in a different world, and she'd need a secret password to get in, if she even wanted to enter.

7

The Favor

June 14, 1974

Iris arrived at the front door of the Langley's house five minutes before seven o'clock and rang the doorbell. The mother ushered her in and made the introductions. Sherry was eight and Andy was six. Once the parents left, Iris turned her attention to learning more about the kids and providing the evening's entertainment. They seemed very reasonable, volunteering what time they should go to bed, telling Iris the limit on how many cookies before bedtime; they were out of popcorn. Sherry talked a lot, but she followed directions without protest. Iris was accustomed to having to go into kids' bedrooms several times to calm them down but when bedtime rolled around, these kids needed no reading or singing. Fifteen minutes after Iris left their rooms, she came back to the doors, standing just outside, and distinguished the low, even sound of sleep breathing.

In the living room, the air smelled stale and heavy. Iris went to the window, and when she cranked open the casement a warm breeze came in the screen. Iris knew that across the street, Rosemary was dealing with that baby. She wished this house didn't feel so strange. When Scott was alive and Iris babysat at the house next door to her own home, Scott would come over sometimes, if she called. Bringing her a book she might have forgotten at home, or a cup of popcorn, if the Youngs had run out. He might stay to watch a movie, until their mom called to remind him that he still had a bedtime, weekend or not.

Finally, Iris left the window and went to the couch, lowering herself down on the vinyl upholstery, feeling the heat and sweat at the backs of her thighs where her shorts ended and her skin began. She started reading her book, but the adventures of Hercule Poirot and friends seemed out of place.

At one o'clock a car pulled up in the driveway, and a man got out. Although Iris was expecting the kids' uncle to show up, she was still surprised by the features that materialized in the spotlight over the garage as he came to the side door. His hair fell to his shoulders; above his lip, a dark, heavy mustache protruded, the hairs thick and coarse. His face was blank as he looked at Iris through the side door window, but he smiled when he put his key in the lock. She heard the clack of the deadbolt and backed up as the door opened.

"You must be the babysitter," he said.

Iris nodded.

He put out his hand. "Karl," he said. "Pleased to meet you."

Iris reached her own hand out and shook Karl's. "Likewise." She laughed nervously. She remembered shaking Sheldon's hand a week earlier. "My dad told me to say that."

Karl threw his keys on the kitchen table and went to the refrigerator, fishing out a beer. "So?" he said.

Iris felt her face flush. "So?" she repeated. His eyes were almost black, and he was looking at her in such a serious way that she felt uncomfortable.

"So, what is *your* name?"

"Oh, sorry – it's Iris. Iris Merchant."

"Like the flower," he said. "Pretty name." Then he smiled. "Pretty girl."

Iris looked down, unsure of how she should address the compliment. She'd edged herself into the corner behind the kitchen table, and she watched him put both hands on the counter and hoist himself up in one flexing motion to sit on the Formica countertop. His body was thin, but his muscles bulged out from under his black Led Zeppelin T-shirt. Maybe he did some sort of construction work. Lifting things.

"So," Karl said. "The substitute babysitter. You're doing this mature job, but you can hardly be more than a baby yourself. How old are you?"

Iris felt flustered. She didn't know what he was trying to say. "Fourteen," she said and immediately wished she'd lied. "And how old are you?" she blurted back.

"I'm twenty-eight," he said. He looked at her for a few minutes longer and then began to tell her about the party he'd been to at the bowling alley and how boring it was, though he'd bowled a 190 and then a 222 game. While he sat there, he took slow sips of beer. His Adam's apple lurched when he took a gulp; his brown-black eyes continued to focus on her face. Iris felt warm and wondered if her face was flushed. She watched him as he drained the last of the beer from the bottle, throwing his head back and then hoisting himself off the counter to take the bottle to the trash can. He walked over to the kitchen table and pulled out a chair. "I know my sister probably told you to stay until they get back. She says I sleep way too soundly to be a trustworthy babysitter." He rolled his eyes. "Plus, I never know what time things will wind up at the alley. But I'm here now," he said, grinning. "Wanna play cards?" Karl's mustache moved when he spoke. and Iris felt a bit awkward as she watched his lips move. But his eyes were friendly and encouraging. The Langleys had told her that she was welcome to leave when he came home, although they didn't know when that would be. Or she could stay, and that would save them the trouble of sending the money to her house later. Iris felt a little uneasy, but she was also flattered at his offer to help her pass a few hours of babysitting. She felt too antsy to read the book she'd brought, and part of her appreciated the attention, the way he talked to her like she was old enough to hear about his day, like she might have something interesting to say in return. "Okay," she said.

He gave a quick, resolute nod. "Good," he said. "You don't talk much, do you?"

Iris shrugged.

"Oh, one of those," he said, rolling his eyes. "Shy," he whispered, and his voice brushed against her skin. He reached over then and touched her chin, forcing her eyes to meet his. "Just kidding," he said. "Shy is fine. No harm, right?"

Iris shook her head and felt a sense of relief as his fingers fell away from her face.

Karl went into the living room. Iris heard a drawer open and items being shifted around. He came back into the kitchen with a pack of cards in his hand. "Can you play poker?"

"If you remind me of the rules and what beats what," Iris said.

He tilted his head and the kitchen light glinted against a red hair in his mustache. "How do you know I won't cheat?" Leaning against the counter, he shuffled the cards, and the blue-and-white pattern of the cards changed with the movement of the deck. Then he split the deck and held the two halves in the air, folding them against one another. Liz's old boyfriend Michael had tried to teach Iris to do that. "Well?" he said.

"I guess I'll just have to trust you," Iris said.

He laughed. "I've never cheated at cards. It's not worth it." As he dealt the cards, he gave Iris the basic rules for five-card draw, reminding her that a royal flush beats a full house, and four of a kind beats a two pair. Iris tried to retain the hierarchy, but the warm air in the kitchen distracted her, and she could feel the sweat gathering under her cotton shirt.

He rose from the table and went to the refrigerator. "Wanna beer?"

She shook her head no.

He looked at her, squinting his eyes until they were barely open. "You don't mind if I smoke?"

He said the words as if he was making a statement, not asking a question. Iris just kept looking at him, not moving her eyes or her head.

Karl reached into his pocket and pulled out a pack of Camels. He struck a match and held it to the cigarette, his eyes squinting as the smoke drifted into them.

While they played cards, the light smell of smoke filled the air. From time to time, a bit of foam from the beer would cling to his mustache, and somehow aware of the residue, he would slide his tongue up and around his lip. Iris couldn't keep herself from staring as he did this, and once he looked up from his cards and caught her gaze. His face eased into a grin.

After he won four out of five games, he suggested that they go into the living room and listen to the stereo. His sister and brother-in-law had eight-track tapes, he said. Iris told him she would be there in a minute. After he left the room, she straightened the kitchen chairs and wiped the table, especially the rings his beer sweat had created on the table. She wanted to stay in the kitchen, sit at the table and read her book, maybe pour herself some of the pop she'd found earlier in the refrigerator. But she knew he was waiting for her in the living room; she didn't know how to tell him that she didn't need him to entertain her anymore.

Iris stood in the doorway leading to the living room. Behind her, the kitchen light spilled from the yellow and orange linoleum tiles onto the dark gray shag carpet of the living room. The sound of hard plastic meeting hard plastic came from a corner of the room as Karl knelt over the box where the eight-track tapes were housed, searching for a particular one.

Iris murmured something about remaining in the kitchen. Karl's head turned as the first word came out of her mouth, her voice hollow, tentative.

He cocked his head. "What?" he asked. "You don't like music?" His eyes blinked softly into a droop as he sat back on the carpet in a relaxed way. "You'd rather read," he guessed, the pitch of his voice a faint challenge.

Iris stepped from the kitchen into the living room and sat down in the corner on the black vinyl couch. Karl popped a tape into the deck, and as Janis Joplin's voice came out of the speakers, he sat in the middle of the sofa. Iris exhaled and looked toward the picture window. Outside, on the corner, the streetlamp cast a subtle light on the road and a red car parked there. In the distance, a dog barked, not a deep mature bark, but an edgy yipping.

She tried to concentrate on Janis Joplin's voice. Although she didn't look right at Karl, the tip of his cigarette glowed from the place that might represent his mouth. He then transferred it to the ashtray. "Her voice is so strange," Iris said. "So wailing and scratchy at the same time."

Underneath her fingertips the vinyl of the couch was slick and smooth. Iris flattened her hand and rubbed it against the armrest. The couch moved, and then Karl's face was next to hers. Before she could turn her head away, she felt his lips next to her mouth and tasted beer. Squirming, she slid down the back of the couch to avoid his face, edging away from him, her hips inching off the couch as she tried to slip out from under him. "No," she said, and her voice came out sounding much heavier and fuller than she expected.

"Wait," he said, his fingers wrapping around her upper arm, brushing against the fabric of her shirt next to her bra.

She inhaled and then cringed as she felt her small breast rise next to his fingers. He moved his hand to the front of her shirt, cupping the air around her breast, the fabric itself.

"No," she said again, and this time her voice was a pale whisper, but at the end of it she could hear something strange. She closed her eyes in shame when she recognized a half-sob.

He sat up, pulling his hand and his face away from her. She tried to breathe without making a sound as she slid onto the floor and crawled away from the couch to the window. He leaned back against the couch, picking up his beer. "I bet you've never been kissed before."

She didn't say anything, but she stood up and walked toward the kitchen. She didn't want to leave the kids, but she would if she had to. She would position herself by the kitchen door, and if he came toward her, she would open it and run.

He looked at Iris standing in the doorway of the kitchen, and though she tried to look composed, he must have seen the panic on her face, because he gave out a hoot. "Sorrrrrrrr-rrrryy," he shook his head, "but you sure were giving off signals."

"No," she said.

"Yes," he nodded, his voice stern all at once. "Yeah, you *were*, babe." He looked at her, his gaze traveling over her, like his eyes had become his hands, wandering over her pink shirt and shorts. She felt chilled, but her back was soaked with sweat from the vinyl of the couch.

He shook his head in disgust. "Well, I'm heading off to bed, then." He finished his beer and set the bottle down on the table with a heavy clunk. He stood up and took a step toward Iris, rolling his eyes as she backed further into the kitchen. "You know how to work that thing?" He gestured toward the tape deck.

Iris nodded.

He turned around and headed for the back hallway. "Nice meeting you," he said.

After he left, Iris moved from the kitchen back into the carpeted living room, sinking onto the floor. Although her clothes were hot next to her body, the backs of her calves were cool and tingly. Across the room, the round, silver knobs on the eight-track player appeared luminous in the dark, suspended in the air, thin disks of silver coin that one might place in the eyes of the dead. The music drifted out of two large stereo speakers on either side of the couch, a screeching, mourning song. In the corner, the green Lazy Boy chair sat open, the leg rest suspended as if someone still reclined there, propping his feet up to rest after a long hard day at work. As Iris stared at the chair, she realized that it was not a solid green, that it contained swirls of black buried deep within the green; she felt desperate to trace the pattern of the swirls, to determine where they started and where they ended.

Next to the chair, a plant cast a shadow on the living room floor. Iris's stomach tensed as the shadow altered until she realized that in the back hallway, Karl was moving from his bedroom to the bathroom door. She sat in silence, watching the shadow, waiting for the light to fall on the dark gray shape again, altering the form. After ten minutes the shadow moved again, and she heard a slight click as Karl's bedroom door closed.

A cool breeze blew through a side window, but a bead of sweat still drifted down the back of her neck. She put her hand underneath her hair to wipe away the bit of moisture. On the wall in front of her, a large picture hung, a sailboat in the middle of the open sea, and Iris concentrated on the height of the mast, which stood out white and glowing in the midst of the dark landscape. She stood up and went to the window, opening it wider, even though her shoulders were chilled. Yet even as she opened the window, she felt a sudden urge to slam it shut, afraid of the darkness from outside, the sound of cars on the gravel road, creeping down the street in the middle of the night to who knew where for what purpose.

8
Beyond Midnight
June 15, 1974

Once at home and in bed, after the Langley parents had returned at three o'clock and driven Iris home, she forced her mind to the nights when Liz had come home late from work the previous summer, before Scott died. When she worked the late shift at Richland Dairy back then, Iris would stay awake until she arrived home just after midnight. Liz sauntered into the house with her red- and white-striped ice cream jacket thrown over her arm, and Iris would follow her to the bathroom and sit on the toilet seat while Liz soaked the jacket in Tide, pouring dish detergent on blotches of ice cream. When the jacket became covered with spots of ice cream by the end of a shift, the red-striped coat took on the hues of every flavor from orange sherbet to blue moon, two of their brother's favorites.

Iris never asked about what Liz did on her off hours away from home. Instead they talked about work. As Iris sat on the toilet seat, raising and lowering her legs in an exercise she'd seen on Jack Lelane as a child, Liz would scrub at the ice cream and tell Iris how many guys had winked at her and made sexually loaded suggestions, how many children had changed their minds about flavors after she'd already begun filling the cone, and how many dollars the cash register was over or short when she checked out. Packing ice cream was harder than you'd think, she would tell Iris. If the ice cream were soft, it was fine, though a bit messy, but sometimes when they'd just brought out a new gallon barrel from the back, the ice cream would be so hard and stiff that Liz would scrape her fingers on it. Liz would tell Iris all this while her hands moved through the water, which soothed her scraped and sore fingers as she worked with her garment, touching it softly as if it were a baby. After she treated all the stains she saw and rinsed out the soap, she'd pull the soaked coat out of the sink and the two of them would hold it over the bathtub, turning the ends in opposite directions and watching the water twist out as knots developed in the fabric from the wringing. They would laugh and play a mock tug of war until one of them nearly fell over in the small bathroom, and they shushed each other so they didn't wake anyone in the house. Iris had admired her sister so much then but had also felt like an equal. Liz valued her then, even if it was only to help squeeze the water out of her work clothes.

But now Liz was in bed, asleep, and it was Iris who came into the house late and filtered into their bedroom. As Iris tried to sleep, tossing and turning in her bed, she willed her sister to be awake and even contemplated sitting next to her bed on the floor. Maybe if Liz sensed her sister's presence, she would open her eyes, and Iris would speak in a quiet whisper, telling Liz everything that had taken place at the Langley's house, their two faces in shadow, save for a few thin rods of light from the moon which filtered in on the sides of the curtains. Yet Iris couldn't leave the bed in which she twisted the blankets and tugged on the sheets; she and her sister were nearly mortal enemies at this point, no trust between them. And without their younger brother alive to balance their contradictions and chaos, or serve as the third leg of their stool, Iris and Liz were frozen in their opposition. If Iris talked to Liz, would this second summer feel different, she wondered? She wanted Liz to listen quietly, staring at the ceiling as Iris talked and then, rolling on her side, to look Iris straight in the face and say, in a voice not heavy or tired, but maybe half-disappointed and a little bit outraged, "Oh, Iris, it shouldn't have been like that." She wanted Liz to reach her fingers out and touch Iris's hand, beckoning her closer and smoothing her hair like a mother would, pushing aside the covers to let Iris in, swaddling her so the shivering would stop.

9

Catalyst

June 16, 1974

On Sunday, when Iris called Rosemary late in the afternoon, she learned that Rosemary had gone out with her father somewhere. "Errands, I think. Try back later," Rosemary's mother said. And then she paused. "I hope you're having a good summer, Iris."

Iris didn't know what she would have said to Rosemary anyway. She felt too uncomfortable telling her what had happened with Karl, yet she wondered if Rosemary had met him yet, what kind of things he'd said to her, if he'd been to her house, had talked to her father tinkering on a rowboat in the side yard.

Iris wanted to be at the beach, to hear the quiet of the water and shake off the frightening feeling that remained from that Friday night. It had been almost a year since she'd allowed herself to have that yearning for the water, allowed herself to think maybe she could step foot into that beach park again. Rosemary wasn't around to go with her. Iris always thought the first time she walked in through the gate since Scott's death, she'd be with Rosemary.

She arrived at the beach as the last swimmers were leaving, a family of four, the lips of the children bluish-purple, their shoulders stiff and shivering under the towels they'd thrown over them.

The air was finally beginning to turn breezy after the hot day, and Iris didn't have a sweatshirt or sweater. She was glad she didn't have to use the new key her mom had purchased which she'd shoved in her pocket before leaving home. It was bad enough that she was entering the beach park; even being in that space felt like a betrayal to Scott.

She wasn't ready to sit on the swings, so she went away from the sand play area in front of the water and the swingset, instead choosing to go past the boat launch ramp and over to the willow tree on the corner of the property, to the vacant bench positioned next to the trunk of the tree. The willow's fronds had already grown out from their wintering state, each rope of greenery draping down to the ground, like the tree was a hand, and each long thin finger had reached for the earth to anchor it, creating a canopy under which a person could sit and enjoy the view, peaking between fronds. Iris watched the sun as it began to depart from the sky, patches of pink and orange slashed across the horizon, like swatches of sherbet on her sister's work jacket, until the color slowly sank into the lake, folded in, a garment subsumed in washtub water. Iris wanted to absorb the quiet, listen hard to the crickets, to see if she could count them by their songs, listen for the flap of a small fish jumping up and then splashing back into the lake. Forget for a moment the face of her brother. Forget, too, the smell of beer on Karl's breath, the slap of cards on the kitchen table, his hand on her shirt, next to her breast. Did she want him to touch her? Was that what she wouldn't let herself perceive, some buried desire for a touch, anyone's touch? Did she secretly forgive him for knowing that she

64

hadn't been kissed, that his lips, his mustache, would be the first to find the lips on her own face?

Every time her conscious mind drifted to thoughts of Scott or Karl, she made it swerve away, and thus she played a constant game of distraction.

Night had fallen. Iris knew she should head back. Her parents would wonder about her. She tired of playing the distraction game. She was ready to rise from the bench and climb up the hill when she heard voices from the road above, beyond the gate. She shrank back into the shadow provided near the trunk of the tree, watching above as a group of four figures approached the gate from further down Destan. The streetlight hadn't illuminated the street yet, but Iris heard Sherry's voice. "So, this is the beach," she said, as if she were giving her uncle a tour.

"Your mom has told me about it," he said. "And you two plan to come here every day, once your family buys a key?"

"Every day that it's not raining," Andy said.

"It's a great place for kids." The female's voice was so quiet that Iris almost couldn't hear it, but she looked up through the willow branches and recognized the relaxed stance as Rosemary's.

"And maybe you and Rosemary can bring us here some time," Sherry said.

Iris inhaled and sank to her knees behind the tree trunk, her hand touching a patch of rough, sun-dried grass. The four figures stood beyond the gate looking down at the water, their bodies clamped together in an array of shadowed heights. Iris watched as Rosemary reached up two hands, her fingers closing over open diamonds of chain link, resting there lightly at first, then gripping harder, raising herself off the ground to hang there, as if she might decide to scale the fence and enter. Karl put his arm around his niece and nephew and cocked his head to the side, his eyes on Rosemary, who created a light metallic bounce as she jumped back from the fence. Iris's heart beat faster, her knees aching, hands numb as they pressed against the willow trunk, until the figures stepped away from the beach entrance and turned back toward the direction from which they'd come. Iris sat down then, resting the side of her head against the tree. She knew immediately that Karl was a catalyst, that something from this night would trickle through the rest of Rosemary's life, and maybe even her own, but she didn't know how yet.

10

Mall Diplomacy

June 17, 1974

Iris and Sheldon were outside in the driveway, cleaning brushes and shaking out and folding drop cloths when Liz pulled up to the house. She sat in the car for a minute, and Sheldon and Iris exchanged a look. Iris didn't know what her father had told Sheldon about her relationship with Liz. That they couldn't be in the same room together? Her parents still made the two of them eat and wash and dry the dishes together, but beyond that, they maintained distance from one another, at least during the school year.

Liz got out and looked at the house as if she were assessing it, evaluating their work. Iris wanted to say, "We're painting the inside, not the outside," but she stayed quiet. Liz walked up the driveway, and as she approached Sheldon, her lips turned into a natural smile like the one Iris's mother wore for strangers, the one she seldom wore for Iris anymore, even to be polite.

"Howdy," Sheldon said. "Here to pick up my right-hand gal?"

"Our mom wants me to drive her to the store to get some shorts," Liz said.

"How about some pedal pushers?" Sheldon said. "Clam diggers? You know, all those things will one day come back in style."

Iris winced at the deadpan response on her sister's face, but Sheldon kept smiling, unfazed by Liz's lack of enthusiasm. "Well, we're done here. You can have her." He looked over at Iris and winked, and then he reached over and patted her on the shoulder. "Buy something psychedelic!" Even Liz laughed at the way he said the word. Sheldon held up a finger to motion "wait" and then pulled his wallet out of his back pocket, retrieving a ten and a twenty.

"You paid me on Friday," Iris said.

"I'm giving you this money in advance," Sheldon said. "I'm going to work you hard this week." Iris smiled a thank you, followed her sister down the driveway, and waved before climbing in the front seat.

In the car on the way to the mall, Iris studied her Liz's profile, the fine blonde hairs that contrasted with her growing tan. Iris opened her mouth several times to start a conversation, but nothing came out. They were on the shortcut path to the mall, driving past the new Wave Pool the township had created a few years earlier. Iris remembered making fun of it, talking about how lame it must be compared to being in a real lake, but she knew that Scott had secretly wished to go, just to see what it was like. A long line formed outside the door, and a young boy with his mother and sister brought up the rear, his face both rapturous and innocent. Iris had to look down; she was relieved when the light changed, and she and Liz had passed the pool entrance.

Finally, Iris said, "Are you paying attention to the news about the murders?" The minute the sentence was out, floating in the space between them, Iris knew that it was the wrong subject to bring up.

Liz looked over at her. "How can I not?" she said. "On Sundays, people come to the dairy to get their milk and their newspapers. We have stacks inside the door. *The Detroit News. The Free Press.* So even though I'm not at home most nights to see the news when mom and dad watch it, I hear people talking about it, and I've got to keep those damn papers stacked neatly inside the door so that no one trips on them."

"I'm sorry," Iris said. "I didn't realize it was your job to deal with newspapers." She could hear her father's voice in the "damn" Liz said. Her mother's, too.

"The door opens, the wind blows in, the edge of the papers lift, the circulars fly. It's supposed to be easy for the customers to grab them. You want to make sure they grab at least five things when they're visiting your store. And whether you're scooping ice cream behind the case or standing at the cash register where people are lining up with their milk and the newspaper, they're talking to the person standing in line next to them about how sad it is. It's a constant reminder."

They were nearing the mall, and Iris couldn't wait to get out of the car. She couldn't read her sister's voice, but she knew there was something else beyond Liz's frustrations with the job tasks, and she wanted to either shut her up or make her scream. Liz put on the blinker and turned into the mall, heading for their favorite spot by Montgomery Wards, and Iris couldn't help herself, she had to put something out for Liz to chew on. "Well, at least Scott is dead. He can't die again, so we don't have to worry about some child killer coming to get him." The worst thing was that Iris knew he really would keep dying for both of them. Over and over again.

The fountain in the center of the mall's main wing always drew Iris in with its swish and patter of water. She sat on one of the round concrete stools next to the large, marbled oval. The flecks of white in the black granite were like the pieces of coarse salt that covered the cinnamon pretzels the shop at the corner sold. Yet the surface was smooth to the touch, the edges of the pool's rim rounded to discourage people from sitting right next to the water; stools were provided instead. Since it was still early in the day, there weren't a lot of shoppers walking the gleaming floor tiles, and for the first time, Iris could really hear the quiet without her thoughts pecking and squawking like in Alfred Hitchcock's *The Birds*.

One of the last times she and Scott were at this mall together, he'd asked her about why the stream of water transformed itself from small droplets to continuous rivulets and back to droplets again. Together they marveled at the arcs created by the separate strands coming from the center. He'd had an appreciation for the way things worked, the movement of objects through time and space. Their father had always said he would be an engineer when he grew up. He made that comment with a kind of certainty and pride that Iris never heard in his voice when he talked about her or Liz. It was the guy thing. But Iris knew he loved her. Wasn't his getting her the job with Sheldon proof of that?

Or, perhaps he felt like he shared some of her guilt also. She'd fallen asleep, but he'd been away at work. Neither one of them had taken care of him. Yet Iris felt sure that she wanted to keep the fault to herself. It was hers to bear alone, she reminded herself as she stepped away from the fountain and went toward the stores to complete the errand her mother had assigned her. She was so ready to take responsibility for her mistakes, if only they would talk to her and admit their anger.

At three o'clock, Iris was back by the black-and-white marbled fountain pool with two bags in her hand, one from Marianne's and one from Hudson's. A cheap pair of shorts and an expensive one. One plain navy and one psychedelic. Iris willed herself to relax and hear each droplet as it fell. At the bottom of the pool lay the pennies that passersby threw, some coppery orange, others a dull brown.

Fifteen minutes later, Liz had still not shown up. Iris sighed, even though no one was around to hear her frustration. Liz was probably at the make-up counter at Hudson's, so Iris traipsed down the length of the mall and wandered around the display cases of Estee Lauder and White Shoulders, rows of Almay mascara wands, a strong scent of musk following her as she searched for Liz's pony-tailed head. On the way back to the fountain, she ducked into Marianne's, but although there were lots of teens crowding the aisles in the store now, Liz wasn't one of them.

Iris felt relief when she approached the fountain and saw Liz's slim body standing there, back straight, not slouchy like her own. But when Iris saw her face, she dreaded the ride home.

"Where have you been?" Liz's head was lowered, and her words formed a growl.

Iris was glad she hiss-yelled the question instead of shouting out loud. "I was here, right at three o'clock. I waited for almost twenty minutes on that stool over there, and when you didn't show up, I went to look for you."

"You couldn't have been here, because *I* was here," Liz said, each word clipped. "Right in this spot." She pointed her toe to illustrate, the sole of her sandal slapping the floor tile.

"I was over there," Iris said, pointing to the opposite side of the fountain. She tried to listen to the water to calm herself. "We didn't see each other," Iris offered.

Liz shook her head, and Iris looked away. A blind older woman moved through the mall with a long stick out in front of her, tapping on either side of her, the taps creating a pattern in opposition to the rhythm of the water in the fountain.

"What was I supposed to think?" Liz said, her voice now shrill. "What if someone had taken you?" She let out a long, wavering sigh.

Years later, Iris would understand what her sister was really trying to say. Liz wanted to blame Iris for the mix up, because she knew, deep down, that if something happened to Iris, she would be at fault. And that was the dilemma, because when something horrible happened, there needed to be a reason why, a person at fault. Circumstance didn't have a clear enough face, no eyes into which an accuser could stare. A single individual needed to bear the blame. Maybe it shouldn't be that way, but it was. And that individual wanted the inquisition, needed to be brutalized by the accusers, made to feel shame, so she didn't have to listen to the voice inside that spoke in a needling, insistent way. "Maybe if someone carted me away, you'd all feel like justice was done." Iris said. They were headed back to their car in the parking lot now.

"Oh, God," Liz said in disgust. But her taunt sounded faint because Iris had hurried ahead of her, striding through the lingerie department at Montgomery Wards, trying to keep the tears from sliding down her cheeks.

They drove home in silence, and Iris kept thinking about cause and effect. Years later, she could have told her sister that the clearest of dangers more often than not was benign; what was deadly was the inconsequential act. Or the omission.

Iris walked the path of regret that all failed protectors walked, avoiding and then finally knowing, never forgetting, that the blame for her brother's death lay with her. She wasn't there to save him, and then he was gone. Looking back, Iris could see without haze the two versions of herself those summers, integers on a number line. One who still had a brother, a girl who danced far off into the summer eve, hopeful, brave, splendid in her innocence. The other stepping heavily to the left, wandering, mired, and then, unexpectedly, at a precipice with only a plunge to anticipate. Iris needed to call to them from the wings, tell them to move to the center. To watch in awe as they negotiated the survivor's pas de deux. She needed to be able to decipher what they could learn if they moved together.

11

MIAs

June 18, 1974

Iris sat on the floor, a drawer next to her, pulled out from its position at the bottom of the bureau. She and Liz shared a large dresser, and their mother had asked her to please empty one of her drawers because her sister was a growing teenager who needed more space.

The room they shared was cramped now that they'd given up bunk beds. Scott's room sat unoccupied, but no one talked about getting rid of his things or moving Liz or Iris into that space.

The drawer Iris tackled was her junk drawer, which seemed easier than a clothes drawer.

Her mother called her a packrat and a squirrel because she hid random things in her deep bottom drawer. It wasn't that she was hiding them – she really did just squirrel them away, and she wasn't as effective a cleaner and organizer as her sister. There were a few of the older Jackson Five posters she'd cut out of the *Tiger Beat* magazines, which she'd replaced with newer photos. Random song lyrics and poems that she'd written on the special shopping list paper that their dad had purchased in rolls from the Whoopee Bowl. Letters from her old friend Laurie who had lived behind them on the non-lake side of Destan and moved away in elementary school. They'd reconnected by letter when they were in sixth grade and wrote to each other about the Mary Stewart books they both read.

And the whole package of POW-MIA material she'd sent away for a few years back.

When Iris had purchased one of the POW-MIA bracelets, they'd sent her a package of bumper stickers, flyers, and decals along with a letter explaining their goal of raising awareness about the plight of POW-MIAs and how they were part of the forgotten casualties of the Vietnam War. Rummaging through the bag of decals, stickers, and buttons, Iris knew she wouldn't be able to bring herself to throw the material away, but she felt guilt about not distributing it. When she'd originally gotten the packet in the mail, she had every intention of passing out the materials, but when she'd tried with a few neighbors, Noelle, and then the Youngs, she felt tongue-tied and confused. Liz was the only child in the Merchant family who'd done door-to-door sales. Texas Fruitcake for the high school band, for which Liz was the only female who played drums. She was so good with people – like their mother, she could make conversation easily. When Iris had tried those few neighbors, talking about captivity and disappearing off the face of the earth, she didn't know how to complete her sentences. She wasn't asking anyone to buy anything, was she?

Iris knew a few kids from school whose older brothers were drafted. And there were some second or third cousins, her mom said, whose families send pictures at Christmastime, their sons in uniform. The last draft was at the end of 1972, beginning of 1973, around the time she'd sent away for her bracelet.

Colonel Patrick M. Fallon. That was her MIA's name, with the date of July 4, 1969. That's what she knew about him – his name, rank, and the date he went missing.

It was only a few months or so after she got her bracelet that she lay on the beach – that summer before Scott died – and Rosemary told her about her own cousin.

"My mom heard that Vic is missing," Rosemary said, after they'd been at the beach for a while and had decided to switch from lying on their backs to lying on their fronts.

"Who is Vic?" Iris said

"My aunt's son. My mom's sister's son. My cousin."

Iris tried to think about people she'd seen at Rosemary's house over the last couple of years. They'd known each other all the way through elementary school, but they didn't really talk much until they'd started taking the long bus ride from elementary to junior high school. Iris remembered only a sister that visited Rosemary's house sometimes. "Missing from where?"

"He's a soldier. He's missing from war. Missing in Action."

"Oh, Rosemary," Iris said.

"I didn't even know he was in the war. He was a lot older than me. My aunt lives in another state, and I only saw them at family reunions. We used to see him a long time ago, but when he got older, we didn't see him so much."

"So how did you learn he was missing?"

"My mom and my aunt have been talking. I guess my aunt got a letter from the government, and then I guess his dad got one, too, and there's a girlfriend, so my aunt got a letter from the girlfriend. I'm just not sure what to think about it."

"I'm so sorry," Iris said.

"I need to learn more about it," Rosemary had said.

They had talked about it a few times, but then Rosemary said her mother and her aunt had gotten in an argument, so the aunt didn't talk to Rosemary's mother anymore. Then Scott died, and Iris felt like she and Rosemary had gotten further and further away from each other, like taffy pulled past its stretching point. They went through the school year in different wings of the junior high building, waving slightly in the hall on the way to the cafeteria, and then barely even lifting their hands anymore.

Cleaning the junk drawer was harder than Iris had thought it would be. She should have picked a clothes drawer after all. She packed the mailer back up with the flyers and bumper stickers and buttons. Opening the underwear drawer, she wedged the bag into the corner. She carted the other things from the junk drawer to the basement, to a spot on the rusty industrial steel shelves where she had a section of other things she wasn't ready to let go of yet, opened a big shoe box she'd left there and jammed the papers in.

When Liz got home from her shift at Richland Dairy, Iris said, "That drawer you wanted? It's empty now. Cleaned it out, dusted it, put some of mom's drawer liner in it."

Liz sank into a chair, unbuttoning the last two buttons of her ice cream jacket. "Thank you, Iris." She sounded just like their mom after they'd finished their chores, her voice infused with gratitude at the moment she noticed the scent of Windex, or the gleam of a chrome towel rack, but not quite as warm and gracious. She and Iris were wary of each other again after the mall visit.

Iris went outside in the backyard and sat next to the lilac bush that formed a partial border between their yard and the neighbor's. The lilacs were mostly gone, but she could still smell a tinge of their sweetness. She lowered herself onto the grass.

She'd worn the bracelet for so long that she barely noticed it anymore. She left it on when she did dishes and took baths. The letters of the name were engraved in the stainless steel. She'd never talked to Scott about the war. How was that possible? Maybe he'd never been around when their parents talked about it, or maybe she hadn't been paying attention back then. She suspected he'd been too young to have an opinion about it; she'd had an opinion about it only in the last year. Scott had tried her bracelet on once, just after she'd received it in the mail.

"Will you wear it for the rest of your life?" he asked, rubbing his finger over the engraving. She'd told him she didn't know, but as she ran her finger over the engraving, she realized that some things did get etched on your life just like letters on a bracelet, and you couldn't rub them out or wash them away. They were indelible, an imprint you couldn't escape.

12

Protecting the Innocent

June 19, 1974

The next evening, Iris's mother waited until they were at the dinner table, pushing their pork and beans from side to side on their plates. Iris could tell from the way she looked around at their faces expectantly, almost nervously, that she had something to share. Perhaps Liz had spoken with their mother about the mall issue, but when she looked over to Liz's face, it seemed passive, resigned, if not slightly bored. Iris suspected her mother had decided that they needed some normalcy in their routines – a return to the conversation, even the squabbling that had characterized mealtimes before Scott died.

"We had an incident at the center today," their mother said. She set her fork down next to her plate, leaning in to get their attention. "A crazy lady in the bathroom."

Their dad chewed slowly. "How did you know she was crazy?"

"This young mother who had been at one of the programs earlier with her two young kids came to me and asked where the bathroom was located. The kids really had to go – bad. But she was back at the desk five minutes later because when they went into the bathroom, this lady in a silver dress was standing in front of the mirror, yelling at herself. Waving her hands, jumping up and down. The younger woman said she thought the lady was angry, crazy angry, so she was going to drive the kids home to use the bathroom, but she wanted me to know."

"Did you see her?" Liz asked. Their dad was still chewing, a little faster now, louder, too. Iris tried to make her own lips quiet as she chewed, so she wouldn't interrupt the story.

"Rita told me to check it out, so I grabbed my purse and went in there, like I was just a regular patron using the bathroom, and there she was, in front of the mirror. She was yelling all right, but just as I walked in the door, she jumped, and her leg sprang out from underneath her dress at this funny angle before she landed."

"Were you afraid?" Iris asked.

Their mother paused and took a sip of her milk, slowly reaching her hand up to pat at her lips with a napkin. "Not at first, but she got so quiet, and as I sat in the stall, trying to really go to the bathroom, so she wouldn't be suspicious, I couldn't hear a sound. It was eerie. Then there was this burst of angry gibberish. *You shouldn't have done that. You shouldn't have done that.* I didn't know if she was talking to me. When I came out, she was just standing there, putting on eye makeup. She turned around and looked at me. She held this blue eye shadow wand in her hand. Then she turned back to the mirror."

Their mother sighed, picked up the glass lid to the baked beans, scooped some out, and clattered the lid back onto the top of the serving dish. "I felt bad. I hate to judge people, but what could we do? The building manager said to call the cops, so I did."

"And they took her away? Just like that?" their dad said. He put down his fork, his eyes squinting at his wife like he was trying to understand something.

"I mean, we saw them putting her in the squad car less than an hour later." She looked back at her husband, waiting for a response.

"But she didn't do anything," Iris's dad said.

"She was scaring people out of the bathroom." Their mother exhaled loudly, like she used to when they were kids and she'd have to explain something for the third time. "It would have been one thing if she were just mumbling, but she was agitated. She had that look in her eye."

"What look? The I'm-a-psychotic-killer-with-a-knife-in-my-purse-so-don't-cross-me-or-I'll-puncture-you look?" Their dad didn't grin when he said it. After he spoke, he took a huge bite of his hamburger. Liz almost smirked, but when Iris tried to catch her eye, she turned her head.

"This is serious," their mother said, her voice insistent. "This woman presented a clear danger to herself and others. And for God's sakes, the building is a community center. You can't have crazy people running around – there are kids in and out of there all day."

"Some little old lady wants to do the Hokey Pokey in front of the mirror, and she gets arrested." Their dad shook his head.

"She was middle-aged. And not senile, but crazy. We have a responsibility," Iris's mom said, her voice rising, almost incredulous. "And since when are you an advocate for the misunderstood? Jesus!" she said, sliding a look at Iris and Liz. Then she said more quietly, "Jesus, it was just something that happened."

"I thought you said it was serious," her husband said.

"Serious for me, and certainly for the woman. And I'm just trying to share with my family a moment from my usually humdrum day that was maybe a little more exciting with just a little something to talk about because, Lord knows, we don't have much to talk about."

Iris's father rose and picked up his plate, crumpling his napkin and dropping it in the center of the dish. Iris wanted him to leave the table. She wanted them all to leave the table, one by one, like everyone left the church on Maundy Thursday, silently, heads bowed, not saying a word to anyone else. Across the table from Iris, Liz stood up, the chair leg scraping the floor.

When Iris's father passed her mother, she reached out her hand and grabbed his freckled forearm, pleading with him. "I didn't want an evaluation or a judgment or approval of my actions and reactions; I just wanted to tell you something about my day. Is that so horrible?" She whispered. "Why can't we talk about anything?" Her brown eyes pleaded with him.

Iris thought she understood her mother's sadness and frustration at her father's analyzing the situation from the outside; she didn't understand why her father was so bent on making her mother the bad guy. At least she had reacted – watched the world, made an observation, and then did something. Iris wasn't sure the rest of them could. They felt numbed by the mistakes they'd made in the past and couldn't see the dangers they needed to guard against. Iris wanted to follow her father into his sawdust haven in the garage and tell him that he was wrong, that you had to be on guard, that her mother was right for keeping her eyes open. Iris wanted to flip the switch on her father's table saw, hold her hand above the blade, and yell to him over the whine of the spinning disc that she could just as easily die from a crazy lady in hiding in a public bathroom as she could from an accidental amputation.

Before Scott died, when the parents had a fight, Iris would go to Liz and they would talk about what their parents had said, sometimes examining each line. They probably came to all the wrong conclusions, but it was their way of putting things right again. The process somehow helped make things seem lighter. But now, Iris was afraid to go anywhere near her sister. And maybe even more afraid because even if she could, she didn't know how to make sense of the wobbly connection between her parents.

Liz cleared the rest of the table without speaking. Iris filled the sink with soap suds and was about to plunge her hands in when her mother touched her shoulder. "I'll wash," she said, her face weary. "Do something fun. An old project you'd like to finish? Or look through the recipe file – a new cookie?"

Iris grabbed her favorite cookie book and headed toward her room. She sat on her bed and flipped the pages. Rolled cookies. Drop cookies. Refrigerator cookies. It made no difference. Scott wasn't around to eat them, and she finally realized the biggest problem with dinner and food in general. None of them was hungry.

13

Extinction

June 20, 1974

The next day, Sheldon taught Iris to paint trim. He was fairly certain she was a natural, he said. She would probably just need to be a bit more meticulous. Up until that point, Iris had mostly been cleaning walls throughout the house, moving the stepladder around each room and climbing up and down. Setting up fans to speed the drying process if Sheldon wanted to tackle a room before the walls were dry. Iris had actually worked on trim a bit also, but in a limited way, mostly scraping it, or taping around it.

What Iris liked best about paint was not the smell, though there was something distinctly sweet and faintly hypnotic about it, but the way it looked, just after you took the lid off; thick and gluey; it was like a failed Jello pudding, failed in a marvelous way, not thickened but still creamy. It offered a clean slate. Sheldon said you didn't stir it like cake batter, fast and furious, but slowly, like you were dragging the paint stick through mud, feeling the resistance. He showed her all the colored paint sticks he'd collected for the house – avocado greens, corals, sandstones, purples, and buttercups.

"Since you paint the trim first, in some ways you can mess up as much as you want," Sheldon said. "You can always clean up the stray marks when you do the wall coat. But I try to view it as a challenge. If I can make the trim coat almost perfect, then I've got a head start."

He started Iris on a lower window, so she didn't have to deal with the ladder at first. "I have to confess: this green is not my favorite color," Iris said.

"Mine either," said Sheldon, "but I just think to myself – *Key Lime Pie*."

"I've never had Key Lime," Iris said. "My dad likes lemon meringue. Everyone else likes Dutch Apple. Except Scott. He likes...pumpkin," Iris said, and then more softly, "Liked."

Sheldon nodded, ignoring the correction. "One of my favorites, too. There's a diner a bit north of that other place I'm working on – owners are from Florida. In the summertime, Key Lime is one of their specials." He stepped down. "Missed a spot. Nice even coating, though." Iris made her brush glide back over the spot he'd pointed to.

"So, the diner is by the house where the widow keeps making you come back because she likes you?"

He rolled his eyes, and then grinned. "You weren't supposed to pay attention to that remark." He sighed. "Really, she's just lonely; I can't hold that against her, can I?"

"But if she makes you do extra work," Iris said. "Just to keep you there?"

Sheldon shook his head. "I put an end to that. Last week I told her I'd stop by with milk once a week. She likes buttermilk on Wednesdays."

Iris made a face.

"So, I get the buttermilk and a box of cookies, and it's the old folk's version of tea." He chuckled, took his hat off and wiped over his bristled head. "I think somehow – God knows how – I've made her realize that that's as far as it will go. Buttermilk and cookies, once a week. And of course, if the vandals spray-paint her garage door again, I'll re-do the deer mural."

"Do you ever get tired of painting deer?" Iris asked.

"For years I painted fruits and flowers and then portraits. Then I did all that experimental stuff – lines, geometric shapes. After all that, it's not so bad to paint a deer or a few chipmunks. So what if I'm not in the National Gallery? At least you can find me in your neighborhood."

He brought Iris a chair so she could stand up for the top of the window molding. "And now," he said, "my passion is fishing. Today we must wrap it up early, because I'm heading off to a fishing derby to throw my hat in the ring, so to speak." Tossing his painter's cap in the air, he bounced a bit from his knees, and then groaned. Iris loved to watch him do stuff like that. He looked so goofy, childish almost, like a bumbling waiter who couldn't get anyone's order right, and then, in the midst of the chaos, started juggling everyone's dinner rolls, just to get a laugh. It was something Scott would have done.

"So, I had a key made for you. I'll clean up with you today – that window trim looks terrific, Iris – and day after tomorrow, I just want you to come check on things. Don't paint or anything, just look things over. I'll be back in a couple of days. And maybe I'll be able to tell you that I won a prize. Salmon. I think that's what we're going for this time around. Salmon. Sometimes I don't even pay attention to what the derby is, and when I get there, I find out that my bait's all wrong. But that's fine; it's just for the sport."

He sat down on a rung of the stepladder, nodding his head approvingly as Iris poured only a small amount of turpentine in a coffee can and began swishing the brush around. "And really," he said, "what I want most is just to see a cisco, and there aren't many around anymore."

"Why not? And what's a cisco? A fish fried in Crisco?"

"Cute," he said. "You're really loosening up, starting to give me a taste of your lousy sense of humor." He winked. "Cisco is a fish that used to be plentiful here in Michigan – in Lake Huron and in Lake Michigan. But no one's seen one in Lake Huron in a while, and they're thinking maybe the fish is extinct. The lampreys ran 'em out."

"What does it look like?" Iris watched as the turpentine water turned to frothy lime. "And how do they make a decision about when something is extinct?"

"The blackfin cisco is the one I'm talking about – black fin, obviously, with silvery scales and a black stripe. As for the extinct part, I don't really know how that's decided. I think people just don't see a particular fish or animal for a while, and then one day someone scratches his head and says, 'When's the last time we saw one of those anyway?' And then the experts talk to the plain old fishing Joes and the plain old fishing Joes talk to the experts, and then they finally figure out that Ed Hawkins over there on the south side of Lake Michigan pulled one off his beach one day, in the spring of 1960." He exhaled. "You're such a nice girl to let an old man like me rattle on, Iris."

Iris tried to think of something funny to say or maybe an odd face to make. He always did the eyebrow scrunching thing when he tried to make her laugh. But she couldn't. She wanted to tell him that sometimes, when she listened to him ramble on, she lived in a different town, on a different street, but in this house, where she could spend her days hearing the tinkle of wind chimes in the lake breeze. She wanted to live anywhere but where she really lived, wanted to erase her past and make a new life with new surroundings.

Instead Iris gave him a weak smile, and he didn't say anything, just smiled a bit as well and said, in a teacher-like voice, "And what, then, do we do with our turpentine? Do we leave it in a coffee can? Put it in front of a window in the line of the noonday sun? Dump it in the lake?"

"We put it in the specially marked container Sheldon brings for sad old turpentine, and Sheldon carts it away to turpentine heaven," Iris said. "We would never leave it in front of the windows – not turpentine, brushes, or rags, because you just don't know when you might get spontaneous combustion."

"Bravo," he said. He let Iris tap the lid on the paint can with his rubber mallet. Then, after they'd checked all the rooms, he watched her as she locked the door with her new key. Climbing into the car, he offered a brief salute and said, "Wish me luck in the wild!" before he pulled out.

Iris sat on her bike for a long time after his station wagon rattled down the road. Then she put the kickstand down and walked around the side of the house toward the back. They'd be putting a deck in soon, Sheldon told her. Right off the kitchen. And then, whenever they wanted to, they could bring their coffee, their tea, their pink lemonade, their buttermilk out the sliding glass doors, sipping it slowly as they watched the lake, their wind chimes clanging in the breeze. Iris stood there and watched the waves play gently against the sand. Closing her eyes, she remembered herself at the beach, the sun on her eyelids making her drowsy. But then her body tensed up. She longed for the sort of ease she used to feel with the sun on her face and the sound of lapping waves lulling her to sleep or deep relaxation. But she felt like that lullaby from her past was something she would never hear or feel again, the rhythms and sounds lost forever.

14

Family Album

June 22-24, 1973 and June 21, 1974

With Sheldon travelling away for his official summer vacation, it was hard for Iris to avoid thinking about the previous year, when they had gone to Sleeping Bear Dunes near Traverse City just after school let out. It wouldn't be as hot as it would be in August, but their Dad liked getting a long summer weekend in shortly after Memorial Day. On the first leg of their journey to Sleeping Bear Dunes that summer they sang all of their favorite dish-drying songs: "Edelweiss," "Henry the VIII," and "Finnegan," until Scott put his hands up to his ears and complained to their mom that he was being tortured, and at the same time Liz remembered that she was a mature teenager who shouldn't exhibit too much zest for any one activity.

Their father wanted to travel along the water, so he told their mom they'd take I-75 to U.S. 10 all the way to Ludington and then catch the coast road. That meant they started early. After Ludington, they stopped frequently, buying smoked fish, cheese, and crackers at a small back door shop for lunch, eating them at the peeling picnic table they found at the next rest stop, their father swatting away the bees who came by the food, until their mother reminded him of Scott's allergy and told him not to make the bees angry.

Once in Glen Arbor, the three kids fought over the roll-away bed, of course, each of them assuming they'd prefer the lumps, the sinking, indented mattress, the feel of a metal bar underneath their backs to the cold, clammy limbs of their siblings, the sharp toenails, the arm flung into their face in the middle of the night. They could sleep in a double bed any old time: a rollaway was novelty. Scott won, which was predictable, if only because he was a boy, but Liz and Iris still did the groan, making the requisite comments about how he always got everything.

They hadn't called far enough in advance to get a motel on the lake, but the one their father had picked was within walking distance of Glen Lake, so when he said, "How about a moonlight stroll," they all agreed that that was the thing to do, donning their windbreakers and spilling out of the slatted and screened motel room door. Though the motel sign sported a neon "No Vacancy" indicator under its name, the evening was quiet around the small area of the motel grounds. The way to the lake was marked by a path next to the road wide enough for two to walk abreast. Scott and their mother went first, Scott picking up a short, thin tree limb from the grass and offering it to their mother as a walking stick. Liz followed, close enough that she could hang her head forward into their conversation, close enough that Scott could reach back and swat the air in front of her face to pay her back for whatever dumb comment she made. Their father and Iris brought up the rear. First her father asked how she'd enjoyed the ride up; then he fell quiet as they approached the lake and the path turned to gravel. Their feet made shushes and pings in the gravel, and an occasional stone flung itself up to hit the back of a tennis shoe. The lake was still, quieter even than their lake at home, much quieter than Lake Michigan, which they'd passed on their way into town and were returning to in the morning.

They woke up that first morning in Glen Arbor to reports of rain on the portable radio their father had brought along. Weighing the weather reports and their options, Iris's parents decided that they'd better skip the dunes for the morning, at least until the weather became clear. They would hang around the lake instead. Iris's mom sent her dad up the road to one of the markets they'd passed for a half gallon of milk and some kind of coffee cake confection. They still had apples from their trip up. It wasn't a gourmet breakfast, or even a healthy one, she said, but if they wanted to get any fun out of the day, they'd have to forego a restaurant experience.

An hour and a half later, they were all on the beach. Their dad had hauled down the lawn chairs, and their mom had called dibs on the best one, a recliner. She put her red plastic hat on her head, the one they made fun of because it looked like a driving bonnet from earlier decades with its gauzy flaps that she tied at her neck. Their father sat in his chair for a good forty-five minutes reading the local paper while Scott and Liz and Iris danced in the water. Scott kept going further and further out until their parents called him back. When Iris walked out, though, she understood the draw. Iris walked for yards and yards, but the depth of the water remained the same, up to her knees, so she kept walking, waiting for a drop. Gradually the water deepened, but like Scott, Iris was a long way from shore. When she came back in, she told her parents how the shallow water worked, but she didn't tell them how isolating it felt to be out there, so far from shore but only up to your knees, knowing that if the bottom did drop all of the sudden, you could fall practically to the other side of the world and they would never see you stumble and fall.

Another family from the motel had joined theirs at the beach, armed with an arsenal of shovels and pails. The father, like theirs, took a seat and began looking at the paper. But as his two sons and daughter began building a fortress, he squirmed noticeably in his chair, looking over the edge of his newspaper at their progress. Finally, he folded the paper and walked over to stand above them, bending down on one knee to point out how a mixture of wet and dry sand made for a better packed bucket. At first Iris admired the calm, careful way he showed the young boy how to load the pail. She remembered the first time her mother had taught her to make chocolate chip cookies, telling her how important it was to pack the brown sugar. But then the father began directing, suggesting, ordering, and directing even more until finally the kids were scurrying around, dumping bucketsful of sand wherever he pointed.

Their own father stood up then, looking at his offspring's rows of brown sugar, bucket-like pillars of sand. Walking around the structure – a dam and an underground tunnel, not a fortress – he knelt and admired their handiwork. With a look at the other family's castle, he said, "Maybe you could try..." and then paused, his voice trailing off. Their mother looked straight at him, shaking her head. "Maybe you could let me know if you want some help," their dad said.

"Sure," Scott said. "You can be water boy."

Thus, their own father became water boy, bringing them pail after pail of water, while the engineer across the way designed a better world of sand for his children. And even when pail after pail of water evaporated too quickly in the sand, their father kept bringing it, and finally, when the dam worked, even though they lost a few tunnels to collapsing bridges, he sat down on his heels and smiled a wordless smile at Scott and Iris.

The rain hit just after one o'clock. They felt the wind picking up on the shore, making their mother's red plastic hat, which was now untied, tumble off her head. Liz got sand in her eye and wince-blinked. Their mom said okay, okay, they needed to get back to the motel and make some lunch plans. The sky suddenly turned gray, then a dark and funny brownish-green, and their father, collapsing the lawn chairs, said they'd better scoot. The other father stood over his family's fortress as the first spatters of rain came down. He was a king, Iris thought, witnessing the downfall of his kingdom, watching as the rain made heavier imprints in the fortress walls.

The driving rain turned their lunch into another makeshift operation. Their dad crept down the road in the station wagon to the same hole-in-the-wall market and bought some cooked hot dogs and a block of cheese, which they ate with crackers. They spent the afternoon playing Euchre on the bed, Liz and Iris cross-legged, their parents pulling up motel chairs. At home, when they played Euchre, their father loved to fling his card on the table when he knew it would take the trick. Iris wondered if he was disappointed not to hear the slap that the card usually made when he peeled it out of his hand and flung it onto the table. The bedspread made no noise; the card fell, taking the trick without a sound. They tried to teach Scott, who'd never showed an interest before, but he was clueless, not able to understand how this thing called trump could change from game to game. "But I thought it was hearts," he said at one point.

And their mother just smiled and said, "It's a new game, Scott – Liz called suit this time and it's spades." Finally, he went over to his cot and grabbed a book out of his suitcase, and Iris knew he must have been desperate. She made a vow to herself that she'd try to teach him Euchre later in the summer. And next time he could play her hand.

They went to bed knowing the next morning would be iffy, the weather reports suggesting that the rain pattern could stick around another day or maybe clear out by noon. It would be their last day, their last chance to climb on the dunes. In the early hours of the morning, as rain spattered against the tin motel roof, Iris felt Liz's knees against her back. Both of them, unused to sleeping in a double bed, kept rolling over the imaginary center line they'd drawn, more as a joking reminder of how they'd shared vacation beds as kids than as an actual need to mark their sleeping territory. But still, her knees were a problem, and as Iris rolled from her side to her back, she felt a sharp stinging pain at the back of her leg. A warmth spread across her flesh, followed by a sharp pinprick sensation in her leg. As she lay there, the stinging sensation grew worse, and in a panic, Iris bolted upright and said what she suddenly realized must be true: "Spider, I've been bitten by a spider!"

The light next to her parents' bed clicked on and her mother raised her hands to her eyes to shield them from the light, her brown hair damp around her face from sleeping in the heat. "What?" she said.

"Something bit me. A spider," Iris said. And as she looked down at the sheets where she'd done a few frantic swipes with her hands, she saw the dark shadow of something crawling over the edge of the bed. She felt her voice rise again, "There," she said, pointing. By then, her father was up and stumbling over to the bed, pulling his glasses onto his face. Liz had sat up as well, though Scott was still a lump on the cot in the corner.

Their father stuck his head under the bed and peered around. "God, it's dirty under here," he said. "I don't see anything crawling, though." He motioned them out of the bed, and Liz and Iris got up and stood by the bathroom door.

"Are you sure you weren't dreaming?" Liz asked.

"Look," Iris said, pointing to the back of her thigh, where she felt a welt rising at the hemline of her pajama shirt.

"That's not your leg, that's your butt," Liz said, smirking. She looked closer. "But you're right. You're getting a little bump."

Their dad peered over the top of his glasses to look at Iris's injury. "It's definitely something," he said. "But I've been through the sheets and there's nothing there that I can find."

"So where are we supposed to sleep?" Liz asked.

"In the bed," her dad said, his voice deadpan, though Iris suspected he was enjoying the humor of the situation.

"But it's probably still in there," Liz insisted.

"I checked the sheets once, and I'll go over them again," their father said.

"But you could have missed it," Iris said.

"But I'm inspecting them again," their dad said, in his trying-to-be-patient voice.

Their mother sat up. "Forget arguing with them," she said. "We'll switch." She grabbed her pillow and housecoat. "You sleep in our bed; we'll sleep in yours."

Liz grabbed her pillow and went to their mother's side of the bed. "You can have the snoring side," she said, pointing to where their dad had been sleeping. Iris rolled her eyes, pulled her own pillow off the bed, and moved to the place their father had just vacated. Then she stopped, thinking of the spider still at large. She held the pillow up to the light, exploring the crevices for a dark, hairy body. Liz did the same thing with her pillow while their father leaned against the wall, his arms crossed, grinning faintly at their search.

Back in bed, Iris felt the welt at the back of her leg where her thigh met her butt. The site had grown and was now almost a nickel in size. When she pressed on it, she felt a sharp point. She rolled on her side. She could tell from Liz's faint, even breathing that she was once again asleep – she clearly hadn't suffered too much anxiety at the thought of a spindly-legged spider clenching its teeth or pincers or whatever they were called into Iris's flesh. Their mother coughed and a sleep sigh escaped from her mouth. In the corner, Scott's body was still a huddled mass on the cot. He had slept through all the commotion. A breeze came in through the small motel window, making the edge of the Venetian blind clank lightly against the window frame. Lying in the dark with the faint light from the motel sign glowing against the wall, Iris felt the shame of being the one who called out, the one whose cries in the night woke the world. There in the dark, she saw the value of keeping things to herself, however misguided that thought might have been.

The next morning, Liz and Iris were in the car's back seat, their hair still wet from their showers and the rain. The game plan was to eat a big breakfast at a local spot and then come back to pack up their stuff. Once they left the motel, they'd hope for a break in the rain so they could visit the Sleeping Bear Dunes. Their mother sighed and leaned her head forward, peering out the rain-drizzled windshield. "I wish they'd quit their lollygagging about." Occasionally, she pointed out to their father that the males in the family were the ones who kept the rest of them waiting. Their father once told Iris he hated to acknowledge her mother's point, but deep down, he knew he was a slow poke.

The motel door opened, and Scott came out, a windbreaker held high over his head. He took big leaping steps to the car, pretending to jump over non-existent mud puddles. When he got in the car, he flung himself in the back seat with a flourish. "Wait until you hear," he said.

Their dad opened his car door and got in quickly, attempting to keep the rain out.

Scott poked at Iris with his finger and their father gave their mother a wry look. "Guess what we found next to Scott's cot?" their father said.

"A big fat bee," Scott said, not wanting their dad to get the punch line.

"You're kidding." Their mother looked at their father, who nodded in confirmation.

"Here's your spider," Scott said, and he reached over Liz and dropped something down the back of Iris's shirt.

Iris felt the thing wriggling down her back but didn't know she was screeching until she heard Liz say, "Cut it out, Iris, you're killing my eardrum." She wanted to quiet down, but she knew she couldn't stop making noise while the hairy-bodied insect was next to her skin.

"Scott," their mother said sharply and glared at him. Iris pulled at the shirttails tucked into her shorts as Liz looked down the collar of her shirt.

"It's just a piece of paper," Scott crowed.

It took a second for his words to sink in, and then Iris stopped fumbling. "Paper?"

"Crumpled up," Scott said, "so it's nice and scratchy."

Liz took her fist and thumped him on the thigh.

"You jerk," Iris said. Then she reached over and thumped his thigh, also.

"Hey," their dad said.

"Hey, nothing," Iris said. "It wasn't funny. He wasn't even awake last night."

"But I heard your squealing in my dreams," Scott said. "A spider, a spider," he mimicked, making his voice into a shrill falsetto.

"Mom," Iris said, "make him stop."

"That's enough, Scott," their mother said.

"Asshole," Iris hissed at him.

In the front seat their parents, who had been trying to have an ongoing discussion about where to go for breakfast, fell suddenly quiet. "Iris Merchant," their mother said, speaking in that low, ominous way she had of talking when they were really in trouble.

"Liz swears all of the time," Iris said.

Liz looked at Iris indignantly. "I do not." Then she shrugged her shoulders. "Sometimes I get grounded," she offered.

"It is *not acceptable* to call your brother what you just called him," their mother said.

"My throat hurts," Iris said. She leaned her head back and tried to shrink her body so no part of it was touching Liz.

In the fuzz outside of her brain she could hear her father saying something about whether they should consider washing her mouth out with soap and then Scott groaning with disappointment when their mother said, "Oh, please." Iris's throat felt dry and scratchy, and she realized she'd had a dull ache at the back of her neck all morning.

"I don't feel well," Iris said quietly.

"Likely story," Scott said. Then he added, "Maybe *you* are allergic to bee stings."

"I don't feel well," Iris repeated. She knew her voice sounded whiny. She was tired and angry because she knew Liz swore at least two or maybe more times a week, but they gave her more latitude since she was a teenager. And mostly she just felt bad because her head hurt.

They pulled up in front of the restaurant, and their mother said to their father, "She does look a little peaked." Then she turned and said to Iris, "We'll talk about this later, Iris. Your brother was definitely antagonizing you, and I'm not going to pretend to be shocked by a little swear word." She turned to glare at Scott and then looked back at Iris. "But I do *not* want you to get in the habit of swearing whenever you feel like it, and I did *not* care for the venom I heard in your voice when you spoke to your brother."

Iris was silent.

"Iris?" her mother said, waiting for an acknowledgment.

"Yes, mother," Iris said finally. Scott smirked.

"Now, let's try to enjoy our breakfast," their mother said, turning her voice pleasant.

Iris tried not to say anything at breakfast to display her ongoing simmer, though she said, "Pass the butter, please," once because she wanted more butter on her hash browns. Amid the clang and clatter of the dishes in the restaurant, their dad talked about the last time he'd been to the dunes, and their mom reminded them of the Ojibway legend behind the Sleeping Bear Dunes.

"All of Michigan was actually Native American territory, not just Sleeping Bear Dunes. The land in our state once belonged to the Ojibwa, also known as the Cherokee, the Potawatomi, the Huron, the Menominee...."

"She could go on," their father said.

"There's a lot of powerful history there. Some rich legends," their mom said.

Once they made it to the main attraction, the place where most people walked on the dunes, they stayed in the car for a few minutes assessing their surroundings. Their father said it was hard to predict what the rain would do to their climbing efforts. "In some ways," he said, "it will be easier to dig your heels into wet sand than into dry, hot sand. But even so, stepping into the wet sand will take a toll on your calves."

"Are you sure you're up for this, Iris?" their mother said. Iris nodded. "Does your head still hurt?" their mother asked.

"Not as much as my throat."

"All right," she sighed. "Just let me or dad know if you can't make it."

The climb that brought all the tourists was only a small slope. Despite the weather, the parking lot was full of cars, with various groups of people scattered at the base of the hill preparing to climb. From the parking lot, the climbers looked like pegs in a Lite Brite set with windbreakers and raincoats of red, yellow, green, and blue. One block of yellow shirts appeared to belong to a youth camp group. As they approached the base, they could hear laughing groans from midway up the hill. "Oh, they're already killing me," a woman said, rubbing at her thighs.

Scott and their father got a running start, but Iris, Liz, and their mother took a more cautious approach. They'd climbed for only a few minutes when the clouds broke and Iris felt a blast of heat on the back of her neck, making her head swim. They climbed in silence, and though Iris tried to breathe quietly, a slight pant escaped from her mouth with each step she took.

Scott and their father were three quarters of the way up the hill. Scott turned around and waved, and then stuck out his tongue. A second later, as if deciding he should be a bit nicer, he put out his thumb pointing upward, to let Iris know he thought she was doing fine. Their mother had stopped a few paces ahead of her. "Phew," she said. "This is hard work. Are you okay, Iris?"

Iris nodded and tried not to chuff as she said "Yeah."

The last few yards were the hardest. And when the sun came out again, flirting as it went in and out of hiding, Iris felt like she was a bear cub, wet and tired, certain that she wouldn't make it. But a few steps later she was there, her throat aching, her head tense with pain, and Scott was crowing that he was the first one up, what were they, a bunch of old ladies? Iris didn't even care what he said as she hung her head between her knees, inhaling the damp, gritty sand.

But Liz, who had kept her pace slow and steady, was the one who asked for more. They'd done the tourist climb, but there was another one, their father said. A group of young guys climbing next to him had mentioned it, and they'd already headed that way. A downward slope ended at the water, and the challenge was climbing up after a long, freefall run to the bottom.

Liz was determined, and though their parents murmured about getting something to drink and resting their aching legs, Liz crossed her arms and said, "Oh, come on. I'll do it. You can watch."

The walk over the rolling path to the more challenging climb was hazy in Iris's mind. But she remembered the look on Liz's face a few minutes later as she threw her arms up in the air and let out a whoop while galloping down the hill – straight toward the group of boys their dad had mentioned. The rest of the family members parked themselves on the crest and watched Liz take her shoes off at the bottom and rest on the sand, her elbows propped on her knees. One guy with a baseball cap walked over and said something. Her lips spread in a smile. Then the three other guys came over, and you could tell that they were exchanging names and hometowns.

After fifteen minutes they started up the hill, and Iris watched as Liz strode quickly at first, then fell behind. But the guy with the cap dropped back, too, and when he reached out his hand and Iris saw Liz place her own in his, lifting her head and angling her neck in that flirty way, Iris felt cold and angry. Still, she watched as Liz laughed at the things the guy called back to her, the way he used the full weight of his body as an anchor to bring her forward. And when Liz made it to the top and introduced the guy to their parents, Iris couldn't look at her; she could only cast her eyes downward and turn away.

Then Iris felt a sharpness behind her eyes, and she couldn't stop herself from turning back and in a final fury, croaking at her sister, "What about Michael?" her throat aching as she said his name. Her mother reached her hand out as if to prevent Iris from saying more. She needn't have. When Iris turned away again, her tennis shoe slipped. She went down, sprawling in front of everyone. Her cheek felt wet grains of sand, and she heard her sister laugh.

That sand and that laugh had remained firmly lodged in Iris's memory about their summer vacation the previous year, a vacation they took just a few weeks before Scott's death. She tended to think about the humiliation she'd felt at the climb, the frustration of the middle-of-the-night insect bite, the searing pain in her throat, which turned out to be strep. The lousy weather. But as the anniversary of her brother's death approached, she kept seeing the other sand, not the grains that met her face when she slipped and fell while croaking at her sister, but the sand she'd shared with Scott while building in the sand, their thin hands dusted in part by soft, dry grains as well as the wet ones, clouds above them gray, not white, no bright light from the sun, but the hands, his hands and her hands, together in the pail. Or even Scott's hand, reaching down the back of her shirt with the scratchy paper, her pride ruined by the prank but his hand warm. Hands. Sand. She didn't think she could bear it.

15

Soothing

June 22, 1974

Liz came home in early evening after a long day at a special promotion for Richland Dairy. For much of the day, she'd been in the parking lot of the ice arena, which was owned by the same people who owned the dairy. Her face was bright red from the sun, but as she threw herself on the couch where their parents were sitting, two pillars on either end, it was her legs that she drew attention to. "Look" she said. "A thousand and one mosquito bites." She reached down and scratched one. "They're driving me crazy. You'd think those morons who arranged the promotion would bring a can of mosquito repellent or something," she said.

"Use your knuckles," their mother said. "If you use your nails, they could get infected."

"You can't work up a good scratch with your knuckles," Liz said.

"That's the point."

It was one of those times when Liz and Iris could ignore each other without their parents really catching on. Iris was in the dining room, doing a paint-by-number picture she'd resurrected from a shelf in the basement. She could hear everything they were saying in the next room, but she didn't have to contribute anything.

"Your father and I are going for a walk," their mother said. That was a euphemism for "Your father and I are going somewhere you won't hear us so we can argue." Iris and Liz had grown accustomed to it over the past year, so neither of them responded. "I'll make you a bowl of baking soda paste and leave it on the table."

"I hate that stuff," Liz said. "When it dries, the white stuff falls off like dandruff."

"Who's going to see?" their dad said. "You think your family can't live with a few flakes of baking soda on the floors?" He shook his head and went toward the bathroom.

Their mother clanked around in the kitchen for a few minutes, then brought a bowl to the table. "It's right here," she called into the other room. Then she grabbed her pack of cigarettes and went out the door, followed a few minutes later by their father.

The small bowl of white, wet powder looked like the finest, whitest sand plastered to the side of a bucket. In the other room, Liz's sigh was followed by the sound of more scratching.

Iris picked up the bowl, then, and walked quietly into the family room. The television was still on at a low volume, but Liz wasn't watching. Her head was back, her chin pointed toward the ceiling, eyes closed, legs stretched out in front of her, feet on the olive ottoman. In her lap she held one of the old, mismatched couch pillows, the one that Scott had adopted as his own, smashing it beneath his head every time he watched television. Iris stood there for what seemed like a long time, and then quietly sank to her knees. She picked up a spoonful of baking soda and dribbled it on Liz's shin where a group of bites had wealed up. Liz's body jumped at the feel of moisture against her skin, but she kept her eyes closed. And

Iris smoothed the paste on each bite, touching each welt with her finger.

16

Heroism

June 24, 1974

Iris didn't even need to talk to Rosemary about the night she had seen her with Karl. When Rosemary called a few days later and said the neighbor's cat was missing, would Iris help her search for it, her voice sounded so normal that the events from the weekend Iris babysat felt remote and gauzy, like they'd taken place behind some filmy curtain.

Iris hadn't remembered a cat at the Langley's house, so she figured it belonged to some other neighbor. When she arrived, however, she saw Sherry and Andy with Rosemary in her back yard. They waved, and Iris felt her heart start to thump louder in her chest; she wished she'd thought more about trying to help out Rosemary.

"Their uncle is down the road, talking with some other neighbors," Rosemary said. "I thought maybe you and Sherry could cover half of the block, and Andy and I will cover the other half with their uncle, Karl." She paused. "You've met him?"

Iris nodded wordlessly.

"Oh, that's right. You babysat that one night. Well, the cat isn't theirs – it belongs to someone from Karl's work. He's cat sitting, and he'll be in big trouble if he loses it."

Iris let Sherry take the lead. Though she was many years younger than Iris, she was much more social and friendly, and this was her street. She had a speech all prepared for each of the neighbors whose doors they knocked on. With her dark brown hair in curly pigtails high up on each side of her head, she appeared child-like and enthusiastic, but Iris suspected many of the neighbors might be learning about her precocious, organized side as well. "We're searching for a cat – could you help us? He's mostly black with a bit of white on his face and tail. Here's our number." Sherry handed each neighbor a slip of paper. "Would you mind if we looked in your back yard?" She gazed at whomever so sincerely, brown eyes wide with concern.

They'd visited ten houses when they stopped to take stock. An open field filled the space on the right side of the road – three vacant lots belonging to some out-of-state property owner. Thick with trees and brush, the land was a popular spot for winter exploring when the foliage thinned out, but it was a heavy mass of green in the summer.

"We should look in these woods," Sherry said.

"Poison ivy?" Iris questioned.

Sherry shook her head confidently. "I know poison ivy," she said. "Besides, there is a path we can follow." Iris wanted to resent her for being so steadfast and deliberate in her purpose, for feeling so comfortable in this neighborhood to which she'd recently moved, a neighborhood Iris had known her entire life. For having such a sense of grace. But Iris bent over and pulled her socks up as high as she could, motioning for Sherry to do the same. If Sherry could be the certain one, Iris could at least be the practical one. They found an opening and entered the woods.

Immediately, the air was warmer, closer, and Iris thought of movies she'd seen of tropical rainforests, macaws squawking overhead. "Tick-kulls," Sherry called in a high singsong voice.

"I though you told those people the cat's name was Tiger?"

"Tiger is his real name, but Tickles is what Uncle Karl and I call him."

"Does the cat know that?" Iris asked.

Sherry rolled her eyes and then poked Iris in the ribs with a finger. "Of course," she said, turning back toward the trees. "Tick-tock Tickles," she called.

"Tiger?" Iris called firmly, trying to ignore Sherry's look.

"Tickles, Tickles," Sherry called. Iris stepped on a fallen branch, and a loud crack filled the air. Then they heard a faint meow.

When they finally made it through the heavy brush to where the meows came from, it was clear that Tiger/Tickles was terrified, caught high up in the branches of a tree.

"We have to get help," Sherry said. She turned around and headed out of the thicket.

"That's a good idea," a voice said from behind them, and Karl emerged from another part of the woods, parting the branches of two thick bushes. Sherry stopped then, turning back.

"Go ask Rosemary and Andy if they can bring that ladder from the garage. Not the big one, the small one. I think I can reach the cat," Karl said.

"Wait," Iris said to Sherry. "I'll go with you." She looked up at Karl then, watched the same mouth she'd seen last in shadowed darkness, his lips curve into a reassuring smile. Iris's feet felt heavy, but she tried to move them as she said again to Sherry, "Wait."

"Why don't you stay?" Karl said, as he motioned his niece on with his hand. "I bet you could sweet talk this little cat down. I'm not much good at that kind of thing. Go ahead," he said to Sherry, who looked back at Iris with her open, curious face. "Go ahead."

And then Iris could hear Sherry crashing through the brush, not paying attention to poison ivy now, just eager to save the cat. The opening where they stood was small – if Iris reached her arm out and leaned forward, she could easily touch Karl's face.

"Stupid cat," he said softly.

"He's afraid," Iris said.

Karl took a deep breath. "I suppose."

Iris looked at the ground, trying to think of some way she could escape, knowing he wouldn't do anything – he'd walked away when she babysat, hadn't he? For several minutes they were both quiet, breathing evenly in the enclosed heat.

"So, you and Rosemary are close?" he asked. He took a step back and folded his arms.

Iris felt braver. "Yes," she said. "Pretty close."

The cat meowed, a small bleating. "It's okay," Iris said softly, her voice wavering.

"Like you tell each other everything?" he said. Iris knew what he was getting at, but she ignored him, instead moving closer to the tree, until she could almost feel the cold, damp bark.

"It's okay," Iris said again to the kitten, this time stronger. Then she turned around and looked at Karl. "Yes," she lied. "I tell her every little thing."

He stepped forward then, grabbing a branch of the tree and giving it a little shake. The cat's meow became loud and insistent as it made clawing noises against the tree. Iris put her hand up to steady the branch.

"Don't," he said and shook it again.

"The cat's afraid. Leave him alone."

In the distance, they could hear voices, the sound of a large object smashing into brush, some giggles from the kids. "We're almost there," Iris could hear Sherry say.

"Finally." The sound of Rosemary's breathing came from a distance, loud and a little labored; Iris guessed that she carried most of the weight of the ladder.

Iris looked at Karl, straight in his dark brown eyes so much like Sherry's, wanting to hold his stare until he backed down, like she used to do with Scott for their staredowns, but knowing she wasn't strong enough with this stranger who made her so uncomfortable.

"Don't tell her," he said, shaking the branch again, smiling when the cat meowed louder.

"Tell her what?" Iris replied quickly.

Then the crew arrived in the small clearing, and Rosemary helped Karl figure out the logistics of setting up the ladder, holding it carefully for him as he climbed up, his voice a soft wheedle as he repeated the cat's names over and over again, a seductive lament that keened through Iris's ears. By the time they got back to Rosemary's house, Karl was the hero, and even Rosemary's mom came out to congratulate him, watching as her daughter doused cotton balls in hydrogen peroxide and dabbed them up his arm, cleaning the scratches that the bushes had made. Rosemary bent her head over his arm as if it were a loaf of bread she was tenderly kneading, and Iris watched as Karl's glance lingered at the hollow of Rosemary's skin near the top of her shirt.

Iris stood up and muttered, "I have to go." She nodded at Rosemary and tried to ignore her funny look as she turned to trudge down the street.

17

The Power of Staredowns

June 25, 1974

To distract herself from the awkward cat rescue, Iris cleaned the bathroom. It had almost been a week, anyway. As she scrubbed at the blue sink, she wondered what Scott would think of Karl, if he would find him intimidating. She wanted to believe that Scott would be unimpressed; instead of feeling some odd mixture of fear and powerlessness when Karl tried to lock eyes, Scott would just be determined to outlast any power games. He would focus his brilliant blue eyes on Karl's, and Karl would become like Iris herself – tongue-tied and unsure. The staredowns with Scott were what Iris missed and remembered most. She and Scott started the routine maybe when Scott was eight, a young child, without guile, but still playful and charming. They'd seen it on some television show, and Iris explained how some of her friends did it in school. You made a challenge, and you tried to lock gazes with the other person and hold that stare until someone looked away or laughed. Blinking was allowed; it was about the composure. If you couldn't concentrate well enough, or if you thought too much about what you were trying to do, you inevitably burst into laughter.

Whether it was a power play or a fun diversion, what nobody told you, Iris often thought, was how much you could lose yourself in someone's eyes. That was the way to win. You took yourself out of the moment and put yourself right into that gaze.

Looking into Karl's eyes in the woods had frightened her, almost made her angry, but now she just felt sad about not looking into her brother's eyes again. Her family needed him. They needed his humor, the strange things he would do or say that would make their parents sigh and then laugh uproariously when he was out of earshot.

In that spring before he died, Scott was apprehended for playing strip poker with four neighborhood girls. Apprehended not by the authorities, but by the parents of one of the girls, who'd reportedly overheard some timbre of burgeoning sensuality in the tittering and giggling of the children playing in the backyard playhouse. Scott was the only boy involved, which made him, in his parents' eyes, rather vulnerable to various sordid charges.

Shortly before dinner one evening their mom got a call. Iris and Liz could tell from her clipped "Uh-huh's" and the way she sighed and kept glaring around the room that someone was in trouble. Scott was oblivious to the impending danger. When their father arrived home a few minutes later, Iris tried to send him a guarded signal.

Scott chomped his way through dinner without realizing that he was the target of the cold freeze their mom had started. Iris and Liz knew they were off the hook when she started smiling at them and offering them extra helpings, while glaring at Scott's bent head. After dinner, Scott was summoned to the living room and Iris and Liz were told to make themselves scarce, a command which they ignored, dallying in the kitchen in order to overhear the conversation.

Their mom started out by saying that kids did all kinds of stupid things when they were growing up, but some things were more dangerous than others. It took her only ten sentences or so to work herself up to a higher, louder pitch, which ended with her nearly shouting at him, "And how could you be so foolish as to play strip poker with four girls who will probably be going through puberty any day now?" In the hallway, Iris and Liz exchanged glances. Iris thought Scott probably sat buried in the deep avocado armchair, pushing the backs of his thighs against the fabric of the cushion and squirming every few minutes. There was a silence as their mother waited for him to explain himself. Their father cleared his throat.

"Scott, what your mother is trying to say is that you've shown a real lack of judgment here and could have gotten yourself into serious trouble. What if one of those girls had taken all of her clothes off?" Apparently, the facts of the case were clear: no significant clothing had been removed. "What if one of them had claimed that you touched her?" He cleared his throat again. "Touched her inappropriately?"

Iris and Liz strained to hear Scott's mumbling.

Their parents were also straining. "What?" their father said. "We can't hear you."

More mumbling came from the other room.

"What do you mean 'dresses and jewelry?'" their mother said.

"I said we put on extra clothes," Scott said, his voice now loud and irritated. "Carol had some of her mom's and her grandma's

121

old clothes and some busted up jewelry. We put that on over our clothes, and then we played strip poker."

Iris pictured Scott in the dust of Carol Wenger's playhouse attic, swathed in an old shirtdress, maybe a peach print, with a tasseled belt. Around his neck hung a large string of orange beads, which he occasionally picked up and put in his mouth, rubbing his tongue along the surface until one of the girls looked up at him and winced, saying "Gross." From time to time, he would reach up and tug on the large orange button-like earrings clipped to his ear lobes.

"Oh," their mother said. "I see." The silence intensified in the room around the corner from where she and Liz hovered.

"Dresses, Scott? Really?" their father said.

"Come on, Dad," Scott said. "Just dresses and jewelry."

"Well, don't do it again," their father said. He sounded distracted, and Iris and Liz looked at each other as their mother's voice, now with a hint of laughter, repeated their father's words.

"Yes, don't do it again," she said. Iris and Liz grimaced, knowing he was getting off easy because he'd caught them off guard. Their parents were all worried about the dressing up thing now, sidetracked. It was clear he was going to escape without any real punishment.

Two minutes later he sauntered out of the living room and into the kitchen, heading for the cookie jar. His face was triumphant, and he came back to stand in front of them, waving his cookie and his grin – wide-set blue eyes, a rash of freckles on his nose, a sharp chin.

"You bum," Liz said. "I would have been grounded for at least a week." She looked over at Iris and suddenly her eyebrows lifted. Iris could see her edging closer to Scott. "I think we need to help you out," Liz said. She spoke slowly, enunciating each word.

"Now that you've discovered fashion, you need to be introduced to a *new* world." She motioned to Iris to grab his arm. "The world of make-up!" she hissed.

They dragged him to the bathroom, where Liz kept a little basket full of cosmetics. He was a strong kid, but together Liz and Iris were stronger, and they'd caught him off balance. As they half-yanked him through the hallway, he kicked in a desperate attempt to escape.

Once they'd closed the toilet seat and thrown him on it, Liz twisted back toward the counter and grabbed some peach blush. "Let's see," she said, "this looks like a good color for your complexion." While Iris held his arms, she brushed it on his face, which he was twisting from side to side. "We'll pass on the mascara." She winked at Iris.

Their mother called out from the living room. "What's all the racket in there?"

"Nothing!" Iris yelled. She thought her brother might yell out to their mother for help, but Scott was silent, focusing all his efforts on escaping her grasp.

Liz stepped back and shook her head. "I wish I had some orange lipstick, Scott. You'd look terrific in orange." She grabbed a tube off the counter. "You'll just have to settle for pink!"

Some of it found its way to his lips, but most of it landed around his mouth in an uneven band of color to make him look like a young version of Caesar Romero's Joker on *Batman*. Within seconds he'd worked himself free and flew out the open door, scooting past their mother in the hallway, who'd come to investigate, knowing that *nothing* meant *something*.

"What gives?" their mother said, looking at Liz and Iris carefully, examining their flushed faces and labored breathing. "Was that make-up on his face?"

"Yeah," Liz said flippantly. "He wanted to complete his *ensemble*. She dragged out the last word. Then she glared into their mother's eyes. "For the next time he plays strip poker."

Their mother was about to say something. She put her hand on Liz's shoulder and her lips parted, but Liz kept staring her down and said defiantly, "Well, *you* weren't going to punish him, so we did it for you." She shrugged out from under their mother's hand and stalked away.

The tenor of things had changed, and Iris realized then that Liz had been really angry. For her, it was more than just a forceful prank, and Iris had unknowingly been a party to the exercise of her anger. And their mother didn't push it. She just let it rest, not saying a word as she helped Iris wipe some pink smears off the counter next to the bathroom sink. Part of Iris still felt indignant on Liz's behalf, but most of her felt bad for what they'd done to Scott.

He came into the family room a half hour later, his hair still wet from where he'd scrubbed his face. When he came around the corner, he gave Iris a blank look, and it seemed certain that he was going to ignore her, make her suffer for her actions. But when he kept looking, Iris knew he was about to engage her in a staredown. The blue in his eyes turned darker and deeper, and he kept looking straight through her, focusing so hard that she knew her mouth would quiver soon, and she would laugh. His face was so straight, his eyebrows so fierce that for a moment she felt another strong tug of guilt, ashamed that she'd helped to smear his face with pink and orange. The specks in his eyes seemed unforgiving. It was probably only twenty seconds or so that they locked gazes. Iris was ready to look down when his face fell into a grin, his eyes filling with light. "You guys," he said, shaking his head. He snapped Iris with the wet towel he'd been holding behind him, and she was nearly over-joyed to experience the sting of the soggy terrycloth.

Iris missed her brother's good-natured intensity and the ways in which he could be braver than his age, comfortable in his naïve fearlessness. If he'd been there, in the woods with her, he would have scrambled up the tree to get the cat, laughing at Karl and his attempt to be menacing. As Iris stared into the toilet bowl with it's blue on blue – squirt of blue cleaner on the blue porcelain, she tried to summon energy from those moments she'd spent mesmer-ized in the blue of her brother's eyes. "Help me figure this out," she said to the toilet bowl. She grabbed a brush and began scrub-bing around the rim, swishing the water and the bubbles from side to side.

18

"I Want You Back"

June 26, 1974

Iris spent the morning painting in the humidity at the Lake House on Destan. According to her parents, the day would be sticky hot, and when she arrived, Sheldon told her that they'd work for a couple of hours and then set up some fans, because the paint would take longer to dry. She wore her old jean shorts and a stretched-out tank top, hoping to stay cool, especially in the second-floor rooms.

When Sheldon told Iris she could leave for the day, she loaded up her stuff and headed toward Cate's Corner to buy a snack. As Iris travelled down Wertz, she felt in her pocket for the matches she'd stuffed there earlier in the week, when she'd burned the paper garbage in the back yard with her father. She saw Rosemary's father in the side yard, by his boat, and she waved as she turned left on to Rutherford and pedaled up the next hill.

At the store, Mrs. Cate smiled as she entered. Iris walked briskly down the aisles, grabbing the ingredients she needed and then moving to the door's single checkout lane right in front of the store's entrance and exit. She placed her items on the conveyor belt.

"Cookout tonight?" Mrs. Cate asked. Iris smiled a noncommittal answer.

When she left the store, the bag of merchandise loaded into her basket, she followed the path on the side of Williams Lake Road that she usually travelled, whether on bike or foot, but just before the curve where Williams Lake Road veered left, just past the marshy culvert, she looked both ways for cars and cycled quickly across the road to the opposite side of Williams Lake. The shoulder straightened out with the road, and Iris could see that she wouldn't have to ride too much further before reaching the street that led to the New Subdivision.

Once at the New Subdivision House, she grabbed her bag with snacks and the transistor radio and went inside. She wandered about the main floor, gathering small boards and furring strips, the half-ripped wrappers from the sheets of paneling. She tiptoed down the stairs into the basement wearing the flip flops she'd changed into, watching for nails.

After she'd carried the bits of wood and paper down to the basement, she created a pile in the middle of the sand floor. A small casement window opening was framed in on the upper right wall. That opening and the absence of a window or screen would allow for ventilation but likely would not be seen from the road.

Iris knew if she waited for spontaneous combustion, she'd be waiting forever. Her fire was a modest one, by most standards. The paper burned too quickly, and the small brick-sized segments of 2 x 4 refused to burn. But the flames stayed small and intense for about fifteen minutes, long enough for her to sharpen the point of a thin, long tree branch she'd found on her journey from the store. At one point, she looked around and realized that a pocket of smoke had formed in the room like a barely perceptible fog. She hurriedly grabbed a couple of marshmallows and forced them onto the end of the stick, close to each other, with no room in between, the way Scott liked them.

She needed to monitor the density of the smoke, wave it toward one of the other window openings in the basement. She ripped open the graham cracker box and the wax paper that surrounded one of the packages. Pulling the Hershey's Bar out of the bag from the store, she placed a cracker square on the box and layered a few rectangles of chocolate on top of the square. Then she poked her marshmallow-tipped stick into the hot part of the flame. "I'm going to burn these marshmallows to a crisp, just how you like them, Scott," she said.

With the other hand, she turned the transistor radio on, propping it nearby in the sand. Strains from Stevie Wonder's "You Are The Sunshine of My Life" entered the basement in upbeat melodic tones. In the old summer days, Scott's lower face would wear at least a mouthful of graham cracker, melted chocolate, and marshmallow, a food smear he seemed not to register. Iris wanted to eat this s'more sandwich for Scott, maybe even smear it on her own face.

She pulled the marshmallows out of the flame, their white cylinder shapes glowing with the glaze of red, yellow, and blue fire that surrounded them. Iris blew out the flames, looked at the charred marshmallows and laughed. She eased them on to the waiting crackers and chocolate and then layered crackers on top, pushing down gently on the cracker surface so that the marshmallow would flatten and melt the chocolate a bit. She threw the stick off to the side.

She would let the crackers sit while she smothered the fire with the cool, sandy earth from the basement floor around her.

After Iris extinguished the fire, she sat down to nibble at the ends of the sandwich she'd made, knowing the marshmallow goo would cool quickly. When she bit into the layers, the bottom cracker broke in half, and she almost lost the middle, but the cracker half hung in the air, stuck to the marshmallow and chocolate. She kept her hands closed carefully around the melded debris, laughing at the bits of cracker that fell out of her mouth as she tried to chew the three substances at once.

The disc jockey on the radio had finished announcing the last group of songs, and the strains of the first song in the next set started to sound with a downward trill and the rhythm of a base guitar. It was the Jackson Five, and Iris stuffed the rest of the cracker in her mouth and rose to her feet. She wanted to dance. When she heard Michael Jackson's voice, she thought of Scott, teasing her about the posters from a teen magazine taped on her side of the wall in the bedroom she shared with Liz. They were the same age, she and Michael Jackson, and he sang and danced with a joy and lack of inhibition that Iris envied. She reminded herself that she was alone and unobserved in the basement, so she began moving her arms, waving them in patterns around her head, pushing at the air with her two hands to the front and the sides and then flinging her relaxed fingers around in patterns and echoes, her hips moving side to side while her feet stayed put. She closed her eyes and tilted her head from side to side, imagining Michael and his brothers moving in unison on the stage on *American Bandstand* or *Soul Train*. At the end of the song as she chewed through the last bits of the s'more cracker, she tried a twirl, and she made it halfway around a circle when her flip flop shot out from underneath her foot and flew toward the transistor radio. She fell down in a heap on the sand, tired and happy.

19

Fresh Paint

June 29, 1974

A closed door in Iris's household used to mean that someone needed privacy. Someone was changing clothes, taking a nap, or, in the worst of possible scenarios with respect to the bathroom door, having a gut-wrenching bout of diarrhea. But as Iris stared at the swirls in the wood of her parents' bedroom door, the darkened whorls in the center of the stained wood, she knew a closed door had come to mean that an argument was in session. Before Scott died, her parents had displayed freely their discord, like her dad's diamond-patterned boxer shorts waving in the breeze on a summer's day. Not that the parents staged any arguments for the benefit of their offspring, but the offspring often heard the beginnings or the endings, and sometimes, if they were trapped in the car, the painful middles.

Now the parents seemed to feel that because of the family loss, their living offspring couldn't digest any more discomfort or sorrow, so rather than acknowledge their struggles openly, they retreated to the bedroom, trying to keep their voices low. Which meant that Iris learned now, in a way she never had before, the patterns on the door, the dark spots becoming bruises in the wood.

Their bedroom doors were shiny, orangish-brown ones, lustrous, but hollowed out. As Iris tried to decipher and then, contrarily, to block out the rising and falling of her parents' voices, she felt that she stood in front of a tremendous tree, and some cross between a wise, talking owl and a diligent woodpecker would soon poke its head out of the knot and tell her the lay of the land inside. Was peace in sight? Would a truce be declared?

Vacation was what they argued about now. Their mother argued no, even though Iris knew that she had asked and received time off from the library; their father argued why not. "It will do them good," he said insistently. "It will do us all some good – we need to get away."

"You don't understand." Iris's mother's voice came in a hiss. "Everywhere I go, I see him." The words sounded sharp but then wobbled into a near sob. Iris wanted to tell her that she saw Scott everywhere, too.

"And what's wrong with that – don't you want to remember him?" It was almost a taunt, like he was choosing to be cruel.

"Of course I do." Her mother's voice pleaded. "But I get exhausted from remembering."

"So, we skip the Great Lakes. We go to Ohio, or Pennsylvania."

"I can't leave," their mother said.

"You aren't being rational. You can't leave, you can't stay."

"I *can* stay. In this house. But I don't want to go traipsing all around Michigan like we did last year, think about him here and then not here, just like that. Because it was just like that." She paused, and Iris heard her take a breath. What came next was quiet, almost a whisper. "He was here, just last year, here, standing in the doorway, grabbing a towel before his bath. Every time I think about that it just kills me. I can see his hand, reaching for a towel, the fingernails, for God's sakes. I can see his fingernails even." For a few minutes there was silence in the room, and then her mother's voice grew louder. "I'll do that family reunion of yours in August. It'll probably kill me, everyone with their *How are you holding up, really?* I'll do it for you and the girls; you need to just appreciate that. Because I won't go anywhere else."

Iris hoped they embraced, hoped her mother buried her face in her father's neck, the wetness from her eyes collecting on a few small hairs of stubble that the afternoon had grown on his jaw. But she knew that he probably turned away, lowering himself to sit on the bed, shaking his head at her mother's obstinacy.

"It would do you so much good," he murmured, and Iris tried to determine if he said the words in disgust or guarded empathy. But she couldn't feel his mood through the door, his voice impenetrable, and as she heard her mother's footsteps creak on the floor, she moved away from the whorls, the woodpecker-owl who'd told her nothing that she didn't already know.

* * *

Iris needed to escape. She grabbed a few dollars from her money stash and opened the garage to retrieve her bike. When she headed out the driveway, she thought she'd ride to Cate's Corner to buy some Pixy Sticks and Neccos. But at the last minute, she decided to make a stop at the Lake House. Sheldon was still away at his fishing derby. She used the key to let herself in the back door. After being closed up for a few days, the rooms smelled heavy with paint. Iris walked through the main floor, the living room with its large picture window overlooking the lake, the kitchen, the dining room, and the den.

It was a house Iris's mother could love, here in her own neighborhood, but it was above the family's means – much larger than their own house AND sitting on a lakefront lot. Yet Iris knew that once she and Sheldon were finished, the homeowners who'd requested the paint job could sit and look out at the lake every day, watch the waves thrash and dance, watch the swimmers and water skiers bob.

Iris moved up to the second floor room she and Sheldon had been working on, the paint can, paint trays, rollers all neatly lined up. Picking up one of the unused rollers, she held it aloft, then pressed it against the wall, listening to the squeak it made as it went up and down. She hadn't done walls yet. Sheldon said most people thought trim was harder but putting just the right amount of paint on a roller was an art as well.

She had washed the walls a week or so previously and knew they were ready for paint. She looked around for the big screwdriver Sheldon used to pry open paint cans. She found it and the rubber mallet they used to tap the screwdriver head. She was nervous about taking the next step, but she felt drawn to the wall that sat waiting in the quiet of the unoccupied house.

Once she got the lid open, she moved it carefully into a corner, setting it on some newspaper she'd spread out. The green paint on the underside of the lid looked glossy, even though she knew it was a flat paint. It was flat, but it was also wet. She poured a small bit of paint into one of the aluminum roller trays just as she'd seen Sheldon do. Not too much. Better to add more later if necessary.

Taking one of the new rollers out of its plastic wrapping, she set it lightly into the roller tray and watched as a warm avocado green color spread across the aluminum tin of the pan, covering the roller with paint. So vibrant. Wet and silky, the sponge of the roller soaking up paint until the roller itself looked soft, with the textured look of a lamb's fleece. The color would cut a distinct swath over the old beige paint. Like a child with a Styrofoam flyer, Iris dive-bombed the wall, making first a huge "X." Tic-tac-toe. Then a figure eight, the roller squeaking as she turned the curves on the eights. More loops and vees. An "S" for Scott. For ten minutes, Iris allowed herself to create random roller strokes on the wall, feeling a sense of relief each time she dipped the roller back into the pan, rolling it into the narrow pool of paint that gathered at the top of the pan, where a little trough for the paint formed.

A creak sounded from the main floor, and Iris lifted the roller from the wall's surface, holding it aloft. Listening. Her hand dropped from the wall.

"Iris?" Sheldon's voice yelled up the stairs. "Is that you?"

She panicked. In the back of her head, she'd assumed whatever marks she made could be painted over, but she didn't have time for that now. She'd have to explain herself.

"Yes?" she called down. Then she moved from the bedroom to the landing, gripping the roller in her right hand. Sheldon stood at the bottom of the stairs, his face redder than it had been the last time she had seen him.

"You're back," Iris said.

"One day early, due to my wonderful sunburn."

"Looks painful," Iris said.

"The first night was horrible," he shook his head. A deep crease, almost maroon in color, split his forehead in half, and Iris wondered how the sun would have fallen on his face to make the crease. She knew she was avoiding the next few moments, the explanation she needed to create for what she'd done upstairs.

"But what I have for my pain – you can see it if you want, down in the truck, in my cooler – is fish." He grinned, rose up on the balls of his feet with exuberance, and then came down again. "I got the big one, the one that always gets away? I caught him. And his brother, and his sister. Christ, I caught the whole damn family."

"What kind?" Iris tried to sound curious, normal.

"Walleye." Then Sheldon lowered himself to the sawhorse that sat at the bottom of the stairs, balancing in front of the wall. "It's hot in here, we should open some windows. Walleye and a big fat old salmon. I got pictures. Of course," he said, reaching his hand up to wipe a bead of sweat off the side of his face, "I didn't win the derby." He sighed. "Somebody's fish is always bigger than mine. But I'm not complaining. I have plenty to eat, plenty to freeze. I'll fry some up for you, you and your family," he said. "A fish fry. We'll have a Friday night fish fry one of these days. Like the Catholics do. Actually, the salmon would be better grilled." He looked around the landing. "So," he said. "Enough about me and my silly derbies. What's new? Anything exciting happen while I was gone?"

Iris looked at the floor, avoiding his eyes. "Not much," she said. She was ashamed of her silliness with the roller, ashamed that she'd opened the can.

"Come on, spill the beans."

Iris rubbed her thumb against the roller's handle, and it made a slight squeaking noise.

"Are you painting, Iris?" Sheldon asked. "What's that green?"

Iris felt her face flush red. "I was going to clean it up."

"You're painting the wall? But I told you I'd give you instructions!"

"I was excited, so I began painting, just to work off steam, but don't worry, I'll fix it."

"Fix it?" his voice rose a bit. "What do you need to fix, Iris?" Sheldon sounded confused, even frustrated.

"I can wait until it dries and paint it with primer."

"How much paint did you use? That was a special color mix," Sheldon said.

"You weren't supposed to come back until tomorrow."

"Well," Sheldon said. "I'm not sure what that means. I should leave now and pretend I wasn't here?" He bowed his head for a minute, and Iris could see the top, where the skin was white, where he must have had it covered by a hat, since the rest of his face was pink. He cleared his throat. "I'm thinking maybe I shouldn't go upstairs now. I'll admit, I'm confused, but we can wait until another time to have this conversation." He looked up at Iris as she stood on the landing, the avocado-green paint-covered roller in her hand.

When Iris saw his face no longer relaxed after his fishing trip, she felt her stomach sag. "I'm sorry," she said. "I wasn't thinking. I was in this bad mood – weird mood, I mean. I just needed to experiment, see what it felt like." She brought up her right hand, gesturing with the roller. "It's so fresh when it goes on the roller, so rich." Iris had no idea what had made her open the paint, pour it in the tray, dip the roller in, roll it against the wall. Each action had required a movement on her part, and she could have stopped at any point along the way.

For a long moment Sheldon stared at her face, and she tried to keep her chin up, but she couldn't look directly at him, and her eyes felt watery. Then he spoke. "You were excited, huh?"

"Not excited like giddy," she said. "Excited like I had to do something." Iris felt a noise rise up from her throat. "And I'm so sad," she said finally.

She saw him nod. "I bet you are. I get that."

"Today is the day he died," Iris said quietly.

"Jeez. I didn't know what day it happened."

"It doesn't make any difference. I shouldn't have messed up the walls."

"And maybe I shouldn't have come back," Sheldon laughed, and then reached into his pocket and pulled out a cloth handkerchief. "It's clean, do you want it? Do you need to talk? I wish I could do something to help you, Iris."

Iris shook her head. "Can you not," she stopped. "Can you not go upstairs?"

"If that's what you want, I can wait," he said. "But you need some plastic wrap for that roller," he said. "There's some in that box of supplies in the corner of the room upstairs. I want you to put plastic wrap around the roller pan and more plastic wrap around the roller. Wrap both of them like you're wrapping your mom's best casserole to keep it fresh in the refrigerator. We'll clean it up another day, and if the roller is too stiff, maybe you can pay for a new one."

"I'm sorry, so sorry, Sheldon," Iris said again.

"We'll get over it. Go home. Remember we're not working until after the Fourth, so I'll see you that Monday. Don't worry about the walls. They're just walls." His shoulders had been hunched during their conversation, but as she watched, he rolled them backward and put his hands on his hips, growing taller in a stretch. "Fishing is not good for your back," he said. "You heard it first from me. I'm going to leave now, so I'd like you to go put the paint roller in plastic and clean up as best you can and lock up the house. I'll look things over when I get back."

"Thanks, Sheldon."

"You're welcome, Iris. The next time you see me, I'll have had my fill of fish."

Iris watched him leave out the door. She felt a sad kind of relief, like she'd been let off the hook, which didn't feel right. Sheldon was too nice. She looked at the roller she held, the paint starting to lose its glossy look as it dried. She took her index finger from her other hand and wiped it along the edge of the roller, until she had a coating of paint along the smooth side of her knuckles, and then she wiped the finger against her face in criss-crosses, smearing the paint into her skin.

20

House Hunting

June 30, 1974

In both Iris's own neighborhood and in the New Subdivision, some houses were more appealing than others, but Iris hadn't always noticed the differences. Since she planned to stay away from the Lake House in Sheldon's absence, she gave herself the task of biking around both neighborhoods to examine the exteriors and select the most compelling features.

Porches. Iris focused on the porches. She remembered talking to Scott and debating about their purpose. Scott said they were for getting more space and air, and being alone. Iris had pointed out that when you saw people on porches, they were often with other people, even though she agreed that a porch might be a good place for reading. Their own porch was cement, and no one sat there long, because of the hard surface, but the ant traffic sometimes made Iris lose track of time. And when her mother asked her to husk the corn, she liked the porch because she could open up her fingers and let the silk float away in the breeze.

During the previous summer, before Scott died, their mother had persuaded their father to go house hunting. She had a mission. After finding the house of her dreams in the paper, she had convinced their father to go see it. Actually, she had two open houses lined up, and she carried around a face that was soft and pleased with his consent to accompany her.

"Okay," Scott said as he slammed the station wagon door, "If I have to go on this little drive, what do I get?"

"What do you *get?*" their mom said, her voice growing a little testy at the edges. Their dad's mustache twitched. He could have gone either way on this one. If he were in a certain mood, he might have lambasted Scott, but on that day, he wanted to roll with the sun, letting their mother, who was generally more tactful and diplomatic, handle the situation.

"I mean," said Scott, softening his tone, "are there any incentives other than the sheer pleasure of a Sunday afternoon ride, say," he looked over at Iris and made a face as if to say 'watch this,' "an ice cream cone?"

Their mother sighed. "*Not* as an *incentive*," she said emphatically, "but maybe, just maybe, out of the goodness of our hearts."

Scott winked at Iris, who thought then how grown up it was of him to be able to wink at age eleven, like their dad, or like their dentist when he made a gut-splitting joke while their mouths were full of cotton. A wink required confidence, something Scott and Liz shared that Iris hadn't inherited.

On that afternoon, once they left church, Iris looked out the window at the rows of corn their car passed. With the windows rolled down, she could smell the green of the leaves. It was the end of June. "Knee high by the Fourth of July," her grandfather had always said of the corn, and it almost was knee high, or at least close to ten inches. They were "in the country" now, as her mom said, but her dad was slowing the car as they approached a developing subdivision. They drove down the streets slowly, and they observed half-developed houses dotting the dried earth. A big thicket of bushes blocked the end, where the road stopped abruptly, waiting for more neighborhood occupants before the subdivision continued into the trees.

In the Merchant's neighborhood, there were no sidewalks and no paved roads, just the gravel roads that the neighbors lacquered with oil after pooling their resources each summer, then chloride, once oil was banned. Liz, Iris, and Scott had learned to ride in the streets, always watching for cars like their parents taught them, though as they aged, they'd get to the tops of hills and careen down, barely checking for oncoming traffic, wanting to feel the rush of descent and hear the clang of stones hitting the metal bike fenders after being spit up from the tires.

Once inside the first open house, which smelled of new carpet, freshly treated wood, and the heaviness of paint, Scott and Iris wandered around, separate from their parents, opening closet doors, measuring off room size by walking toe to heel, selecting where their bedrooms would be. The luxuries of the house were not lost on them. It had two bathrooms. The Merchants had only one, and it was not uncommon for someone with a full bladder to call through the bathroom door, "I can't hold it much longer."

The luxuries of the house were not lost on their mother, either. In the car, on the way to the next house, she waxed enthusiastically on the merits of the place they'd just seen, and she, too, focused on the bathroom, how nice it would be during the morning crunch time, when Scott, especially, lived in peril of having toothpaste dribbled onto his head as he tried to sneak his thin body underneath that of a hasty tooth brusher stooped over the sink. Perhaps she was tired of hearing them moan like cows about how hard it was to "hold it much longer."

When they pulled into the driveway where the next open house was being held, Iris threw Scott a look that said, "I can't believe Mom is doing this – what can she be thinking?" The neighborhood they'd entered far exceeded their price range. It was a place for doctors, lawyers, entrepreneurs, people who had Jacuzzis in their basements and pools in their back yards, people who had catered parties with appetizers. But when Iris looked at her mom's face and saw the softness of her mouth and the way she held her head up, her eyes quietly taking in the landscaped entranceway, the brick facade, she knew that the other house in the country had been a set up for this one. This house was the dream house her mother had discovered as she sat looking through the real estate guide when Iris had gotten donuts the morning before at the laundromat.

Perhaps their mother needed some of their enthusiasm, their capacity to see a vision for the future, to make a case to their father. Though the house felt out of their league, they probably should have imagined a new league, for her sake. Things probably would have been okay if she hadn't gotten back in the car and turned her whole body toward their dad on the front seat, hardly waiting for him to put the car in reverse and make his way out of the neighborhood before she said, "Well?" in that loaded, expectant way.

Their dad looked out his window at the surrounding houses. "Check out that roof," he said. And then, "I like the front of that one."

Their mom nodded patiently, commenting on a woman watering a garden as they passed by, how the woman lifted a hand to wave. Then she repeated, "Well, what did you think?"

Iris wished their father could have indulged her mother, just for the afternoon, with some discussion of their options, with some eye toward changes they might make in the future. He could do that, her father. He could be soft, indulgent, a spinner of dreams, or if not the spinner, then a willing observer, a Wilbur the pig to her mother's Charlotte. But on this day, he decided to call off the charade, and he did it with a laugh – half bark, half guffaw – that had no less sting than a hand would have had against their mother's cheek. "We can't afford to move," he said flatly. Not "Ho-ney," his voice dropping the second syllable in a note of sympathy, "you know we can't afford to move." Just the flat declarative statement. No interjections, no exclamations.

When Iris's mom was frustrated, she could sputter and fume with the best of them. But when she was hurt, she would go all silent, which is what she did at that moment. Scott leaned his head back against the seat, and Iris wondered if he, too, wished he could climb into the back of the station wagon, lie down, and bury his head to ignore their mother's pain. When their dad pulled into Richland Dairy, Iris could tell from Scott's sigh that he didn't care for any ice cream now, but they would both jump out of the car anyway, grab the couple of dollars their dad handed back without even asking if they needed money. Their mom had rolled up her window, despite the scorcher day, not as hot as August, but still hot.

They dawdled in the store, looking around at the candy and the pop case before they finally got in line at the ice cream counter. As they approached the car, Iris noticed that their mom's window was down again, a hand and a cigarette held out the window, and she heard a sharp tightness in her mother's words, "Why did you even come, then?" which came out the window to join the smoke. Later, Iris would see the spoken words as her mother's plea for deliverance from the waves of disappointment swamping her, but at that moment, she felt the prick of realization that they hadn't purchased a cone for their mother and given her the delight of her favorite summer pleasure.

* * *

That evening, Iris and Scott went out to play badminton in the driveway. Their father stood over his saw in the garage; he measured and marked the piece of wood he was working on, then flipped the switch so they heard first the hum and then the whine of the saw as it met the wood. Their mother had sequestered herself in the basement for the evening. With the washer broken and the laundry done, she had no reason for being there, but the effort of being civil to their father, of keeping her ire under wraps, must have caused her to seek refuge, to reorganize the pantry to make room for the jars of pickles she would can.

Iris was ahead two games to three. A slight breeze made the net dance lightly, and the birds chirped from distant trees. Iris tried to concentrate on the soft whizzing of the badminton birdie as it sailed through the air, on Scott's giggle-grunt as he threw his body up to flail at a clearly out-of-bounds shuttlecock. Next to where they stood in the driveway, the living room fan hummed softly in the window. When they were younger, on hot summer evenings

after baths, they would stand in front of the fan, hair still wet, paja-
maed bodies damp, and sing Mother Goose rhymes, laughing and
giggling at the rumbles and waves the fan made in their voices. No
matter how clearly and sweetly they might sing, their voices came
out in gurgles and warbles. Their dad had flipped off the saw again,
and the garage was quiet.

Through the fan they heard the warble of their mother's voice,
not singing, not talking, but sad, full of soft, quiet tears.

* * *

Iris decided as she circled around the block, that there were
only two good porches she'd seen. One had screens, and though
she could hear the clank of silverware from some table beyond the
porch, she didn't see any people. She liked the other house without the screens because it was so open, and the house itself was
slate blue. But open porches didn't give you any place to hide your
secret sorrows.

21

Barbershop Harmony

July 1, 1974

On Monday morning, Iris pretended to get ready for work at the Lake House as usual. She'd been vague with her parents about Sheldon's vacation, so they knew that he was generally off around the Fourth of July but not the specific details. Liz had already left for Richland Dairy, with an unusual split shift for the day because of co-workers' vacations. Iris heard her mom move around in the kitchen, which meant she must have an afternoon shift at the library. The kitchen counter clock radio still played loudly. Her father set his alarm there each weekday so that it came on at six o'clock each morning, their breakfasts full of news, commentary, and Detroit talk.

Iris waited for her mother to move out of the kitchen so that she could sneak out of the house without explaining why she wasn't going to paint with Sheldon that day. She could hear the radio announcer talking about Fourth of July festivities and what made for excitement around listeners' houses during summer. It was clear that her mother didn't want to go on vacation. It would be too painful to think of that past. Iris guessed that her mother must want to control her summer carefully, rule over the borders, make sure the days of this summer didn't touch too many things from the past.

July for the Merchant family had usually begun with anticipation of holiday festivities at their lake. Before Scott died, Iris liked to ride around the block, especially on Destan – to see how preparations were shaping up. When Iris heard her mom move out of the kitchen and toward the basement, she crept from her room and left out the back door, grabbing her bike and fleeing down the driveway.

She didn't want to take the route past the Lake House where she might see Sheldon's vehicle parked in the driveway, so she went the other way around the block to determine if people in the neighborhood were gearing up for the festival. At the beach park, the benches were nearly full, and several chaise lounges and towels were spread on the hill that sloped down to the lake. Whoops and splash noises rose from the lake. A few doors down, Iris stopped at the Rifkin's house, where Mrs. Rifkin was working in the front yard on her pontoon. When she saw Iris, she tucked the roll of blue crepe paper under her chin, motioning with her other hand, which held a roll of red. "Iris," she said, her voice muffled from chinning the paper, "would you do me a favor and hold this so I can weave it through the railings?"

Iris nodded, jumping off her bike and kicking the stand down.

Mrs. Rifkin smiled as Iris took the roll from her. "You don't have to be home?"

"No, just left. Riding my bike."

"This decorating is probably pointless," Mrs. Rifkin said, gesturing to the pontoon boat that was parked on the trailer in the front yard. "One good wave and it will be drenched and soggy, and the blue will run into the red." She shook her head. "But we've had years when the lake has been as calm as a sleeping baby – not a ripple, so I figured it was worth a shot."

Mrs. Rifkin and her husband were among the devoted pontoon boaters who decorated their boats every year for the lake festival that took place for five days around the Fourth of July. In addition to a pontoon parade there was a barbershop singing event every year in the middle of the lake. Their mom always talked about wanting to go, but because they didn't own a pontoon and none of their close neighborhood friends did either, Iris's mom could only listen to the strains of the songs from the beach. But this year she'd received a call from the new festival organizer who'd had a son in Scott's class. Somebody had told her that Scott's mom liked to sing, and she extended an invitation to Iris's mother. In June, their mom had started to go through some boxes she had in the basement with sheet music and printed lyrics to the songs that she used to sing with her sisters.

Mrs. Rifkin didn't sing, but she told Iris she and her husband lingered around the edges of the circle the boats made in the water, listening for the faint strain of the pitch pipe, then the blend of the rich voices, from bass and baritone to soprano, voices mingling with those of complete strangers from the other side of the lake, in search of the harmony that hung in the air, waiting to be sung.

Mrs. Rifkin motioned to Iris to follow her around the side of the pontoon. "We never win," she said. "But I can't seem to be more creative than this. And I like the traditional look – the red, white, and blue, though I have to get to the store for more white crepe paper." She sighed and dropped to her knees. "You know that one family down the street makes all those red, white, and blue flowers out of tissue paper? Hundreds of them. They must start in May."

Iris admired the way the crepe paper waved in the slight breeze, the stray ends festooning out, then settling back down to cling to the boat like a stray sock might cling to a sweater, coming out of a hot dryer. "But winning doesn't matter, right?" Iris said. "At least that's what adults always say when they're trying to make us kids feel better."

Mrs. Rifkin smirked. "You've got that right. That's what we say. Who knows if we believe it ourselves."

"I'd better go," Iris said. The wind had picked up, and Iris remembered that her mother had asked her the night before to take the towels off the clothesline the next day before it rained.

"Thanks for your help, Iris."

She pedaled as fast as she could over the non-bumpy stretches of road, knowing that the rain could break through the clouds any minute, drenching her mother's towels and destroying Mrs. Rifkin's float decorations. When Iris arrived home, the sky still showed blue in spots, though the charcoal gray was starting to spread across the blue. Yet the clothesline was empty, and she remembered that on the day Scott had died, she'd come home to find the clothesline empty then, too.

Iris told herself that her mother wouldn't mind that she'd forgotten the chore, and yet, she felt irresponsible – the errant avocado green strokes on the Lake House walls, the laundry chore ignored. She was failing at everything. Again.

Liz had to work that night, so Iris and her father were the only ones to walk her mother to the beach for the barbershop event. The rain had held off, and Iris had apologized to her mother for not taking down the towels. Her mother hadn't gone to work that morning but to the grocery store, and she seemed excited, telling Iris not to worry, the towels were all folded and put away. It was dusk as they walked around the block moving slowly down Destan, seeing families dart in and out of houses, collecting lawn chairs from garages. In between houses, the lake was clearly visible, lighted boats floating on the water, some of them strung with Christmas lights, others dark save for one or two lanterns on the port and starboard sides.

When they got to the beach, Iris's mom and dad descended the hill to the catwalk where several neighbors were boarding the pontoon Iris's mom had been invited to join. Iris and her father both shook their heads when the group offered to take them along. "We'll watch from the beach," Iris's dad said. Iris wondered if her parents thought about the last time they'd been on that dock in the water that ran parallel to the boat ramp, or if their mother just kept her focus on song, and a breezy pontoon ride.

Iris and her father spread a blanket on the hill and watched the boats circle around the shore, waiting for darkness, inching gently like caterpillars toward the center of the lake, their crepe paper streamers floating in the breeze. The boats moved in the same way that people gathered to form a crowd around Christmas carolers at a local mall, and the wake from so many vehicles created soft waves that touched the shore, making the toddlers in the wading area raise their fingers from the wet sand and their eyes from the observation of minnows and look up toward the center of the lake. The high school music teacher had already anchored his boat in the middle of the lake and was waiting for everyone else to arrive. Up in the corner of the beach lot, a group of teenagers giggled and called out to another group on the sand below.

They didn't hear the pitch pipe, but a chorus of voices carried across the lake, together in a harmonious blend on the first notes of "Sentimental Journey." Iris's mother's family sang that song at family reunions, Iris's uncles' voices so different but so perfectly in tune. Iris knew that out there on the water her mother beamed out each note, happy to be singing. And her father, who liked a good song but enjoyed a quiet whistle as well, sat still, knees up, hands folded atop them. He listened that way to every song, from "Three Little Sisters" to "Sidewalks of New York," not joining in the conversation going on between the other blankets but listening respectfully. Iris wished her mother could have seen him and the way he honored her desires that night, appreciative and engaged, like she was a diva and he'd spent a huge sum of money for a seat way up in the balcony just to watch her face. In retrospect, though, perhaps Iris gave him too much credit – perhaps he was miles away, his mind occupied in a project. Or perhaps he was in his old boat, on the lake, watching the waves come up and hit the front, feeling the rumble of the floor beneath him. But he seemed to know when the last song was over, because he rose slowly and asked Iris to help him fold the blanket, his face carrying a faraway smile that Iris hadn't ever seen.

At the edge of the beach, a father walked with his daughter, the little girl teasing him about how he reacted to the water, telling him how warm it was. Iris remembered being younger, on family vacation when she walked behind her father at a beach, putting her feet into the wet imprints his bare feet made in the sand, like she did now in the winter when she followed his boot holes in the snow-filled yard to get back to the garbage cans at the end of their property.

The light from the moon shone on the wet patches of the carpeted docks in their sectioned-off swimming area, making shiny the surfaces she knew to be rough, so rough that you scratched your belly wriggling on them hoisting yourself up when the ladders to the docks were broken. Behind Iris, the chains on the swingset squeaked and whined as the last swinger slowed her pace then jumped from the swing with a soft thud, her feet hitting the sand. Next to the beach lot, a fire glowed in the backyard of the neighboring property and the smell of singed marshmallows drifted over the fence. People left the beach in groups, calling to one another as they parted at the gate and walked their separate ways through the neighborhood. The giggling teenagers had gone as well, though one lone figure remained on the bench at the top of the hill, his cigarette tip glowing.

Iris wanted to tell her father how much she longed to take her shoes off and walk in the sand, this real sand right next to the water. How much she missed it, how she'd deprived herself, almost in a punishment. She'd told herself to come to the beach to honor her mother's desire to sing, but she didn't know how drawn she would be to the water that still repelled her because of what *it* had done, what *she* had done.

The last of the boats moved quietly towards the shore now, the owners who didn't have beach property preparing to pull them out of the water. When Iris's mom's pontoon came closer, she saw them there and waved, her face still flush with excitement. They went to the catwalk then and Iris's dad stood right at the end, his hand outstretched, to help his wife off the boat, a gallant footman. Iris wanted to believe that the hand her father offered was a promise, and by accepting it, her mother was committing to a new unity, a shared purpose. She wanted to see them stay linked together throughout the night; she wanted a camera to capture that moment on film so she could look at the picture again and again. But as they walked up the catwalk, their linked hands fell apart, and Iris felt the evening chill settle into the air around them.

22

Desire

July 3, 1974

Iris tried to fall asleep, but her mind kept churning, so just before midnight, when she saw Liz's bed still empty, she finally turned the light on and started reading. From their parents' room, she could hear soft snores; a slight breeze came through the window, bringing the scent of night air. A faint rumbling caught Iris's ear, like the bass line from one of the Barbershop songs, and she realized it was a car's engine idling. Maybe even in their own driveway. She lay there, holding her book, but not reading. She didn't know who occupied the car, if it was in the driveway. Perhaps a friend of Liz's dropping her off.

Then the engine stopped, and Iris lay there, expecting the back door to open and close. Finally, she got up and crept into the living room, going to the side window, where the fan was churning air, and peeking out the window above it, in between the curtains. Their deep, narrow driveway ran from the road past the house and all the way to the garage at the back of their property. When Iris looked out, the car that had just turned off was right in front of the window. It was Michael's car, with Michael's hands on the steering wheel. Her first thought was to run to Scott's bedroom to tell him Michael was back, and she fell back on her heels in front of the window when she realized how her mind had tricked her.

She wondered what he might be saying to Liz – if they talked about Scott or a movie they'd both seen or maybe even a couple they knew from school. Iris rose up on her knees and balanced herself against the back of the coach, being sure to part the curtains as carefully as possible. Across the way, the neighbor's side living room curtain was fully open, the television still on, with light flickering images through the window and into the Merchant driveway, into Michael's car. The car was full of dark shadows, but the wavering light from the neighbor's television helped Iris decipher Michael's hands as they moved back and forth against the wheel, rubbing at the tubular frame, then tapping with his fingers, then rubbing again. Liz sat forward in her seat, her face in laughing mode and then nodding. A strand of hair fell out of the ponytail she usually wore at work. As she reached up to push it back, Iris watched Michael touch Liz's face with one of the hands that had been on the steering wheel. Then he moved both hands to her shoulders, his fingers moving back and forth, from shoulders to her neck. The light from the neighbor's window went darker, gray fading into black until a bright glow from a new television image illuminated the car, and Michael finally pulled Liz's upper body into his lap, cradling her head and her chest between his own chest and the steering wheel, bending over and burying his face into hers.

Iris stumbled back from the curtain and the fan, hurrying to the room she shared with Liz, putting her book on the floor and turning off the light.

Ten minutes later, Iris heard the water run in the bathroom accompanied by the splishing sound of Liz brushing her teeth. By the time the bedroom door opened, Iris had turned toward the wall, making her breathing sound as if she dwelled in a deep slumber.

23

Nothing to Celebrate

July 4, 1974

When Iris entered the kitchen the next morning, her mother was peeling just-boiled potatoes for the salad. She palmed the hot potatoes, her hands quick, fingers dancing as the steam seeped out from under the skins. Peeling already cooked potatoes was the equivalent of walking barefoot over hot coals, but her mother never even flinched, just worked her fingers around the peels. A pile of chopped celery and onions already sat on the cutting board; next to the board was a small bowl of sliced eggs.

Their parents had given them the choice of going to a nearby park or staying home for the day, and, oddly enough, they'd opted for staying home. Neither Iris nor Liz wanted to see fireworks or a parade. They would eat whatever their mother put in front of them.

Liz came into the dining room and plopped into a chair before the makeshift do-it-yourself breakfast. "I'm *so* glad I don't have to work today." She held up her ice-cream chapped hands, "Maybe if they have a rest, they'll start getting back to normal."

"How was last night?" her mom said.

"Fine," Liz said, her voice vague and breezy.

"You came in late," her dad said.

"But I was home by midnight," Liz said, smiling. "Almost." She reached over the table for the strawberry jam in front of Iris.

"Don't reach," her mom said. "Ask."

Liz sighed.

Their mother began collecting dirty silverware. "So," she said, looking down at the crumpled napkin she held. "You said you might ask that new guy over this afternoon."

Liz leaned back in her chair. "I decided not to," she said, then took a bite of toast.

"Oh," their mom said. "You think he's busy?" She looked up at Liz in that polite way she had. Iris kind of felt sorry for their mom. She and Liz had these formal conversations in which their mom kept asking questions and Liz kept giving her the minimum response, knowing she was irritating her mother no end. And the real test was to see how many questions their mother could ask before she sighed an explosive sigh and said "All right, go ahead, keep the details to yourself. Leave me in the dark and make me look like a fool when I wake up some day and find out from one of the neighbors what you've been up to or, God forbid, on the news."

"I don't know if he's busy," Liz said, munching her toast on purpose so she could answer with her mouth full. "I just didn't ask him." She picked up her plate and the knife.

"A piece of toast, that's all?" their mom said.

"I'm not hungry," Liz said. Then, as she walked out of the dining area and kitchen, she called back, "Michael might be stopping by this afternoon," and disappeared into the other part of the house.

162

"Michael," their mom said, looking at their dad, who just raised his eyebrows.

Then their mom let out a long, tired sigh. "I hope *that* doesn't start up again," she said.

"Just don't get involved this time," their dad said. He put the paper down to look at his wife, who made a face at him.

"Easy for you to say," she said. "You're not the one who has to listen to the crying."

"You want her to talk to you, and then you complain when she cries on your shoulder."

"Only because she waits so long before she says *anything* at all, and then she expects me to solve her problems just like that." Their mom suddenly looked around the table and noticed Iris listening intently. "All right," she said. "Please keep what you heard to yourself."

"I like Michael," Iris said.

"Well," their mom said. "Whatever happens between him and Liz, we need to stay out of it." She picked up the strawberry jam and wiped at the neck of the jar with a napkin. Iris knew that she was saying this as much for her own benefit as theirs.

Their parents had always liked Michael. Quieter than any of the other guys her sister brought home, he would listen to their parents when they talked, his brown eyes steady under dark eyebrows. But when her sister teased him, his face broke into a gentle, almost shy smile, his strong jaw angling out from his blonde hairline. He was Robert Redford suppressing a grin in *The Way We Were*. And when he forgot to be quiet, he made them all laugh.

* * *

Iris was in the bedroom that evening when her mother called out with her hurry-up voice from the family room. "Iris, quick, your MIA is on television." Hurrying toward the family room, Iris felt her wrist for the bracelet she wore to remember the POW-MIAs. Her MIA was Colonel Patrick T. Fallon, missing July 4, 1969, and she had bounded three steps into the room before she realized that her mother must have meant they were talking about her MIA on television. For a moment, Iris had thought maybe he was alive, released home to his family.

"His wife," Iris's mother explained. "They're interviewing his wife." It was strange to see this woman talking calmly about the anniversary of her husband's capture, how she still had hopes but each day they were dimming. How she wanted to do this interview to remind people – and the government in particular – that as Americans celebrated their independence, they needed to remember all the men who'd lost their own independence for the nation.

The woman seemed so calm, her voice full of conviction. Iris hadn't known that the MIA name on her wrist all those weeks had a family – a wife, so strong and resolute. And daughters.

Iris had never passed out the bumper stickers the organization had sent her, but she'd spent a lot of time thinking about the man whose name she wore on her arm. Colonel Patrick T. Fallon. She'd read about soldiers, and she knew a few guys from the neighborhood who'd gone to Vietnam in the draft. Since she was a weakling herself, she couldn't imagine being strong enough to fight in a war, and she couldn't imagine being kept behind bars as a Prisoner of War.

164

She imagined a row of gaunt faces, shaggy beards, and sad, hollow eyes. She'd read that some of the POWs created a schedule for themselves, doing one hundred pushups, reciting the Gettysburg Address. Humming random songs, mouthing the lyrics.

Iris was afraid that if she were in the war, she wouldn't be one of the strong ones. She'd be a screamer, a fainter, a coward who died of fright before the enemy ever touched her or made her bleed. Yet she knew now that her MIA was strong, based on what his wife said. Iris was proud to wear his name on her arm.

And now she knew his real story. He was Firefly 26, and on July 4, 1969, he and another Air Force pilot in the 56th Special Operations Wing investigated enemy activity near the town of Jiangshan in Northern Laos. When his plane was hit at two hundred feet by enemy fire, he had to leave the plane, reaching the ground safely. Yet he was surrounded by Lao troops and the machine gun emplacements on the ridges around him. Although he maintained radio contact with rescue teams nearby, those planes couldn't rescue him due to enemy presence. According to the news story, his last transmission was, "Put it all around me, I'm hit."

As Iris lay in bed that night after the newscast, she could see the face they'd flashed on the news, the clean-shaven man in uniform, his bold ears sticking out from his head, his face wearing a wryly distinguished smile. He had landed on the ground alive, but that didn't mean he would stay alive. His wife knew that, but she kept hoping. He was just like the boy captured by the child killer – they called him The Caretaker, now; the MIA stayed alive for a while, and he knew that people wanted to help get him out of the situation he was in. And his parents were like the pilot's wife – they kept hoping that he would be alive when they found him. They were the same, the boy and Iris's MIA, in that moment when they were both waiting to die.

24

Furnishings

July 5, 1974

Iris planned to take three things to the New Subdivision
House when she left on her bike the next afternoon, a day of work
for the rest of her family. The white eyelet pillow Scott always
crushed beneath him or played around with when he was watching television. They used to leave it squashed in a corner, ready to
be retrieved. Whenever Scott lay on the couch, he batted it about
with his feet, sometimes even shedding his dirty socks so he could
transform himself into a seal, juggling with the white eyelet ball,
propelling it in the air to meet the cob-webbed ceiling before the
pillow fell down, plopping in his groin or his face. "Can't you wash
that filthy thing?" Liz would say, but in the months since the previous summer, only Liz had touched it, on that day she lay on the
couch during her mosquito bite recuperation.

On that occasion, when Liz clutched it in her arms, she must
have known at some level that she was embracing the smell of him,
whatever smell was left after a year, whatever oils from his body had
permeated the cloth of the pillow. Since it was always in plain sight,
Iris guessed none of them would miss it. For the second and third
items, she went to his room, waiting until they'd all been gone for

167

a least a half hour, and there was no chance that Liz would come back and find her. She wanted the Detroit Tiger pennant that hung above his desk. Unattended over the year, the pennant felt was fuzzy with dust. Iris plucked it down, and, starting with the longer side, rolled it like a crescent.

The last item was the 1969 red Camaro model Scott had made with their dad. Unlike the trucks he used to take to the beach, dented and rusty from being rammed into things, wearing grains of sand from play, the Camaro was a display piece, although it had a fair coating of dust. Iris wrapped it with a dish towel and placed it in a cloth bag she'd had for the sponge curlers her mom had given her when she was twelve. She would need to take extra care as she biked while transporting the Camaro, especially.

Once Iris had the items, she stuffed everything but the car into a shopping bag, along with a box of cheese crackers. She'd already loaded the transistor radio in the basket; she added the small shopping bag and hooked the curler bag containing the car around the handlebar, knowing she would have to nudge it with her knee to keep it out of the way as she biked. When she rode down the driveway, the car clunked against the bike's frame, and she decided if she saw anyone she knew, she would just wave nonchalantly, and perhaps they would think she was coming from a garage sale, laden with treasures.

She pedaled hard, the wind cool against her arms, sneaking in through the armholes of her cotton shirt. Once Iris entered the New Subdivision, she felt calmer, closer to her goal. At the house, weeds had grown taller in the back yard, purple smudges on top of popsicle-sized sticks.

She carried the bag up the stairs and into the bedroom that overlooked the back yard. The tack she'd brought poked through the material in her shorts pocket and grazed her hip; she pulled it out and pressed it through the cloth of the pennant. Iris pushed the tack and pennant into the drywall next to the window. She lined the Camaro up with the baseboard in a corner and placed the pillow against the wall. Then she lay down on the floor, her head resting on the pillow.

Her mother had purchased new batteries for the transistor the day before, and Iris had installed them that morning. When she turned the radio on, the sound came blaring out, the volume intensified because she'd last listened to Ernie Harwell call a Tigers game. She lowered the volume and changed to an FM station, and Aretha Franklin sang into the room, spelling the word "Respect." Staring at the ceiling, Iris let the song wash over her, nodding her head on the pillow. Then she sat up, increased the volume, and sang through until the end of the song.

After the song ended, the disc jockey talked about an event happening in Detroit in a few weeks, promising another few songs after a commercial. When Iris heard the opening strains to "Build Me Up, Buttercup," she rose from the floor. It was a song she and Liz had danced to for several years, before Liz had entered high school, or met Michael, or began to work in the summer. Liz had a little record player for 45s, and she and Iris would play a few in the basement. They'd started a dance routine to this one. Iris moved her hips from side to side in double time with the beat of the drums, swinging her arms from left to right, elbows bent, snapping her fingers in front of her face the loud way that Liz had taught her. Every time the music built up to the chorus, she closed her eyes, pointed her two fingers in front of her, pulsing them three times for emphasis when the lead singer sang, "Why do you..." in his syncopated appeal to the girl who kept breaking his heart. Iris swung her hips and her hands to the rest of the song, trying to remember the steps they'd come up with, knowing they might not have ever finished their choreography. But when she sank to the ground, she was happy to turn the radio off and just stare at the walls. They didn't wear the vibrant colors of the ones she painted with Sheldon at the Lake House, but at least she could think within these walls in this abandoned house that no one inhabited.

25

Negotiation

July 8, 1974

Iris left the house early before anyone in her family was awake. She rode around the block five times, pedaling hard for the incline of every hill, coasting on the way down. It was getting close to ten o'clock, when she was due at the Lake House to meet up with Sheldon. They hadn't spoken since he'd returned from the trip early and found her, roller of green paint in hand. She didn't know what her thinking had been in the moment when she poured some of the paint in the roller pan. She would like to believe that she'd had a plan – to do the roller work, clean up, let the weird coat dry, and then go over it with white, hoping Sheldon wouldn't notice. But if she attempted to be honest with herself, she would admit that she had not thought through any of those steps; she had merely poured the paint, dipped the roller, and rolled.

Even when she'd seen him on the landing, her first thought had been, "I need to explain what I've done." Her second thought had been that she made a big mistake, but she was trying to figure out why the first thought was so free and innocent. She had practiced five different scripts to deliver to him, like a speech she might have given in civics class, but none of them captured the strange desire that had welled up in her when she saw the wall, so ready to receive the green.

Now, as the minute hand on her watch crept toward the twelve, she pulled into the Lake House driveway and parked the bike close to the house, away from the road. His car was already there, parked. She needed to get it over with.

When she walked in the door, she could smell fresh paint, which meant he'd started without her. She felt more guilt. As she went up the stairs, she called out, "Hello?" to let Sheldon know she was approaching.

"In here," Sheldon called. His voice came from a room other than the one she'd rolled impetuously the week before. She was relieved; she wasn't ready to see her attack on the walls.

Sheldon stood on the stepladder in the biggest bedroom, the one that had its own bathroom. He painted a paintbrush's width at the top of one of the walls. The line of paint at the top was so even that she felt afraid, worried that she would have to copy his work. "I am 'cutting in,'" he said. "'Cutting in' is what you do before you roll a wall. First, you make a frame at the top and bottom with a small paintbrush – the sides as well, although that's not as important. Then you can roll the wall because you don't need to worry about rolling so close to the top, the bottom, or the corners."

Iris wondered if maybe he was planning on talking business. Maybe he would just ignore what happened the other day.

"I will probably have you do some work like this later in the week, but today I'll have you tape the ceiling. You need to have a few years of painting under your belt before you can do this cutting in stuff without taping ahead of time. When I was first learning, my dad always had me put tape down on the corner line of the ceiling so I wouldn't accidentally get paint on the ceiling from the roller."

They were both silent as Sheldon stepped down from the ladder, moved it further down the wall, and climbed back up again.

Iris didn't know what to expect. She wanted a lecture. Or maybe she wanted him to show some anger, although she didn't know what that would look like, and the thought was frightening to her. "I'm sorry," she blurted out. "I don't want to distract you from your work, but I just want to say that I'm sorry for the other day."

"Apology accepted. But I'm not going to let you off that easy. I would like a little more of an explanation," Sheldon said. "And I am composed enough that I can listen to it now, while I'm painting, or we can wait."

"An explanation," Iris said, "like, why or what was I thinking?"

"Exactly," Sheldon said.

"That's the hard part. I don't know."

"Well, that's a start. So, your actions were impulsive."

"Yes, I didn't plan it ahead of time," she said. "I just acted."

"Were you mad at me? Or the world? Were you thinking, 'I'll show Sheldon; I'll just mess up this wall.'"

"No! I would never be mad at you! And I didn't do anything to get attention or make a statement or whatever. I saw the green paint, and I just wanted to pour it out and roll the roller in it. I was sad about my brother, and I wanted to escape the sadness."

"Because when I saw you here, and I saw that roller in your hand, I thought maybe you were a bit like one of those kids who spray paints over my deer murals on garage doors. Doing an ugly deed to make fun of an old man. And ruining someone's property."

"I'm so sorry kids mess up your work sometimes, Sheldon."

"It's not like I need any reminders that I'm not Leonardo DaVinci."

"And it must feel bad to be attacked. Plus you feel like you have to redo it for free."

"Okay, so you weren't mad, and you weren't trying to deface the property. You were sad about your brother. For me, that sort of explains everything. But tell me this. What would you have done if I didn't walk in on you? If I'd just met you here this morning, like we planned?"

Iris couldn't remember what she'd been thinking that day, though she knew it had something to do with her brother and her parents. She'd been antsy, and the paint was irresistible. "I really didn't think about that at the time. But last night I was thinking that if you hadn't walked in, I would have finished whatever rolling I started, and then I would have realized I'd done something stupid. But because you taught me that paint takes a couple of hours to dry, I'm pretty sure I thought in the back of my head that I could do a coat of white over it, because we've done so much white, and I really know how to do white. I can't say for sure, but I think I would have waited and then done a white coat." Iris plopped down on the floor, across from where Sheldon stood on the ladder. "But none of it was about hiding it from you or tricking you, because I would have told you. The next day. I would have told you what I'd done, and maybe you would even see it, because that green paint would show up with only a little bit of white over it."

She reached over to where the green roller lay in a box of supplies he'd clearly brought over from the other room. "But I wasn't mad or anything like that when I painted, Sheldon. I was a weird excited, like I told you. A nervous excited, because I was thinking about Scott. And I can clean this roller."

"Yes," he said. "I'd like you to go to the tub downstairs in the basement and use some turpentine. You probably won't get it all out, but we can still use the roller. I did buy another one this morning. You owe me $2.69 plus tax."

"I brought my savings bank," Iris said.

"I appreciate your explaining, Iris. I wanted to understand. I'll admit that I was frustrated at first. The idea that you would be somebody who could disrespect someone else's property made me sick. And the idea that I could totally read you wrong – the fact that I trusted you and you might just be laughing at me...."

"I would never laugh at you, Sheldon," Iris said. And then she smiled. "Behind your back, anyway."

"And I'm sorry I didn't make the connection to the anniversary of your brother's death. That was insensitive of me." Sheldon stepped down from the ladder. "And now I feel better about this whole green painting situation," he said.

"I do, too," Iris said.

"And I actually already did what you said you would do if I hadn't arrived. I painted a white coat of primer. Not too shabby. Let's go paint the rest."

26

Bird Calls

July 9, 1974

The day after Iris had resolved things with Sheldon, before dawn even, a dresser drawer inched slowly open beside her pillow, which had slipped sideways, half off the bed. Though her eyes were still closed, she could sense the movement, and as a strange feeling of panic and fear made her limbs tense up, she forced her eyes open. Liz was kneeling on the floor, the hem of her baby doll pajamas falling softly around her legs. She extracted a pair of underwear from the drawer, so intent on her goal that she gasped when Iris reached out, touching her hand.

"You scared me." Liz stood and rubbed at her knees, red from the hardwood floor.

"Well, what do you think you did to me? I just fell asleep a couple of hours ago."

Liz stood over her, peering into her face. "I was just trying to be nice. I didn't want to wake you up." Reaching down, she smoothed Iris's hair in an uncharacteristic gesture. "You look awful."

"Sometimes I don't sleep," Iris said.

From underneath the shade only a faint glow of light crept into the room. Iris reached over to pick up the alarm clock from the dresser. It read five-thirty; the last time she'd looked, it was three o'clock. She rubbed at her eyes. "Why are you up so early?"

Liz sat on the foot of her bed and scooted her back against the wall. "Not that it is any of your business, but Michael and I are going bird watching and then out for breakfast. And somehow," she said, holding up the underwear in her fingers, "my underwear keeps getting put in your pile and I'm always short."

"Bird-watching?" Iris said. "As in pileated woodpeckers?"

"What do you know about pileated woodpeckers?" Liz said.

"Nothing, really," Iris said. "I've seen the name in one of Mom's bird books. I think I saw some nature show on TV."

"Michael's new thing is birds," Liz said. "With binoculars and everything." She paused and sighed. "I guess his mom does watercolors of them."

"Oh," Iris said. "I'd like to learn watercolors."

Liz shifted around on the bed and then made a face. "He imitates their calls, even," she said in a voice that dared Iris to make fun of the two of them.

Iris didn't say anything, but Liz's face flushed. "I've always gotten along with animals," she said defensively.

Iris tried to think of something encouraging to say. Liz hadn't spoken to her so casually and calmly in a while. "Cats and dogs," Iris said finally. "Cats and dogs definitely like you. Thankfully we don't know about mice and rats."

Liz looked down at Iris's face on the pillow. "You are weird, Iris."

Iris closed her eyes slowly and then opened them quickly, glancing to the right to make her eyes look creepy.

"I just want to emphasize," Liz said, "that I don't think Michael is a nerd for liking birds or practicing bird calls."

Iris thought then of Michael's face, his tanned jaw, the dark fringe of lashes that framed his intense brown eyes, but as she conjured him up, his eyes turned darker, and then they muddied to a deep black, like Karl's eyes, and then his mouth had Karl's mustache, and everything was fleshier, fuller, and closer. It had been almost a month since she'd been at the Langley's house. Her head felt heavy, though her brain seemed stuffed with cotton. "No," she said finally. "He isn't." Iris felt so tired, and her own voice sounded wooden and faraway. She wanted Liz to leave, so she could go back to sleep, but part of her wanted Liz to stay, so she could listen to her voice as she talked about Michael, the way it warmed at the edges, making nice curves, softer than other times. Iris put her head to the side and her eyelids closed slowly, mouth in a half smile, features safe and comfortable.

Iris wanted at that moment to tell Liz about what had happened with Karl – to see if her sister could help her sort out how she felt about the night and its aftermath. A coolness brushed her thighs from the breeze coming in the window. "Liz," she said tentatively, "I wanted to ask you...." She paused.

From outside the window, a car engine hummed, the sound travelling as the car went down the street. Probably the man down by the canal who worked the late shift at the plant. Liz looked down at her watch. "Michael's going to be here any minute. Can it wait?" she asked.

"What?" Iris said.

"What you want to ask me; can it wait?" Liz tossed her wet hair over a shoulder.

"Oh," Iris said. "It's nothing." Liz came back to the bed, then, her hand reaching down to the covers, finding Iris's knee and patting it. "Go to sleep, Iris."

"Sure," Iris said. "Hi to Michael and the birds."

Liz rolled her eyes and then nodded as she closed the door behind her.

It didn't matter. Iris wouldn't have known what to ask her sister anyway. She just wanted to tell her that she had been afraid that night with Karl, but ashamed, too. That her fear, her shame, and her disgust felt bad, but that in the beginning she had almost liked the attention. Iris wanted to ask Liz if she felt any of that ambivalence with Michael, wanting his touch, but then being repulsed by it, or if she only felt good about it, especially when it was dark and they sat in his car. How could Iris ever tell her sister that she wanted to replace the Janis Joplin static in her head from that night at the Langley's after Karl showed up? She wanted to replace it with some other song, maybe the one she and Liz sang together when Liz was younger and didn't worry about someone seeing her through the windows, the Diana Ross one they sang with hairbrushes for microphones, "I'm Livin' in Shame," the intensity with which they leaned into the brushes when it came time to sing, "*Mama, mama,*" in a soulful, desperate way.

Iris envied Liz's experience with Michael as they drove out toward the country, the car moving easily over the cool pavement of the early morning, Liz would drift off to sleep, her head slipping sideways toward Michael's shoulder, her eyes heavy since she'd worked until midnight. In such a drowsy state, she would feel the morning air come in the window and brush against her tanned, bare arms, cardinals, robins, and meadowlarks filling her head with chirps and calls.

* * *

That previous summer, before Scott had died, they'd gotten into such a rhythm with Michael. Both Iris and Scott liked him, and Liz knew it. One day, Iris and Scott woke up to a note from their mom, asking them to go next door to Noelle's garden and pick some strawberries. Noelle had made all the strawberry jam and frozen all the bags of strawberries she needed for a year, and the family was going on vacation; the Merchants were welcome to take what they wanted. The berries were starting to get mushy on the vine.

Later, as they all sat in front of the television, watching a tennis match, Michael said, "I'll go with them."

"You want to pick berries?" Liz asked.

"Sure, I like strawberries," Michael said.

"But you don't have to. They really don't mind doing it," she said.

"I don't mind, either," Michael insisted.

"Okay, suit yourself." Liz went into the kitchen and soon they could hear the cupboards opening and closing as she looked for bowls. Iris had to admire her sister because she didn't go off all pouty and moody into another room; she wasn't about to sulk. She squared her shoulders and took a seat on the couch, saying she'd watch television until they returned home.

Once in the strawberry patch, they fell to work. Iris and Scott started in one row and Michael went to work on another area not far from them, occasionally saying an older-kid-type comment like, "Remind me what grades you are going into next year?" Occasionally, a large bumble bee buzzed by and they'd weave and jerk their heads to avoid its path, Scott ducking his head into the strawberry greenery each time until Iris reminded him that bees sometimes hung out next to the white flowers as well.

Iris could tell Scott was growing bored. He began to sit back on his haunches and eye each strawberry he picked as if trying to decide whether it was worthy enough, yet when she elbowed him in the side, he put a finger to his lips.

Just a yard away, Michael bent over his row. Scott picked up a half-smashed berry, held it out in front of him, and then pulled it up to his nose as if he were making some chalk line like their dad did for his various projects. Scott looked over at Iris, cocked an eyebrow, and before she could say anything, he whipped the berry through the air. They both saw it hit the back of Michael's white shorts, hanging there, clinging to the material for a second before it fell off, hitting his calf before landing on the ground.

They knew the Michael who gave them rides up to the Richland Dairy in his Opel GT, the one who teased them when they ate ice cream and got goo all over their faces. But with a direct assault, they didn't know what to expect.

Iris and Scott watched closely as Michael seemingly ignored the hit, bending to pick more berries. They shrugged and returned to work, as if pretending that Scott had never pitched the berry. After a few minutes passed, Michael swung around with a fistful of berries in his left hand and grinned wickedly at them, lunging into action as he began to pluck the mushed berries one by one with his other hand, pelting them. Iris shrieked and hit the ground. Scott let out the battle cry he'd been perfecting since he was five and began grabbing more bad berries. Inching along on her stomach, Iris headed for a section of the garden where she would have more cover, but she wasn't fast enough – with a plopping sound, a strawberry hit her back and the slow ooze of juice seeped into her T-shirt.

Grabbing whatever berries she could find, she lifted her head up and lobbed them toward Michael, crouched in his row. Since he was bigger than both Iris and Scott, he didn't have nearly enough cover, and Iris could see that Scott had already gotten in a few good hits. A splotch of red adorned the neckline of Michael's shirt where skin interfaced with white cotton. Scott still scrambled in the vines for berries, and as Iris raised up on her knees, he leered at her, popped his head up quickly and flung two handfuls of mush at Michael.

"No fair – one at a time," Michael called, but Scott just laughed and dove into another row to find better berries.

"Play by your own rules," Iris yelled back at him. The air was quiet, and Iris could no longer hear Michael moving in the greenery. "He's out of ammunition," Iris whispered to Scott.

"Okay," Michael finally called. "I give up. You guys win."

When Iris peeked up, he had already stood and was using the hem of his T-shirt to wipe the stickiness off his face. Scott jumped around, crowing about being a winner and such a good shot. Iris looked down to see her socks and tennis shoes discolored with strawberry soot.

Iris grinned at Michael as thanks for letting Scott have his victory dance, and when he smiled back, his eyes clear, she realized that for the first time all day the pace of her heartbeat had slowed, and she thought that her sister was so lucky to have this normal boy who liked her and took her out in the open air to see birds where other people could be there watching, not into a dark living room in the middle of the night.

And then Liz was right there, standing in the road which the strawberry rows bordered, hands at her hips, arms crooked at the elbow, knees locked back, head tilted down, eyes stern. The bulldog stance, the one their parents used whenever they upbraided the offspring for their willfulness and lack of respect. It was not even their garden. Then Liz's face cleared in a what-the-heck sort of way, and Iris knew she wouldn't read Michael the riot act; she could always hiss at them later. "Kind of a mess?" she said finally, her voice objective, diplomatic, though she raised her eyebrows at Michael, and he flushed red.

She walked into the open breezeway next to Noelle's garage and came out with a handful of paper bags so they could collect the mashed berries. Reaching down, she grabbed the two large bowls of good berries. Then she walked over and touched Michael's cheek, rubbing a finger lightly over the spot where a berry had left a reddish mark. She dangled the beach key in front of his nose. "Here," she said. "You're kind of sticky. Why don't you jump in the lake?"

Their battleground had encompassed five rows of strawberries and each row was littered with half-crushed berries. While Liz went back to the house, they worked quickly through the rows, Michael more productive than Scott or Iris, and in fifteen minutes they'd cleaned up the mess. Scott ran back to the house for beach towels, and the three of them trudged to the lake. Once there, they threw off their tennis shoes and socks and ran down the hill toward the water. The mothers looked at them strangely as they ran into the water wearing their clothes, but since Michael was there, for once Iris didn't worry about what other people might think. After they'd splashed around for a while, scrubbing at their sticky skin and the strawberry splotches on their clothes, they went back to the towels and stretched out under the sun.

Liz appeared at the top of the beach hill next to the gate. Iris was about to grab the key to let her in when someone else opened the gate, and Liz entered with a picnic basket in her hand and word-lessly sat down, opened the basket, and handed around sandwiches and paper cups of lemonade. She and Michael didn't speak, but he kept smiling at her and tickling her thigh with a blade of grass. When they finished their sandwiches, Liz pulled out a huge bowl of berries that she had cleaned and de-stemmed, and placing it on one of their beach towels. Alongside it, she set out a small container of sugar, and they dipped the berries in the sugar one by one as they watched the sun glint off the lake. In the distance, motor boats cut through the water, pulling skiers who waved cheerfully and just as cheerfully stumbled and sank. Iris bit into a large strawberry and felt the sugar crunch against her teeth. Bits of the pulp, juicy and succulent, clung to her lips. Liz and Michael were the pretend par-ents, and she and Scott were the children; they would dally forever, eating strawberries in the sun.

* * *

185

That day at the beach with the strawberries had been the last good moment the four of them had shared. The loss of Scott was followed by the temporary loss of Michael, a different kind of loss. Perhaps Michael knew now that the birds provided another kind of balm with their language of trills, whistles, and quacks, not unlike strawberries and sugar underneath the sun. Iris needed to listen more carefully.

27

Update on the Killings

July 10, 1974

Iris's parents called her in before the news began. "You should probably hear this," her mother said. The lead story featured the still-at-large Caretaker Killer. According to the detectives managing the case, the newscaster announced, the psychologists consulting on the killings had put together a timetable of the killers' murders. The killer had committed a murder every twenty-one days. Keeping to that schedule, he should have murdered the previous week. The police felt a guarded optimism about his actions, speculating that for now, perhaps, the killing had stopped. Parents were still to be vigilant in protecting their children, police advised. And though authorities were pleased that no more murders had been committed, they admitted that the trail was getting cold. With ten thousand tips received on the now infamous blue Gremlin, they still had their work cut out for them, but as of yet, they had pursued no strong leads.

"So, they think this killer has stopped," Iris said, to clarify what she'd heard.

"Sounds like it. For now. The police don't understand why he didn't follow through with his pattern. I guess that's unusual for serial killers," her father said.

"It could be a she," Iris's mother said. "I mean, I don't think so. I think men are usually more violent than women, but you never know."

"Thanks," Iris's father said.

"I'm not commenting on you; I think men are capable of that kind of thing – haven't they proven that, statistically?" their mother said.

Iris watched as his father rolled his eyes at her and then held the paper up again.

"I know you're not young like these victims, Iris, but you still need to be careful. You go off on your own too much."

"I'll watch out," Iris said. She didn't bother telling them that she and Liz had already had words about caution. And Iris still found it hard to be afraid of something bad happening, at least to herself. The worst had already happened in her life.

28

Texture

July 11, 1974

Iris's mother had promised that she'd take Iris to the fabric store on one of her days off from the library so Iris could buy some material to make halter tops. Iris's chosen fabric was in a sale section, on a bolt of thin cotton fabric, tiny red tulips splashed onto a white background, in ordered rows. She looked at the end of the bolt to see if the material was thirty-six or forty-eight inches wide, when another hand touched the navy print next to her fabric. "Hello, Iris," Rosemary said in a whisper. They'd both had Homemaking that previous year at school.

Rosemary's white-blonde hair was down from its usual ponytail, curled, and brushed softly next to her face. Iris was impressed. Rosemary looked so natural and grown up.

"My dad's in the car, so I have to hurry," she said. "Just wanted to say hello." She dipped her head a little, closed her eyes for a minute. "We need to do something again. Are you around tonight? Can you ride bikes with me to the gravel pit?" She lay her hand on Iris's bolt of cloth, smoothing down the fabric.

"After dinner," Iris said. "Maybe seven o'clock? I can come by and pick you up."

"Great," Rosemary said. Then she winked, and Iris watched the back of her friend as she walked away, legs tan under cut-offs, feet flapping in white sandals.

When Iris arrived at the house, Rosemary was in the side yard, hosing down her bike. "It was really dirty," she said. "I wanted to spiff it up a bit." Iris nodded and watched the water come out of the nozzle in a slow stream. Rosemary kicked off her sandals and stood on tiptoes, a pool of sudsy water building up at her feet. Her toenails were painted pink, but the enamel on the big one was chipped. As Iris watched, Rosemary flexed her toes and then dug them into the grass. Iris envied her long skinny body, her thin frame. Rosemary was tall, but only medium-boned, so she looked much smaller than Iris. A small, foamy soap bubble clung to her kneecap.

The bike had been out of commission for a couple of weeks, so Iris wasn't surprised that Rosemary wanted to go on a major excursion – the gravel pit was three miles away. But Iris was surprised at Rosemary's choice of locations. The gravel pit was an auxiliary dumping location for the local quarry company, so it was a largely unsupervised site where mostly older kids hung out. People called it Kandahar. Liz had told Iris in the past that the pit was a hot location for drug transactions, though she'd admitted that she'd once gone up there with Michael and that a lot of couples went up there to park. Drug transactions or not, Iris knew her mother probably wouldn't appreciate her going there, so she decided not to tell her.

"So why are you so determined to go to the gravel pit?" Iris asked.

Rosemary shrugged, "I heard it's kind of cool."

The day's heat still felt close and sticky, so the warm breeze that moved through their hair and against their legs as they biked provided welcome relief. The air smelled sweet and fragrant as they set off down the bike path that went beyond the Presbyterian Church where one of Iris's friends had taken her to summer Vacation Bible School during their elementary grade days. The trail wasn't difficult, but there were enough bumps and overgrown weeds that they both fell silent as they rode.

Finally, they arrived on a ridge overlooking the pit. Staring down at the large mounds of gravel from the top of the hill, Iris felt small and giddy. "At night, couples come here to park," Rosemary said. "Each car picks a different pile to park next to."

"How do they get down there?" Iris asked.

"See, over there?" Rosemary raised her hand, pointing, and seemed almost to teeter on the edge. "You and I came the fast way by bike, but there's also a road that comes into the bottom of the pit."

"How do you know all this?" Iris asked. Rosemary flashed Iris a quick smile, though her violet-blue eyes darted away, and her shoulders faced the other direction.

"Karl told me," Rosemary said.

"Karl," Iris said. Her voice was uncertain and tentative, even to her own ears. She remembered her first glance at Karl, through the kitchen window at the Langley's, his face looming up out of the darkness, his mustached grin easy and friendly.

"You know," Rosemary insisted. "Mrs. Langley's brother. The guy who saved the cat."

"We found it first," Iris said defiantly. "Sherry and I." She realized how much force her voice carried, so she looked down and kicked at a piece of gravel under her foot.

"But he got it down from the tree," Rosemary said.

"Did he say anything else?" Iris asked. She looked into Rosemary's eyes and the fringe of eyelashes that made them almost sparkle.

Rosemary frowned. "I don't think so. Was he supposed to?"

"No," Iris said slowly. Overhead a solitary crow flew across the gravel pit.

"He's really neat," Rosemary said. She looked out at the piles of gravel; the sun glanced off pieces of shiny flint in the stones. "You know, it's so different here at night," she said.

"You've been here at night?" Rosemary turned away at the rising sound of Iris's voice, her face awkward and embarrassed. "You came here with Karl, is that it?" Now Iris's voice wavered slightly before it was carried off in the breeze.

"Just once," Rosemary said. "The other day."

"Why didn't you just start with that?" Iris said. "You didn't have to drag me all the way up here." Iris stepped back from the edge and toward her bike. "You could have just told me."

"Why are you so upset?" Rosemary asked. "I wasn't going to say anything," she said. "I didn't plan this – I wasn't even going to tell you." She moved over next to Iris, gently tugging at the cloth of her sleeve. "But we didn't do anything, really," she said. "Not anything wrong."

"Well, maybe *you* didn't do anything wrong." Iris nodded. "But maybe *he* did," she said. Iris wanted to tell Rosemary that she believed Karl was unlike any of the younger boys her sister knew who groped around girls' bodies in the back seats of cars, wanting just a touch, a lick. But she struggled to find the words.

"I mean," Rosemary said, "I did lie to my mom and dad and told them I was babysitting." She looked down for a moment, then brought her head up. "But down there in the car--" she gestured to the bottom of the pit. "Down there in the car I didn't do anything, not anything wrong," Rosemary said. "I just want you to know that."

"Rosemary, I know you like him, and I'm happy for you. That's not the problem."

"Well, what is the problem, Iris? Why are you so dead set against him?"

Iris got back on her bike. Maybe she was jealous. Maybe it was all about her own feelings and desires. Maybe she was trying to deprive Rosemary of the kind of affection that her friend needed, especially with Allen out of the picture. Iris felt that Rosemary wouldn't understand if she tried to explain what she meant. "Look," she said to Rosemary, "I'm glad you showed me. It is a cool place. I'd love to see it at night. But let's go back now."

Rosemary nodded, and they began the ride back, the sun setting in the horizon, the air more tolerable, but the day still close, too close.

29

Hookey

July 12, 1974

"Hookey," Sheldon said. He closed the back of his truck and turned to where Iris stood in the driveway, straddling her bike between her legs. "I woke up this morning and thought to myself – that's what we need to do – play hookey!"

"Is it really hookey if there's no one to answer to? I mean it's not like you have some ogre of a boss or a teacher breathing down your neck," Iris said.

"Where *did* you get this tendency to be contrary?" Sheldon asked.

Iris blushed.

"Don't spoil my fun," he said. "I'm asking you if you want to go out and do some exploring. You were planning on working most of the day, anyway, weren't you?"

Iris nodded.

"Good. We'll stop by and let your folks know; grab ourselves a cooler, some ice, and some pop at the store; and be off."

"My parents and Liz are at work," Iris said. "We don't have to stop."

"Okay," he said. "Tell you what." He felt in his pocket for keys. "You run inside and open a couple of windows – one in the back bedroom and the one in the hallway. Now that the rain is gone, I want that paint to get some breeze time. I've got to look through the tackle box."

"Tackle?"

Sheldon joined his two hands up to his right shoulder and straightened his arms out with an arc-like motion. "We're going fishing!"

An hour later they were headed out of town on the road Iris's dad called the "scenic route." Out the window, the houses grew sparser, fields filling the space next to the road they travelled. Iris knew that the town she lived in was a suburb to a bigger town, yet even the main roads in her town had their busy and non-busy sections, and when you drove to the end of the them, the busy parts began to fade, and there was more and more land and fewer traffic lights. She didn't know what qualified as still part of her town and flat-out countryside.

Sheldon seemed to have slowed down the car, and he took his right hand off the wheel and pulled something from the seat behind him. He dropped the packet into Iris's lap. "I don't know when your birthday is, so this is not a birthday present." He cleared his throat. "And it doesn't seem right to give you a present associated with the anniversary of your brother's death. But I wanted you to have this, even though I don't know what the occasion is."

Iris looked down at the package on her lap, a rectangular object with layers of varying thicknesses, all of it wrapped in brown paper and tied up with run-of-the mill string. "Wow, Sheldon. Thank you, whatever the occasion. You didn't have to do this," Iris said.

"You know people say that all the time, right? Are you going to open it?"

Iris pulled at the knotted bow on top and was thankful that it was the kind that undid itself and didn't lead to a string-secured web that was impenetrable without a knife or pair of scissors. She opened up the paper and saw a small stack of large thick books, a package of pencils and charcoal sticks, a package of brushes, and a package of paints. "Oh my gosh, Sheldon, I can't believe you got me all of these supplies! How did you know how much I've been wanting to learn?" Iris said.

"No offense, but you painted on the walls," Sheldon said. "That was a pretty good sign."

"There's so much here! Where do I start?" Iris said.

"I'd do some of the drawing stuff first," Sheldon said. "That one book gives you a few basic shapes to play with, and then you learn about shading, and dimensions, and shadows. Perspective," he said, rattling off the concepts. "After you do a few of those pages, look at the painting books and mess around with the paint."

"I can't wait," Iris said. "But I'll never be as good as you are."

"I'm not sure that the point is about how good you are. I think it's more about how the process makes you feel."

Sheldon put on his blinker and Iris looked up. They were on the road that led to the Whoopee Bowl, their dad's favorite junk store where you could wind your way through the floors of small nooks and crannies.

"The Whoopee Bowl," Sheldon said in his announcer's voice as they approached. "My favorite place to get junk for art."

"My parents used to tell the story of how I got lost there," Iris told Sheldon as they drove along. Their mom carried Scott on her hip, Iris explained, and she and Scott were in a section with plastic placemats, doilies, picnic supplies. Their dad had headed back to the older part of the store where you could find saw blades and drill bits. Iris was supposed to be with him, but Iris and her dad both lost track of that fact, and instead she found herself in a small room stocked with old canning jars full of screws, springs, nuts. On the floor were several coils of jute and sisal, and she kept tripping on them as she wandered in and out of the room, trying to find her father. A blue-haired lady, the mother of the man who owned the place, found Iris trying to tug her sandal out of a pile of rope. "'She was so scared. She thought the rope was going to get her,' the lady told my mom."

"But the funny thing is – that's not the way I remember it," Iris said to Sheldon. They'd just driven past the property. "I don't remember being afraid. I remember putting my feet into two piles and trying to dance."

"Trying to dance?" Sheldon said.

"You know, like hopping in and out – like a hat dance or something, or maybe even some weird kind of hopscotch, where I crossed my feet. But they remember it so differently than I do. They say I was scared."

"Maybe they didn't know you were so brave," he said.

"I'm not," Iris said quickly. "I'm not brave."

"Maybe you are," Sheldon said. "But nobody knows it."

198

"She gave me a Slo-poke. For free. The lady, I mean. Took me to a register in the middle of the store, sent some clerk around to find my father, and gave me a Slo-poke."

"Were they jealous, Scott and Liz? Because you had an adventure and they didn't?"

Iris shook her head. "Scott was way too young to notice, maybe only three. And Liz never said anything to me about it." Iris paused, brushing her hair away from her face, trying to remember the expression in Liz's eyes. "I don't know. But when my parents tell the story, they always say how scared I was."

"Well, I don't know what a psychologist would say, but the fact that you remember it as positive is interesting. Maybe your family is right; maybe you have buried whatever fear you experienced then. But I think it's just as likely that you remember it the way it really was."

"I like the idea that I wasn't really afraid."

"It's your history, Iris. Arguably, you can write it any way you want. By the way, I think we're almost there," he said. "Just have to turn up this road here." He put on his blinker then and slowed to take the turn. Iris saw one of the big brown signs announcing a state park. She began to wrap up the package of drawing and painting books, retying the string and making sure the packages of pencils and brushes were neatly tucked into the brown paper.

"So, you've never been fishing before? Or just a few times?" Sheldon said.

"Once, I think, maybe twice. When we were young, we went to a cabin way up north. I barely remember it, but the guy who owned it was named Stan, I think, and there was this big deer head on the wall. Stan was one of my dad's hunting buddies. I remember being in a boat, my dad telling me to be quiet. It seemed like forever. But then, for years, he kept saying he would take me with Scott, and he never did. Just couldn't fit it in, I guess."

"Having three kids is hard, I bet."

"Now he only has two." Iris didn't realize she'd spoken aloud until Sheldon sighed.

"Sorry, Iris," Sheldon reached over in the air of the front seat as if to offer comfort, and then settled his hand on Iris's head, his fingers warm on her hair, before he pulled them back to the steering wheel.

"It's okay, Sheldon. I can't avoid the truth for too much longer. And it looks like we're here. Hookey land." Iris said.

Iris was glad it was a stream and not a lake. The water gurgled quietly past the spot Sheldon picked out to start their enterprise. Iris opened the two lounge chairs he'd brought for them to sit on, and he went back for the coolers, the big one full of ice with their deli sandwiches from the store and a six-pack of root beer, her choice, and a little cooler full of bait. After Iris opened the chairs she stood on the bank and watched the water, the tiny swells moving over the various-sized rocks and eddying downward.

"I don't see any fish," Iris said to Sheldon as he approached with the coolers.

"You think they jump out and offer to shake your hand?" he said. "Why do you think fisherman are always talking about the one that got away? Fish are crafty little devils."

"What kind of fish are we fishing for?" Iris asked.

"Good question. Maybe small-mouth bass. You'll probably find a lot of the little ones that you'll need to throw back in. You might catch one of those ugly old catfish. And of course," he said finally, "I'd love to see a cisco, but those are lake fish, so I'm really dreaming!"

"Of course," Iris said. "Too bad they're extinct." She made a face at him.

"Well, yeah, sort of," he said. "Here," he handed her a well-worn little pocket fishing guide. "If I don't know what I've pulled out, I start thumbing through the book."

"And you'll put on the bait for me?"

He nodded.

When it was time, Iris turned away as Sheldon skewered the bodies of the night crawlers on the hooks. He'd threatened to buy leaches, but Iris told him she'd throw up for sure if he did, so he said okay, night crawlers and some smaller worms then.

"Didn't know you were so squeamish, Iris."

"It's not that the worms gross me out. It's the act of puncturing them." She shivered.

"Okay, now, once we get situated, we have to be quiet so the fish will bite."

"This is the part I remember," Iris whispered. "My dad kept saying 'shhhh!'"

Sheldon's voice went down to a whisper. "So, we picked this part of the stream because it's up river. We cast with our lines upstream and let the current carry the line downstream; the worms tumble naturally in the current." He gestured to their lawn chairs. "We get to rest sometimes but depending on how fast the river is flowing today, we'll be casting every few minutes. So, it's up and down with the chairs, until we decide to get lazy and just sit."

He nodded at the stream and said, "Watch." He cast his pole to the side and flicked his line, and Iris traced its path under the sunlight, until it settled into the water. "Sometimes it gets caught on rocks, but we'll just deal with that when it happens."

Iris took the pole he'd given her and tried to imitate his motions, though her line didn't land nearly as neatly in the water. But their lines were both in place and slowly moving downstream, so Sheldon nodded to Iris that she could sit for a few minutes.

Red-winged blackbirds flitted in and out of the cattails on the other side of the river in an adjacent area that looked more swamp than river or stream. Iris opened her mouth to ask Sheldon the difference between a river and a stream and then remembered she wasn't supposed to talk. A chorus of peepers sounded off to her left. It was funny how they'd been at their spot setting up for a least a half hour and she hadn't even noticed the peeper noise, which had become a part of the larger river chorus. Iris had taken her sweatshirt off as soon as they arrived and wrapped it around her waist, so she sat back now in her tank top, her bare arms meeting the cool nylon webbing of the chair. She closed her eyes and felt the light breeze move over her face. "You can let your mind relax, but your hand must stay vigilant," Sheldon whispered.

Iris nodded. Let her mind relax. Would she ever again let her mind relax? Next to her right ear a buzz sounded, and Iris's eyes flew open. It was a horsefly, though, and with a pang she remembered that she wasn't the one allergic to bees anyway. Sheldon stood up and cast again, and Iris did the same, pleased to see that her line seemed to be wandering a slow, meandering path downstream.

Iris sat back in her chair again, trying to hold her pole firmly, but not too tensely. "Not like a soldier," Sheldon said, "but like a conductor. Can you see the difference?" Iris wasn't sure. In the pictures of Arthur Fiedler she'd seen on television, his hands moved intensely, almost like he was irritated with the musicians and he was shaking his baton at them. She wasn't sure how much his grip differed from that of a soldier.

Iris felt it then, the tug. Just a gentle little thing, but her posture changed enough that Sheldon sat up, too, watching her line tighten. A few ripples broke the surface of the water.

"Start winding the reel gently," Sheldon said. "Not jerkily, gently."

Iris started winding; it was so easy that she sped up a bit, her fingers excited and agitated.

Sheldon shook his head. "Slow and steady pressure. Otherwise this guy will spit the hook out," he said.

"Shhhhhhhhh," Iris whispered, as she made a face.

"So now you're shushing me?"

"Just doing what you told me."

"You're doing great. Keep the line taut. Can you feel pressure at the end?"

Iris nodded. She couldn't talk. She wanted to save her energy for reeling the fish in. "I didn't know the line was so long," she whispered.

"It just feels like it," he whispered back. Then he said in a normal voice, "We probably don't have to whisper anymore. In a minute this fish is going to be flapping all over the surface of the water, warning all the other fish away. Now, if you want, I'll take over from here, but I really think you can do it, if you're willing. I can talk you through it."

"I'll try."

"Okay," he said. "Now you can pick the pace up a little bit. Don't let him scare you. I'll get him from the end; you just control the line. Hold it taut and keep the tension steady. Whatever you do, don't let the line go slack."

"Don't let the line go slack," Iris repeated.

Just as Sheldon had predicted, the fish soon flipped out of the water, the scales glistening silver under the sun. Then the fish dove back in.

"What kind is it? Did you see?"

"Bass, I think. Keep the pressure steady," Sheldon said. He made his way down the bank with the bucket he'd brought, dunked it in the stream to fill it with water. "Keep reeling."

"It's getting harder," Iris said.

"I know, the last few feet are always hard. Just keep the line tight."

The fish emerged again, and this time, Iris saw a shiny flash. She tried to focus all her attention on reeling in the fish, but she saw Sheldon's hand reach out for the line with a fish net in his other hand. He soon held the net up and then flopped the fish into the bucket of water. Then, with one hand holding the fish, he reached into the mouth with the other hand and pulled out the hook, turning to Iris with a smile of triumph.

Later, at the restaurant, they told the story over again in interrupted fits of laughter and half sentences to the waitress, who was one of Sheldon's friends. "You should have seen her – she was tremendous." Sheldon said it like her dad might have said it, that little catch of pride in his voice. Iris was embarrassed.

That was her only fish that day. Sheldon caught three little ones and let them go, but Iris got the keeper, twelve inches long. And meaty, Sheldon said. They could make a great meal of it.

When Iris had seen her fish in the bucket in the back of Sheldon's truck, she felt happier than she had in a long time, until she remembered the next step for the fish – the beheading, the gutting, the filleting. Sheldon said he would take care of all of that at his house later. Iris looked at the fish's eye, glassy, focused. She didn't know how or if fish thought about anything – if fish operated by instinct and made calculated decisions, or if they just knew how to swim and eat and elude hooks. The photo-taking provided an awkward moment. The fish was still alive, so Iris couldn't hold it in her hands, and Sheldon said it would be weird to take a picture staring down into a bucket. So, Iris stood next to the park sign with the pole to the side, her one hand pointing toward the bucket. At the last minute before he took the shot, Iris puckered up, making a fish face. And after Sheldon took the photo, she watched the look of disappointment kindle briefly in Sheldon's eyes as she told him she wanted to let the fish go.

"He won't survive. His breathing's been compromised," Sheldon said.

"But he has a chance, and I won't be the one who did him in," Iris said.

"You've read way too many murder mysteries," Sheldon said. Then he sighed. "But it's your fish – you're the boss."

He let it go, and Iris waved when its tail flopped in the water. They'd taken another picture before he dropped it in, the fish dark and glossy in Sheldon's hands. And then they went to the restaurant for their Key Lime pie.

The sun was moving down in the sky now, and there was the faint glow of approaching twilight. Sheldon told Iris he'd take her home and she could get her bike the next day. When they pulled into the driveway, Iris's father was on the front porch smoking a cigar, the tip glowing red as he puffed it, then flashing and going gray when he held it away from his mouth. He approached the driveway and nodded at Sheldon as he stepped out of the truck, transferring the cigar to his left hand and offering Sheldon his right. "So," he said. "Long day at work?" He looked from Sheldon back to Iris.

"Well, actually we were going to leave you a note. We played hookey," Sheldon said.

Iris's father nodded. "I wondered. I went to the house and you weren't there."

"Why?" Iris said.

"Sorry," Sheldon said, almost at the same time. "We were going to leave a note, like I said, but since everyone was gone, Iris said not to bother."

"Why?" Iris said again, looking at her dad.

"Why what?" he said.

"Why did you go to the house?"

"I got home early. Thought you might want to go out for a bit." Iris's dad almost never got home early. She felt confused.

206

"Well, sorry again for keeping her out past dinner," Sheldon said. "We just decided to skip work and have some fun."

"Where'd you go?" Iris's dad said. "I was just surprised, you know, that you weren't there, and you're usually working."

"Fishing," Sheldon said. "And you wouldn't believe what your daughter caught. Tell him, Iris." He looked at Iris, waiting for her to say something. "Tell him," he said again.

Her father looked down, the tip of his shoe nudging a thread of cigar ash on the driveway. "Fishing, eh?" he said. His voice was funny, artificially buoyed up, a game show host's. "So, what did you catch, Iris?" he said. And he wasn't Iris's dad anymore, but Monty Hall or Bob Barker or Wink Martindale trying to be clever and friendly.

"Nothing much," Iris said.

"A small-mouth bass," Sheldon said. "Twelve inches long." And then, as if he finally caught the scent of the dynamic between Iris and her father, between himself and his old friend, he said, "You would have been proud of your daughter. It was really beautiful, quite a feat. And she did a great job reeling it in."

Iris's father looked up then, straight at her, and wading through whatever disappointment or displacement he felt, he asked tentatively, "Can I see?"

Iris closed her eyes and felt the elation of the day sink from her face through her body, seeping out in a pool at her feet, all the energy she'd regained gone. She couldn't even speak, so she was glad when Sheldon said quietly, "You know girls, squeamish and all? She didn't want to keep it. Let it go, back into the stream."

Iris's father nodded then, crushed his cigar in the driveway, and said, "Good to see you, Sheldon," before he turned and walked toward the garage. After her father turned away, Sheldon slipped the brown paper package from the back seat and handed it wordlessly to Iris, who shoved it under her arm, close to her side.

It had never occurred to Iris that her father might have wanted to spend a lazy afternoon with her, like the one she'd just spent with Sheldon. It never occurred to her that her father could long for something that involved her, but she understood then, that however much joy she'd felt with the sun on her face and the fish in the bucket, she needed to subtract that amount from her father's dwindling allotment of joy, pushing him into a deep well, absent fish, absent joy.

30

Memorial

July 15, 1974

A steamy rain fell the afternoon of the memorial service, the kind that might take place in a war-torn jungle in Vietnam or Laos, when the troops were at their lowest, mud-spattered, weary, and still the rain came down, relentless. Iris lay across the bed in her bra and underwear, face-down, staring at a piece of lint on the purple rug. "We're supposed to leave in ten minutes," Liz said from the door. "Mom will be pissed if you make us late. Why aren't you dressed?"

"All of my pantyhose have runs in them," Iris said. But she was lying.

"Then you can use some of mine. Or go bare-legged. It's just us; no one will care."

Iris turned her face toward Liz to show she was listening. "I'll be there in a minute." Iris suspected that Liz wouldn't leave until she moved, but finally her sister sighed and left the room.

In the car, Iris watched the rain stream down the windows. Once her mother took the driver's seat, she twisted a plastic triangle around her hair, fussing about the rain. Their father was supposed to come from work to meet them at church. The middle of a weekday seemed like a strange time to be going to church, but the pastor had said the middle of the week was a nice, private time for a memorial service. If they were Catholic, they would have had a few masses said in Scott's name around the anniversary date. Their mom said they needed to do something, so she and the pastor worked out prayers and readings from the red hymnal, which they postponed until after the Fourth.

But it felt all wrong with just the four of them sitting in the front pew, no printed weekly church program on which to play hangman in the margins. And Iris realized how little she'd been there in those pews since he'd died.

Their father kept clearing his throat as the pastor spoke in a quiet voice. All the windows were open, and outside the rain punctured the earth, making the heat rise in steam from the soil. Their mother fumbled in her purse for a handkerchief, wiped at her face, her eyes. Next to Iris, Liz sat like a statue, her body rigid. Iris thought if she exhaled in just the right way, she could make a part of her skirt-clad thigh touch her sister's, making her move, making her body fall out of that attentive posture. Iris kept staring at her sister's skirt, the pattern of black and gray lines, trying to tangle them in her head. She felt panicky, like she couldn't breathe or like she might jump up and shout something or begin sobbing. She wanted to reach her hand out and touch her sister's skirt, feel the substance of Liz's leg underneath her hand, and she didn't understand why she was having such a physical response to the service. A bubble of sound rose up through her throat, and she clenched at the pew, bracing herself with her two hands.

She choked the sound down, transforming it into a retching noise before stumbling from the pew, running down the stairs, through the large open space full of Sunday School rooms made with dividers and back up another stairway to the broom closet bathroom.

And still Iris couldn't stop the noise, half cough, half sob. She knelt on the floor next to the toilet, holding her head over the bowl, willing herself to cry or throw up or empty something out of her body and into the toilet. She screeched a muffled cry into the white porcelain. She thought maybe the tears would come then, but there was nothing.

When she walked back down the center aisle, their heads were bent forward in prayer. If her mother felt disappointed with Iris's absence, her face didn't show it. The pastor moved into a Bible verse: *"Take his yoke upon you and learn of him. For he is meek, and lowly of heart. And ye shall find rest. Ye shall find rest unto your souls.'* May each day bring you a lessening of your own burdens and an opportunity to see the glory of God."

The pastor asked them to join hands, and Liz offered Iris a limp palm. Iris felt the gale rise again in her chest, but this time, it was a storm of anger. Why did they join hands and speak to God when they could barely speak to each other, when they wouldn't even tell Iris the truth about how they felt, when Iris could barely look them in the face let alone speak a word about how much her head hurt some days with the weight of it all?

In the last few minutes of the sermon, the pastor began the Lord's Prayer, and Iris stumbled over the part about the trespasses.

She had never thought about "those who trespass against us." She was one of those people who had trespassed.

When they moved to the aisle, Liz whispered, "Why is it so hard for you to stay in your seat and give mom what she wants?"

Their mother was further up the aisle, so Iris whispered back, "Why are you so sure this memorial is what she wants?" Was she trespassing when she said that back to her sister?

After the service, they went to an all-day breakfast place for pancakes. When the waitress seated them in a booth, Iris realized that they'd been given the plain old rectangular booth, two people to each side, instead of the circular one they used to get all the time, the one in the corner. The one they got when Scott was alive. They put their order in, and then their mom took a deep breath. "Well, I just wanted to say a little something because we've made it over a year now. And that's an accomplishment. I think we should feel good about our progress."

Their dad smiled, and Liz nodded. She was fidgeting with a napkin. Since it was a weekday, the restaurant wasn't as crowded as usual. "I don't know that I've made any progress, though I think that's a positive way of looking at things," Iris said as she looked up at her mother. "I think maybe you've made progress, Mom, because you're not around much anymore and you seem to have a new life at the library. I don't know about Dad."

The waitress brought four orange juices, and Iris could see that Liz wanted to say something. They all remained silent while the waitress put the juice glasses down in front of them. As she walked away, Liz said, "Mom is trying to focus on the positive, and

I think that's a really important step. We haven't always been able to do that."

"I know she is focusing on the positive," Iris said. "That's a good thing, for her. I just don't know about the rest of us."

"You're not saying that I'm moving on, are you?" their mother said. "I'm not moving on yet, I'm still torn up about it, but yes, I'm trying to stay positive. But not moving on, not forgetting him," she said, her voice going off-track, derailed.

"No one is saying that you're forgetting him!" Iris's father said. "We're saying you're doing a good job of looking at things from a healthy perspective."

"You must know that I think about him nearly every single minute of every single day," Iris's mom said.

"We didn't say you didn't," Iris's father said.

The waitress came forward with a stack of plates lined up her arms, announcing the orders as she put them down in the correct places at the table. After she left, Iris said, "We don't talk about things enough." Then she exhaled. "At all, really."

"What things?" Liz said. "What should we talk about? What are we supposed to say?"

Iris could hear the agitation in her sister's voice, and she thought about how easy it would be to back down. "We don't talk about how we're feeling, and we don't talk about what happened that day."

"What's the point of talking about what happened that day?" Iris's father said.

"I agree with your father – what's the point?" Iris's mother said.

"Why can't you just for once be honest and admit that you all think it's my fault?"

Iris's father reached for the coffee pot and knocked a knife down in the booth. It clanged as it hit the floor.

"I don't see any point in continuing this conversation in this direction," Iris's mother said.

"But don't you think I would feel better if you could all just scream at me and tell me it was my fault that he's dead? That if I'd been awake and doing my job, I would have told him he wasn't ready to swim across the lake? That I should have been awake so that I could stop him?"

"Iris, we don't want to go down this road right now," Iris's father said.

"Right now, or ever?" Iris said.

"I can go down that road," Liz said. "I do think it was your fault. I don't want to make you feel bad, but I do think it's your fault, and I don't know how I'm supposed to just hide that. I don't think about it every day, and I don't hate you." She turned to face Iris, as if she wanted to talk directly to her, but then her shoulders rose, and Iris watched as her sister's lips trembled, her face grimacing, and she looked away. "I don't hate you," she said into the aisle, away from the table, "but I do blame you, and I don't know how to stop doing that."

"Liz," their mother said, a note of caution in her voice.

"At least she admitted it," Iris said. "At least I can feel that blame full force now, even if no one ever mentions it again."

"That's enough," their father said. "We need to just calm down and forget about this – eat our food." He raised his hand, beckoning to the waitress for the bill.

Iris's pancakes were cold. She didn't even want them anymore. She hadn't wanted the day to start, and now that they all sat in their miserable booth, she wanted to rise and race toward the door. She picked up the syrup container and poured it on her stack of pancakes, watching as the syrup coated the top, continuing its journey into the open weave of the top pancake's surface while simultaneously spreading to the sides and dripping down those as well, pancakes swamped in the viscous brown fluid. She held the container over the pancakes until she'd emptied it, and even then, she held her hand there, aloft, until her father finally took the syrup out of her hands.

31

The Detroit Tigers

July 21, 1974

Iris's mother had convinced their father not to go to the family reunion, opting instead to do their annual Tigers game event. They'd purchased the tickets before their post-memorial-service breakfast, and though it was only a little over an hour to Detroit, Iris suffered the ride in the car, especially after they got stuck in traffic on the expressway. She tried to read her book, but the movement of the car and the bumps from the road underneath them made her dizzy. She remembered that the year before, Scott had been sitting next to her, throwing a baseball into his mitt, the rhythmic slap of leather against leather creating a lulling sound.

But this year Liz sat beside her, making a braided chain out of gum wrappers.

That previous summer marked a time when Scott had started to become interested in baseball, so he was eager to sit next to their father and understand the game. The two of them had begun a dialogue, and Iris had felt a bit left out when her father had started to bond with Scott, forgetting that Iris had followed baseball with him for several years already.

Their father wasn't a sports fanatic, but he respected the game of baseball, and he enjoyed recreating the excitement of that 1968 season when the Tigers won the World Series.

Iris remembered the wins. She didn't remember all their names, and she couldn't claim that she'd been an avid Tigers fan every season. But she remembered the wonder of that 1968 season, the excitement in early fall when she'd entered fourth grade and all the boys had been talking about the Tigers, saying their names in a shorthand, familiar way: Kaline, Horton, Cash, Lolich, Freehan, McLain. And the day they'd won the World Series, she'd walked around the block with her transistor radio close to her ear, listening to the game from St. Louis broadcast on WJR, standing near the evergreen hedge right next to Mrs. Humphrey's yard on that day. She stood in the middle of the road and let out a hoot to no one.

It was quiet in the car as they drove along, and it was almost like their father needed to spin out an old story or some history, maybe as if Scott were there in the car with them, and he could continue the education he'd started. If only Iris had been born a boy. Traffic started to move again, and as they drove closer to the stadium exit, their father began talking, like he was picking up where he left off. "No matter what happened in the World Series that year with Lolich, no matter what happened in 1970 with all that Mafia business, in 1968, you just had to love Denny McLain," their father said. "That summer everyone watched him – the whole city, the whole state, and maybe even the whole nation." Their father's voice carried a note of awe as he told the story, his hands moving in front of him as if to sketch out a diamond and put the players on the field. "Three days before they won the pennant, he pitches his thir-tieth win for the season. And then when they won the pennant on September 17, everyone went wild." He paused to look at his wife, beside him in the front seat. "It was their first pennant since 1945. There were over 46,000 fans at Tiger Stadium that night." Their mother looked over at him, smiling pleasantly, and Iris suspected she was pretending to listen.

As they got off on their exit, Iris leaned forward to watch where they would park the car, how much of a walk it would be to the sta-dium. Once they took their seats in the bleachers, Iris tried to work up enthusiasm about the results of the game, but she felt as if she'd lost interest in the sport, found it too tedious to truly enjoy, yet she respected how much her mother tried to make things festive, offering to run to the stands for anything the other three wanted.

Liz and Iris ate two hot dogs apiece. The Tigers were losing, which their dad said wasn't terribly surprising, but they could tell that even he had been hoping; he kept making comments about the team's promise at the end of 1972, saying if they could only get back some of that momentum from 1968. Iris sat in her seat and closed her eyes, feeling the warm breeze play over her face. Someone must have spilled ketchup in the row behind them. As darkness began to fall, the stadium lights came on; Iris counted ninety-six bulbs in each set of lights, though a few were burned out. The field below her was lush, green, and summery. When the opposing team hit a home run, the announcer's voice rose to a higher range as he informed the listeners that the ball had gone over the stadium wall and onto the roof of Brooks Lumber Company. Iris wanted to wish, for their father's sake that they were living in the time of the 1968 pennant race, when history was made by men who might be rife with both talent and folly, famous and wonderful in spite of their flaws. But she knew her heart couldn't get behind that kind of wish.

On the way home, their father turned the radio on in the car, the volume low, to one of the stations he and their mother listened to sometimes, and Iris hoped she could fall asleep. Liz said, "I'll be honest. The whole evening was kind of hard without Scott."

Their mother spoke up, "Oh, I know, honey, but let's not get into that again, okay?"

"Wait," Iris said. "We can't just pretend it didn't happen. Don't you think it would be a little easier if we could get all of the negative feelings out there in the open? Kind of like Liz did at the restaurant?"

"Don't blame anything on me," Liz said.

"But who has negative feelings?" her mother said. "It was a mistake, plain and simple."

"A mistake I made," Iris said, and she looked at Liz in the growing darkness. "I'm not blaming you for anything."

"Not you, necessarily," her mother said. Outside the window, the lights from the buildings in Detroit twinkled around them, the air coming in through the windows they'd cracked with little whooshes.

"Well who, then?"

"Iris, I don't blame you at all," her father said. "It was just a series of circumstances."

"I fell asleep," Iris said. "I was supposed to be watching him!" She was trying to keep her voice calm, because she wanted to have the conversation even if it meant that she felt worse afterward. If she was going to get the punishment of their wrath, she wanted it now; it would be so much better than the long, lonely periods of avoidance.

"What he means to say, Iris, is that I should have been watching Scott," her mother said.

"Or maybe I should have been there," Liz said.

"No, your father wanted me home. He didn't want me to take that library job," their mother said.

"I didn't ever say that," their father said.

"You didn't have to," Iris's mother said. "It was plain as day. As the nose on your face," she said. And then she laughed. To Iris's ears, it was a bitter cackle.

"I don't know what your mother is talking about," their father said.

"I dared to want something. Some things, actually. I wanted some time on my own, away from the house. I wanted the income so that maybe I could think about living in a different house." She pushed in the lighter on the car dashboard. "The universe punished me," she said. "So no, Iris, like your father, I also don't think Scott's death was your fault." The lighter made its popping out noise, and Iris saw her mother lift the red heated coil toward the cigarette propped between her lips.

"I have to get up early tomorrow for work," Liz said. "Can we drop this for now?"

They were on Woodward Avenue, and soon they'd be heading back down Huron and then M-59. Iris remembered that their father had wanted their mother to quit her library job after Scott died, but she said no, she couldn't bear to stay home all day and see

221

his empty room, especially once school started. She hadn't known the burden her mother must have carried. Like all the cigarette smoke filling a car, it must have filled every room in the house and lingered there, in the air, surrounding them, dissipating but never really going away.

Iris knew the danger of paralysis, knew why everyone else in her family tried so hard to stay busy. Wasn't it a failure to act that had gotten her into trouble in the first place? But you could take the wrong step, too, when you acted. Iris knew that, and in that moment, she just wanted to escape the car full of people afraid to talk and retreat to her room, wade through the images in her head, wonder how the Sleeping Bear felt when she wasn't there for her cubs. Wonder how the parents of the dead children could live with themselves and their decisions to let their children walk out of the doors without protection. Wonder how the child killer felt and whether he had an inkling of remorse. Wonder about Rosemary's loneliness. Iris made herself conjure up Scott's face at the moment he took his last breath, eyes wide with terror and then clenched shut in fierce concentration, chin pointed up to produce more air from his lungs, face tilted like he was listening to some song, waiting for the crescendo, ready for the release that would startle him into joy. Remembering him in this way, Iris worked to pay for her transgressions, the strong smell of death keeping her awake, vigilant. When the car pulled into the driveway, she jumped out as fast as she could, wondering where she could go to escape the loaded silence that surrounded her.

32

Parcel

July 24, 1974

A few days later, when Iris felt that the Merchant household had gone back to the polite, distant form of communication that had characterized the atmosphere since Scott's death, Rosemary called. She'd returned from a family vacation and found a package waiting for her. "It's really amazing," she said. "I want you to see it. The package came while I was gone."

"So, you had a good time," Iris said, thinking of the sun-tanned Rosemary she knew from summers past, relaxation loosening her features.

"I got to look at a lot of water and eat a lot of lobster stew," Rosemary said. "It was okay. But you need to see the package from my cousin's girlfriend – you have to see what was in it."

"Okay," Iris said, "I'll be down in a few."

Rosemary sat on the side porch waiting for her, sunglasses perched halfway down her nose, her hair in a ponytail. "Ta-dah," she said, pushing out her hip. She picked up the brown thing at her waist and held it out – a dark chocolate suede purse with a voluminous pocket to carry a million things – nail polish, sanitary napkins, toys for babysitting. The sewing looked pretty good, the seams virtually invisible. It was the kind of purse they'd longed for in the past. The big wide flap hung over the buttonless, zipper-less closure. But the best part was the fringe. Six inches of fringe hung from the bottom of the purse, and more from the flap. Fringe like the kind with strung-on beads for those room dividers you saw on episodes of the *Mod Squad*, when Peggy Lipton, Michael Cole, and Clarence Williams III entered one of those drug havens, making sarcastic quips at the people lounging on bean bags smoking cigarettes, having just stashed their pot or heroin underneath them.

"Can you believe his girlfriend actually sent it to me?" Rosemary said.

"Karl's?" Iris said in amazement.

"Not Karl! My cousin's." She gave Iris a strange look and then said, "Karl doesn't have another girlfriend. My aunt, my cousin's mother? I guess she actually paid the girlfriend to make it because the girlfriend's trying to make money."

"Oh." *Another girlfriend.* Iris touched the fringe, the suede soft under her fingers. "Is there any news about your cousin?"

"In her letter with the purse, the girlfriend said that their other friend told her the governments are supposed to be talking to each other, and all the sides are supposed to list their MIAs to help account for them. But it's a slow process."

"I'm sorry, Rosemary," Iris said. "In the beginning, after you told me, I didn't know what to say. I still don't know, but I know what it's like to miss a brother, even though he's not missing in the same way as your cousin."

Rosemary shrugged. "I feel bad, but it's not like I ever knew him that well. His girlfriend almost acts like they were married, and she wants to know me. It's been so long since we heard from her," she said. "And out of the blue, she sends a package and a letter. *To me*," Rosemary said emphatically. "His girlfriend Mary." Rosemary plopped herself down on one of the two chairs that took up space on the narrow side porch. "I think maybe she's just lonely."

"It's a beautiful purse," Iris said. She rested her back against the porch railing across from her friend. Rosemary was more charged up than Iris had seen her in a long time. "I'm so glad your cousin's girlfriend wrote to you. Will you write back?"

"I already did," Rosemary said. She lifted her sunglasses. "Want to go for a walk?"

They walked from Rosemary's house down by the canal to the beach on Destan, trudging to the place where the road ended not too far beyond the beach. Rosemary understood, she said, that Iris didn't want to go into the water yet, and the air had grown cooler today anyway. But would Iris just swing? Iris was quiet for a few minutes, and Rosemary began digging through her purse, pulling out a beach key. Iris teased her about carting her purse to the beach, and Rosemary summoned a faint smile, the color in her cheeks rising.

They traipsed down the hill, and Rosemary found an ant-free patch of grass on which to plunk down her purse. They sank into the swing seats and began to pump. For a moment, Iris experienced an intense queasiness, and she tried to shut down the panic she felt in her throat, reminding herself that already that summer she'd sheltered under the willow tree, walked the beach shore with her father, ushered both parents down the catwalk to put her mom on the pontoon boat. Her breathing evened out. As they climbed higher, the chains squeaked and groaned with the movement of the swings, the metal anchors high above them complaining, and Iris felt the air whooshing by her as she fell through it after reaching a peak.

For a long time, neither of them said anything. When they slowed their swings and Rosemary finally began to talk, she whispered, even though no one was at the beach. Karl had come home early the night before when she'd babysat at the Langley's house. She told him all about her cousin and the girlfriend who'd sent her the purse, and they sat on the couch talking for a long time. He listened so well, seemed so understanding, she said. Rosemary slowed her swing then, and said in a blurted rush, "Iris, I went into his bedroom, and it was awful." She inhaled a long breath. "What if I get pregnant?" The last word was a hushed sputter.

Iris slowed her swing. "Rosemary, did he make you go into the bedroom?"

"No!" Rosemary said. "I mean, I wanted to go, but I just thought we'd be doing other stuff, you know, kissing, and …. Not that." She stopped her swing, too, and she stared down at the rut underneath the swing where the gravel was worn through, sand appearing underneath, her blonde head nearly upside down. "I didn't know we would be doing that. I wasn't ready."

Iris wished that Liz were there, or their mother, or the woman who made the purse. A woman who could listen to Rosemary's secrets and say some wise words, someone who could listen and hear the truth. Iris didn't want to be the responsible one.

"But you can't tell anyone," Rosemary said. "I just can't – my mom can't know. It would be horrible for her. You can't tell anyone."

Rosemary didn't know that Iris had her own secrets to keep hidden, secrets that, if laid bare, would be like raw or sun-burned skin. But if they kept it between them, Iris thought, with no adult to offer counsel or express outrage, they would never really know how to measure the transgressions that took place, a stranger's or their own, how to negotiate the murky way of attraction, the debris-strung path of poor judgement.

33

Interlude

July 26, 1974

According to the note Liz left, Michael was coming over at three o'clock that day. Liz would work an early shift, from eight o'clock to one thirty. Then she would come home, take a nap. She would shower right before Michael came over. She just wanted Iris to know the plan.

Liz was in the shower when Iris heard the heavy clunk of Michael's shoes on the front walkway. She let him in, and he said, "Hey, can I go look in the refrigerator and bum some Faygo if you've got some?"

Iris nodded. "My mom always says, 'make yourself at home.' You know that." She returned to where she lay on the living room couch, staring at the ceiling.

Michael paused before entering the living room and looked up. "What do you see?"

"Nothing," Iris said, blushing at his serious attention. "You know that Liz will be out from the shower shortly, right?"

He nodded. "I know she's tired. Working late, working early, not sleeping very well."

Iris resumed her focus on the ceiling for a moment, then closed her eyes. "Scott used to say we should never dust the ceiling, just let the cobwebs and spider webs build up, create a whole colony. He thought ceilings had potential." Iris bent her chin to her chest and opened her eyes. She couldn't see Michael, but she heard the quiet whip of his pant legs moving together. "How do you know she's not sleeping well?"

"She told me," he called from the kitchen. Then he came back in with two glasses of orange juice. He handed one to Iris and sat down in the chair across from the couch. "I guess this is healthier than pop," he said.

"She doesn't tell me much," Iris said.

He shrugged. "I'm her boyfriend."

"Is that official?" Iris asked. "On the other hand, I am just her sister. Her only sibling now." Iris's voice caught, but she held her chin stiff.

"I know that," Michael said quietly.

"I'm sorry," Iris said. He was firmly planted in the chair, his hands propped in his lap, holding the glass of juice. The pattern of the chair sprouted underneath him – orange, green, and yellow flowers. He looked out of place inside their house. She was used to seeing him outdoors. "Remember the strawberry fight?" Iris asked.

Michael grinned, but his eyes were sad. "He had a wicked aim."

Iris closed her eyes again but let her face remain angled toward the ceiling. "I spend so much time thinking about him and things he said or did. Nobody here wants to talk about it, though, and sometimes I get so sick of it, thinking about him and seeing his face all the time." Iris paused. "I want him to go out of my head, but then I hate myself for wanting to chase the memory of him away," she said, mumbling. "My father talks about Nixon, and Watergate, and tapes, but he rarely says Scott's name."

Michael set the glass on a coaster on the table in front of him and slid down in the chair, resting his head back. He put his head to one side, and Iris noticed the way his ear lay just perfectly in the center of the orange flowers on the chair behind him. It was a small ear, not big, like Scott's. A little red at the tip, maybe sunburned.

"Has Liz told you that it's my fault?" Iris surprised herself by saying the words aloud, wondering if she'd gone too far.

"Because you were there, at the beach?"

"Because I was supposed to watch him while Mom was at work. Did Liz tell you that?" Iris's voice started to crack. Michael must have heard it, too, because his face became soft, and Iris felt a tug in her chest. The skin on his jaw was smooth, and Iris wondered how he felt when Liz trailed her fingers down the side of his cheek and chin. And the guilt surged into her throat and then her face, and when Michael leaned over and put his hand on her arm, his fingers landing gently, saying "Iris," in a voice filled not with passion but empathy, Iris felt the fire and light of five sparklers tingle and glow against her skin.

When Iris raised her eyes to the doorway, Liz stood there, her look taking in not only Michael's hand but also Iris's face, its shadows of confused longing, pain, and mute desire, and Liz turned and walked quickly away. Iris couldn't read the message in her sister's shoulders, if she just wanted to avoid Iris yet again, or if she believed that Iris had betrayed her, with her thoughts, if not her actions.

34

Candy Run

July 30, 1974

It was time to go to the New Subdivision House again. Iris was sad about the job with Sheldon nearing its end. He didn't talk like it was the end of their connection, but she realized that it likely would be, especially since her father had already told her that Sheldon tended to work down in Florida in the winters. But she knew that however appealing the Lake House on Destan might be, the New Subdivision House was the place where she could be closest to Scott. She'd already loaded a small bag with the books and art supplies she'd gotten from Sheldon but wanted to buy some snacks. She rode her bike down Cumberland and headed down the back roads and onto Williams Lake Road to get to Cate's Corner. Her bike wobbled on the shoulder of the road, the gravel spitting out from under her tires as she hit a heavy spot. The cattails were tall in the marsh where the lake ended next to the road. Brown furry-tipped, velvet-looking like a puppy's coat. Iris reached out and tried to grab one as she passed. The bull frogs choked out intermittent "Ga-rooms," and Iris wondered how many lived there.

Mrs. Miller, the other cashier, sent a distracted smile at Iris once Iris was in the store and traveling through the aisles. She didn't know Iris well enough to say anything, but she knew Iris's parents. Iris spent a long time going up and down the rows, working on her nerve. When she and Scott used to build forts in the backyard with old tarpaulins and worn out air mattresses, they stocked up on Cracker Jack and cheese corn and chocolate pudding that their mom let them make in a special shaking container. But that was a long time ago. Iris decided to get a package of Good and Plenty and a roll of Neccos, knowing she'd have to throw the pink ones away. Maybe she'd float them in the swamp, little miniature lily pads for the frogs, the girl frogs, but she couldn't remember if frogs were both boys and girls. She'd circled through the store and carried a couple of items. She picked up a box of baking soda and some bananas with spots that perched in a corner in the small produce section.

As Iris neared the front of the store, she looked up to the large mirror that hung in the corner. There was one section of candy she could access if she reached in from the last row that few people visited. As a customer approached Mrs. Miller at the front, Iris took the opportunity to reach her hand in from behind the mirror, snagging a box of Good and Plenty and a paper-wrapped cylinder of Neccos. She slipped each item into the side pockets of her pants, jamming them deep into the opening.

Then Iris walked up to the counter to pay. Mrs. Miller had finished up with the previous customer and told Iris the cost would be $1.96. Iris handed her two dollars and she gave Iris the change. Then Iris lingered at the piles of candy next to the door while Mrs.

Miller's daughter waited on the lady behind her who hadn't gotten a price sticker placed on the meat she'd asked for at the butcher counter. While they walked down the aisle to call back to the butcher for a price, Iris yelled good-bye and walked out the door of the store.

The bell jingled behind her, and her heart pounded. She stood in the parking lot, feeling almost numb with some weird mixture of fear and exhilaration. She was about to get on her bike when she heard a voice call from the window of a nearby car. "Iris!" the voice said, but it sounded odd, until she realized it was the Young family, whom she'd only seen from a distance hanging out in their yard. The kids sat in the back seat of the car, one of them unrolling the crank window further down. Iris approached the car.

"Hey," she said. "Long time, no see."

"Oh, Iris," Mrs. Young said. "We think of you all of the time. How are you doing?" She looked at Iris in an open, direct way, inspecting her face.

Iris was startled. People didn't usually come right out and ask her. Except Sheldon. "Fine," she said. "I'm fine."

"We miss you," the two kids in the back said in unison.

"They don't like the new sitter much. Someone our friends use. But we've been outside in the yard, and we see you in yours sometimes. And the kids know that it's just best for us to wait until you're ready. Just make sure to let us know," Mrs. Young said.

"Let you know?" Iris repeated.

"When you're ready to babysit again." Mrs. Young looked out at the traffic on the road and said, "Oops, it's getting busy and someone's going to want this spot. I'd better get a move on." She looked at Iris as she put her car in reverse. "Just let us know, give us a call or something. And give our best to your parents."

Iris stepped to a spot next to the store and watched the car back out and prepare to turn left on Williams Lake. The kids were in the back seat waving, so Iris lifted her hand and waved, more furiously than she intended. She thought of playing hide-and-seek as a young child. "Ready or not, here I come!" In that game, there was the seeker and the person found. She didn't know if she was ready. She wasn't ready for Sheldon to leave. She didn't think she was ready to be found. She knew she wasn't ready to be alone.

Iris sat on her bike, watching the traffic go by. Then she parked her bike and walked into the store again. In a back aisle, away from the mirror that captured reflections at the back of the store, she pulled the Good and Plenty and Neccos out of her pockets and put them on a shelf of pickles and other condiments, scooting them behind the jars. She went around to the cash register by the front door again, pulled another candy bar, a Snickers, off the shelf, and plopped it on the belt in front of Mrs. Miller.

"You're back," Mrs. Miller said.

"Still feeding my sweet tooth," Iris said, smiling as calmly as she could.

When she left the store, she got on her bike and rode fast to the marsh. Then she put down the kickstand and sat there by the side of the road, even though her parents told her to hurry through the dangerous curve where the road and the gravel narrowed. Iris sat down in the dusty gravel and ate her Snickers Bar slowly, trying to savor the chocolate.

35

Impeachment

August 9, 1974

A week or so later, Iris lay in the bedroom with a book on her chest, when through the wall she heard her father crowing as he watched television. The book was a Nero Wolfe detective story, and though Iris was curious about her father's hooting, she didn't have the energy or inclination to go and investigate, choosing to stay put. But the crowing returned when he came home from work the next day in an almost jubilant, celebratory mood. Iris was glad to see him so happy, almost relaxed, even if it took a few minutes to learn that the cause was an event that would ultimately have only a fleeting impact on their emotionally turbulent household, in spite of its significant and long-lasting impression on the nation. Settling into his chair, he held up the paper with a flourish and sighed loud enough to garner his family's full attention. "You need to read this, girls," he said. "This is history."

"What?" Liz said. "What's history?"

He turned the *Detroit Free Press* to flash them a view of the front page. "Nixon Resigns," he said. "Remember the day. August 9, 1974."

"Because of all that Watergate stuff?" Liz asked.

"Yes," their father said gleefully. "Because of all of that Watergate stuff. Listen, this is from some New York journalist named Reston," he said. "'In the long ironic history of America, events have kept unfolding contrary to the expectations of her greatest leaders and thinkers, but seldom has there been such an example of the irony and incongruity of political life as the case of Richard Milhous Nixon.

"'The journalists have now written his political obituary and passed him on to the historians – who will probably treat him more kindly – but he remains a tragic tangle of contradictions, and will have to be left in the end to the dramatists, novelists, and psychologists.'"

"Ha," Iris's father interrupted himself. "Like anyone would want to write his story."

"Why do you hate him so much?" Iris asked.

"Does mom hate him as much as you do?" Liz added. Their mother was in the kitchen, making biscuits to go with the chicken she'd prepared. It was the first elaborate meal she'd made in weeks, and from all the cheery clanging and clattering in the kitchen, it sounded as if she shared their father's euphoria.

"He's a lying bastard," their father said. "Isn't that reason enough?"

The air in the room was muggy. Liz had flung herself on the couch and fanned herself with the television guide. "Why is she making such a hot meal on a day like today?" she said to no one in particular.

"This is what he said on television," their father said. "' I have never been a quitter,' Nixon said. "'To leave office before my term is completed is abhorrent to every instinct in my body.' Abhorrent – ha!" Their father rattled the paper to emphasize his disgust. "Your craven yellow belly slimy instincts are what got you in trouble."

Liz and Iris couldn't help sneaking a grin at one another. In the kitchen their mother had started to hum. It felt good to be a family again, allied in their dislike for Nixon.

They flung open all the windows in the dining room and then sat down to dinner. Iris watched her father as he lathered butter on his biscuits, poured their mother's chicken gravy and dumplings over them, chomping furiously and quickly as he tried to explain what they didn't understand about the Watergate story, as if anyone could really understand. Their mother said little, just smiled and kept passing the plates to him. And Liz and Iris somehow knew just what questions to ask to keep him going, almost instinctively choreographing their lines. It was an anti-Nixon extravaganza they had in their dining room that evening, their father holding sway throughout dinner, and then throughout the entire weekend, and for those two days, the air in their household was charged with more positive energy than they'd known in over a year.

That Monday morning, after a weekend of Nixon stories on the radio, on television, and in the newspapers, Iris and her father set off in the early morning fog. He was to drop her off at the dentist's office, where her mother would pick her up an hour later. They rode in silence. A bike emerged out of the hazy mist carrying a shrouded figure. The intersection appeared empty until their car crept to a stop, and then, through the fog, other headlights became visible. Iris repeated a line she'd heard several times over the weekend, "I guess old Tricky Dicky got what he deserved."

Iris's father turned to look at her, his eyes clear, intensely green. His gaze lingered on her face, and she felt that perhaps, for the first time that summer, he could really see her. He smiled gently, reached over and patted her arm in a strange, absent-minded way. "Really," he said, "I guess it doesn't make much difference one way or another in the long run." And then his eyes went dim again, like they'd been for most of the year. It wasn't them against Nixon then. They *were* Nixon, Iris and her father, Nixon and Denny McClain, and any one of millions of people who'd made mistakes, whether calculated or not, dumb ignorant clods just blundering through.

36

Indebted

August 12, 1974

Because the streets were still wet with potholes of watery dirt road sludge after the night rains, Iris agreed when her mother offered to drop her off at the Lake House.

"I'll be home from the library before dinner; don't worry about starting it." Iris's mother peered out of the two openings of clear glass near the bottom of the fogged windshield. "You've been a lot of help this summer, Iris. With the meals and laundry. We don't thank you enough."

"I don't need thanks."

Her mother nodded again. "Still."

"Okay," Iris said. She opened the car door. On the ground next to the car, a soggy ant hill showed signs of lethargic activity. "See you at dinner."

Sheldon was nowhere in the house, but Iris heard noises on the back porch. She went out the sliding glass door and found him on the deck, cleaning his brushes. "I wanted some fresh air," he said. "Isn't it gorgeous?"

"A little humid," Iris said. "I'm glad the sun's out now, but the air is so heavy."

241

"The sun's even breaking through the haze over the lake, see?" Sheldon gestured. The water's edge rested just yards away, small gulps lapping at a nearby boat tied up.

"Well, aren't you Little Miss Sunshine." The remark, which Iris meant as a joke, turned out to sound a bit nasty at the end.

"And you would be whom? The grim reaper? What side of bed did you get up on?"

"Sorry," Iris mumbled.

Sheldon shook his head. "No problem."

For a minute they were both quiet, looking out at the water. Because of the warm morning, the lake teemed with recreation. Speedboats sliced around the edges, carting skiers from various catwalks to the middle where the boats had more of a chance at a clean stretch to pick up speed, the young boaters anxious to dump their skiing passengers just for the joy of hearing them howl as they went down. A quarter of the way around the lake Iris could see their own beach, the blankets and towels in colorful rectangles on the sloping hill. It looked like they had a new dock for the adults. Last year's had black barrels and a mustard-colored carpeted surface. Iris remembered the burns she'd gotten on her stomach from hefting herself up on the carpet from the water once the ladder broke. This new dock had blue barrels and a clean white surface. Iris hadn't been on one of those docks all summer. She narrowed her eyes against the sun, wondering if Rosemary lay on one of the coral towels, her hair a wet tangle.

"Well, Iris," Sheldon said. "Our gravy train's coming to a stop. We're nearly done here."

"What?" Iris couldn't figure out what he was talking about. So often she needed him to explain his expressions. Today she felt annoyed at his way of talking.

"The job," he said. "We're almost done with the job."

"No way," Iris said. "There are still two rooms – the kitchen and that other bedroom."

But even before Iris finished, Sheldon started shaking his head. "Turns out she's going to change the kitchen. Rip those cabinets right out, put in an island, new Formica."

"She told you that?"

"She was here yesterday. They're back in town."

Iris closed her eyes, digesting the news, at the same time trying to see the kitchen the way the owner might see it – the old kitchen with its beige walls, worn Formica. Would she make it yellow? Yellow would be horrible. Too bright. Although the goldenrod color they had in the back might not be bad. Pink would be worse. Iris couldn't envision the perfect color in her head, couldn't see at all the way the owner might envision it. "And the little bedroom?"

"Wants to add a closet, so I shouldn't bother to paint now. She'll call me back in September or October once it's done." "So we still have what to do?"

"That dinky little bathroom in the corner upstairs, the one with all the trim?"

Iris nodded, unsure of what to say.

"So, this week is it. Are you with me, Iris?"

She felt her silence seep into the room, so she smiled her agreement and cleared her throat. "What will you do next?" she asked.

"After the house is done?" Sheldon took his painter's hat off, scratched his scalp. "Oh, I don't know. There'll be more houses, I'm sure, a few more garage doors. Maybe someone will even commission me to do a portrait."

"Why don't you just travel, go fishing? Can't you retire? I mean, I guess I've been wondering why you keep on working. I get body aches from doing some of this stretching and ladder lifting, and I'm not as strong as you, but I'm a lot younger. Seems like you should get more days off."

"Thanks for reminding me of my age, youngster." Sheldon knelt on his haunches, dried paint splatters crackling on his pants. "Did your Dad ever tell you why I paint? Paint houses, I mean?"

Iris shook her head.

He nodded. "I should have told you. Hell, almost told you last week, when we were fishing. There was just never a good time." He looked straight at Iris's face, like he didn't want to have to repeat himself. "I'm still painting because I've got bills to pay. Big bills. My wife died of cancer about five years ago. She was sick for a while, and I still owe money to the hospital." He tilted his head, squinted one eye shut, and looked up at Iris with the other one.

"Five years ago," Iris repeated.

"Yep. The balance has really gone down a lot, and I actually negotiated with them to reduce it a bit, which they did. My wife and I always patched together artist-hobo type jobs, and we never had great insurance. I feel bad about that. But now I just can't bring myself to skip out on the debt.

"In the beginning, I wanted the distraction. I was so sad after she died, I wanted to stay busy, and painting people's houses kept

244

me exhausted, distracted. Now I find it more tedious, but the balance is coming down, pretty fast actually. And I really want to pay it off, even if it's only for a silly reason like promising my wife that I would do it. She wouldn't care if I just ripped up the bills, but I know in my heart that I owe the money. Besides," he said, standing up, making a face as his knees creaked, "the work keeps me busy. Keeps me focused on something. And someday, when I'm out of the red, I'll have time to work on my magnum opus. Paint the big cisco. Or maybe even catch it; there's got to be one out there in those Lake Michigan waters, one that has eluded the fisherman after all these years, right, Iris?" He put his cap back on his head, tugging on the bill. He looked at her questioningly, and Iris knew he was nervous about her reaction.

"Why didn't you tell me sooner about your wife?" Iris said, trying not to sound accusing.

"I just did," he said. "It's been five years, anyway."

"But we've been working together for a big chunk of the summer," Iris insisted. She felt her chest start to rise.

"Five years is a long time," Sheldon said. "You build up some protection, and then one day you realize you don't need to tell stories anymore about that part of your life."

"Are you saying you just don't need to talk about the person who died anymore? Like she never existed?"

"Not exactly," he said. "The people in your life who knew about that person – you still talk to those people about the things you miss about the dead person. But when you meet new people, maybe you don't tell that part of your life story as much. And for someone like me, it kind of becomes this secret that you enjoy when you're alone."

It occurred to Iris then that he was just like the rest of them, keeping things to himself, just pretending to be open. "I don't want to be that way," she said. "I don't want to pretend my brother didn't exist except for when I'm with family. They can hardly say his name. Who will I talk with about Scott? And didn't you think that maybe I'd want to hear one little story about your wife? Nobody tells you what you're supposed to do with all of the memories!"

"No, they don't tell you. That's for sure." Sheldon said firmly. "You have to figure it out for yourself."

"Did my father tell you about me? Did he say, "Hey, Sheldon, I've got this kid who's a little screwed up because while she was supposed to be watching her brother, he drowned?""

"Your father doesn't always divulge a lot of information," Sheldon said.

"He didn't tell you, then."

"Tell me what, again?"

"It was my fault, Sheldon! Scott's death was my fault! I was supposed to be awake and watching him, and I fell asleep." She stood in front of him, her hands held out to the side, wanting him to be shocked, appalled, offended.

"Iris, I'm sure your parents don't hold you responsible for what happened to your brother," Sheldon said, "And I wish you'd stop beating yourself up for whatever role you played in this death." He sighed.

"Yes, they do," she said. "Or maybe they don't. I don't know. But yes, I hold myself responsible!"

"Iris, it doesn't do any good to keep blaming yourself," Sheldon said. He stepped back and sank down on the porch step.

"People keep on telling me that, but other people ARE blaming me, so why wouldn't I blame myself?"

"Okay," Sheldon said. "Let's slow down. Seventh inning stretch – now I know your father must have taught you that expression. Iris, one thing I am convinced about is that my wife sure would have liked you." He laughed, and then his face got serious again. "Look, I'm guessing it really hurts to feel like people blame you for your brother's death. And maybe you need to think about it and ask some people for forgiveness. But chances are they're blaming themselves as much as they're blaming you. And maybe you're the one you have to forgive most of all."

Iris opened her mouth to say something, but he held up his hand before she could speak. "Also, I want you to know that I am sad about wrapping up my time with you, and maybe I was a bit cavalier when I made that announcement just now, because I didn't want to admit the sadness. I'm sorry. And for that, I beg your forgiveness."

Iris nodded, trying to keep looking at his face. She put her knuckles to her eyes and mumbled, "It's okay. I knew we were winding down. I didn't want to admit it either."

Sheldon smiled. "Okay, I already opened the paint, so let's do a bit of the trim in the small bathroom, and we'll keep talking."

A shout and a squeal resounded from the water, followed by a jeer from someone in a boat. As Iris looked out at the lake, a young man flung a large inner tube into the water at the fallen skier, and an arm came up from the waves, a hand curving over the tube.

37
Natural and Unnatural Cycles

August 15. 1974

When Iris picked up the phone that day, Rosemary's voice was low and quiet, a truck rumbling on a distant highway. "I only have five minutes," she said. "Maybe ten. Can you meet me by the main road, close to where the New Subdivision entrance is on the other side? By the Murphy's house, the people with the three poodles?"

Iris went out the front door, so she didn't have to see her father tinkering aimlessly in the garage. The day was cool for once, not steaming like the last three weeks had been, and as Iris trudged down the dirt road, chimes from someone's back yard peeled and clanged in the breeze. Mr. Young was out clipping his hedges. He gave Iris a salute as she walked by.

At the poodle house next to the main road, Rosemary was pacing, her face flushed. When Iris reached her, Rosemary looked down, took a deep breath, and allowed her shoulders to settle in a sigh. "Don't hate me, Iris." She folded her arms around her middle, almost like she was shivering, though it was a warm breeze that circled them. "Don't hate me," she said again, "but I have to talk to someone." She looked down at the ground, then around in the street to see if any bicycles were going by. "I think I'm pregnant," she whispered.

Iris didn't say anything; she just waited. She saw one of Sheldon's deer painted on a garage door. She couldn't believe she hadn't noticed that one before. They were everywhere.

"Iris," Rosemary said. "Did you hear me?"

Iris nodded.

"I don't know for sure. I just keep waiting, but nothing. No period."

"Did you tell Karl?" Iris asked.

Rosemary shook her head. "I haven't seen him all week."

Iris nodded again. She tried to think, but every time she closed her eyes, she envisioned them together, two bodies transformed into one. "When was it supposed to start?"

"Monday – that was five days ago."

"Could it just be late – from something else? I don't know – stress? Didn't they tell us in gym class that there could be several things going on, and not to panic?"

Rosemary shrugged her shoulders. "I don't know."

"Tell him. See what he thinks."

"No," Rosemary said, shaking her head vehemently.

"You're afraid of him," Iris said.

"No," Rosemary said again. "I like the way..." she paused, looked hard in Iris's face. "No," she said. "Really, no." When she saw the shadow of frustration on Iris's face, she must have had second thoughts, because she said quickly, "Tell me, Iris, why don't you like him?"

Her question hung in the air for a minute. Iris knew she should tell Rosemary. That he flattered her, made her feel special. That he would do the same thing for any other girl, like he'd done for Rosemary. Maybe Iris could end the cycle of bad things happening if she just spoke up. But she was afraid Rosemary wouldn't listen, would think that Iris herself was just jealous because they both wanted someone to make them feel special.

A kid rode by on his bicycle on the shoulder of the road, no hands. Iris watched him continue on down the road. She could hear the metal of the frame rattling, the chain clicking, and for a moment, she could block out everything: Rosemary, Karl, Scott, her sister's face, mottled with anger.

"Iris?" Rosemary said again.

"I don't want to make you feel bad, Rosemary. It was that night that you asked me to babysit. He didn't do anything horrible – he drank beer, we played cards, we listened to some music and then he tried to kiss me."

"That happened to me, too," Rosemary said. Her eyes filled with tears.

"But when I thought about why I left the kitchen to go into the dark living room, I realized it was because I didn't know how to say 'no,' and when he kissed me, I realized that it didn't feel right." Iris reached over and held Rosemary's shoulders. "He's way older than we are. There's something wrong with that."

Rosemary snuffled, and more tears came down her face.

"I felt so stupid because he knew right away that I'd never been kissed, and I was so embarrassed," Iris said. "But why should I be embarrassed by that? I'm only fourteen!"

251

"What should I do?" Rosemary said. "I just don't know what to do."

"Can't you try to talk to your mom?"

"No," Rosemary said. "She'd kill me. I need to think. I just need to think." She turned to look at Iris. "But don't tell anyone," she said. "I need to figure some things out." She shook her head. "I can't believe I thought he found me so fascinating. It didn't occur to me that he tried something with you." She stood up straight and sniffed. "Thanks, Iris. I have to go now."

They both turned in opposite directions, and Iris could hear their separate footsteps move along the road. A pattern of crunching. Iris turned around. "I'll keep trying to think of something, Rosemary," she called. Around her, the evening insects quivered with song in the fields and the tree canopies, the melody changing as summer marched ahead, oblivious.

38

The Roll of the Dice

August 16, 1974

The following night, Iris's father was attending a retirement party for one of his General Motors friends. Iris's mom told her during their Saturday laundry trip that they'd have the evening to themselves, since Liz had made arrangements to spend the night at her co-worker's house after their late shift. Maybe she and Iris could go to Dog 'N Suds for hot dogs and root beer. And she'd seen in the television guide that a great movie was on.

Iris was relieved that Liz wouldn't be around. She'd left the house before her sister on most days, during a week in which Liz had a lot of late shifts, which made her bedtime much later. Liz had been brave, Iris thought, to admit that she blamed Iris for Scott's death. But that didn't mean Iris wanted to talk about it or the moment she had shared with Michael.

At Dog 'N Suds they sat in the car with both front seat windows down. Iris's mom let her have a foot long with lots of onions and a large heavy mug of root beer, and Iris felt almost guilty eating all of it. Scott would have been jealous. And when they got home, with a peppy flourish and wide, snapping eyes, Iris's mother pulled the Yahtzee game out of the closet. Everything about her was so keyed up and dramatic. By the time they were forty-five minutes into the game, Iris's mother had filled her score card up with lots of goose eggs, but she'd left her Yahtzee row open. "I always have luck with five's," she told Iris. "I know I can do this." She'd collected three and had one more roll. Blowing on the dice, she threw them in one hand and shook them in the air, her hand held straight over her head, as if leading a cheer. Then she flung them across the table with such intensity that Iris was sure one would slip off. And it did. The one on the table landed a five, and as their eyes widened, they stared at the clacking noise of the other die finding a spot on the floor where it could land. They stood up, leaning over the table to find it, and when Iris spotted it on the floor, the five black dots showing on the face of the die, she grabbed her mother's arm and let out a whoop.

Iris's mother beamed a big grin, and Iris was sure she would scream or jump up and down or wave her arms, but slowly her smile started to fade. Her eyes became small and she sat down on the chair with a thump. "I'm not sure it counts," she said.

"What do you mean? It's a five!"

"But it fell off the table. I'm not sure it counts."

"Come on, Mom," Iris said. "You always used to let us take it if it fell."

"No matter," she said. "Your turn." And she smiled brightly that fake smile which meant she had closed herself off again. Iris tried several more times to get her to take the Yahtzee, but she shook her head, smiling breezily. Iris watched as she filled in a big zero on her score sheet, the pen going around and round again. Then she got up from the table and walked away, into her room, and after Iris waited for twenty minutes, she finally put the Yahtzee game away.

Later, after Iris's mother emerged, they sat in the darkened family room in front of the television, and Iris watched as her mother put a few pieces of popcorn to her lips. The movie was some light romantic comedy: boy meets girl; attraction takes place; misunderstanding occurs; misunderstanding is cleared up; couple lives happily ever after, sometimes with money, sometimes not. Iris's mother chuckled in all the right places, but the laughs were hollow around the edges. And even though she must have felt Iris looking at her, she didn't turn her face toward her daughter. Iris wanted to reach over, take a small pile of the popped kernels, drench them in the butter that coated the bottom of the pan, and place them gently in her mother's hands, giving her a gift of the glistening yellow treat, maybe a small promise of the future. And if Iris did that, would her mother recognize the lonely look on her daughter's face? Maybe Iris had been right in the car on the night of the baseball game, maybe her mother really had moved into the world of good feelings where even the sad songs had a little lilt, a resonance that felt safe. If she dwelled there now, who was Iris to call her back?

Later that night, after Iris saw the light go out in her parent's bedroom, her mother attempting to sleep, her father still away at a party that would go all hours of the night, she pulled on her shorts and tank top, found her house key and the beach key, and walked out the back door. Loud cricket harpings scraped her ears. Up under the streetlamps, flurries of small gnat-like bugs jittered and danced. As dark as it was, Iris knew she could walk the streets with impunity. There was some logic in the world that said no matter how many bad things could happen, only one horribly bad thing could happen directly to a person. Scott's dying was like life insurance. If the child killer were parked on some nearby street, he could spy on Iris all he liked, but he could never touch her, and she walked briskly with that understanding.

She stood at the gate to the beach for a long time, wondering if Rosemary had ever been there with Karl and the Langley kids, if they'd spread their towels out in the best spot, the one Iris and Rosemary had discovered as creating the perfect angle to meet the sun, the perfect exposure to the faint lake breeze. Iris put her key in the gate lock. She wanted to go in and sit on the hill. And then, when she worked up the courage, she wanted to go down to the water, where it lapped the shore, dark under the dusky moon. If she could just put her toes in the water, she would be taking a huge step; she knew that instinctively. She'd been on the inside several times this summer; she needed to take that extra step.

Iris turned the key and heard the faint squeak of the gate as it pulled away from the fence. Above her, the leaves from the oak fluttered faintly as she stepped into the property area.

Iris wanted to be soothed by the quiet water, by the lights that pierced out of the darkness from the other shore, and if truth be told, she wanted to walk the shore and look for remnants of her brother. Something he had with him, that nobody knew about, something that would smell more of him than of seaweed or sun lotion or mosquito repellent. A small patch of him.

Yet Iris couldn't move beyond the hill. Not tonight. She returned to the gate, opening it and letting herself out. She listened to the gate clang shut, and leaned up against the fence, pressing her face deeper and deeper into the criss-crosses of metal, winding her fingers around the chain links, angry at all the people who walked in there with bright towels hanging from their necks, the beach key dangling. Not even thinking about what it meant to walk into the water.

39

The Fourth Wall

August 17, 1974

It's really dark here. I brought your flashlight, and I even took that good one of dad's that he keeps way up in the cupboard. I'm glad I'd already been here a few times to figure out how to get in. I'm not going to lie to you. It's kind of creepy at night, but once I go up the basement stairs and get to the main floor, I won't be worried so much about spiders. What's the worst thing that could happen, really? The child killer decides to camp out here? Karl decides to bring his latest conquest here? God, I didn't think of that.

It's not the kind of house mom would want, but it will do for us, I think. I want you to see the family room – there's this little nook, almost like a sectioned-off play area with a railing about waist high, and I keep thinking how much you would have liked it a few years ago. Remember when you collected all those cars and all that orange Hot Wheels stunt track stuff, and we couldn't walk through the house without stepping on it? You made that funny sound – not like *vroom, vroom,* but *ahhhhh-shoooom,* the *shoom* when the car began a descent. Little red Camaros, Ford Mustangs, Olds Cutlasses, big fire trucks, ambulances even.

This room is the one I picked out for myself. I like the air that comes in that window over there. That's why I picked this corner. My sleeping bag fits perfectly, and as I lay here, I can feel the breeze move across my skin. I really thought the quiet would get to me, but I kind of like it. And it's not really *that* quiet, what with the frogs croaking in the marsh across the way and down the street. I do hear some cars at those houses that are done. I don't even need the flashlights, really, since the moon is so bright. A man just walked by, with a dog on a leash. He didn't even glance in this direction.

Remember the time you ran away? You were five, I think. And you packed your suitcase full of cars and stuffed animals, and when you went to Noelle's door – you didn't run far – she tried to talk you into going back home. But you just kept shaking your head, those brown, buzz-cut hairs of yours that used to glint under the lights. And later, Noelle told mom she had to bite her lip to keep from laughing when she looked inside your suitcase. No underwear, no toothbrush, just cars and stuffed animals.

Just so you know, I didn't pack any underwear, either. This isn't running away, what I'm doing here. It's more like camping out, sort of to prove something. I've kind of had this theory that you would be more comfortable here. It's so lonely at home now. Even when they're present, they're all absent. No one wants to live in that space because you're not there. But I want to say to them, *Where does that leave Scott? Where does he get to feel comfortable?*

I'm not starving, but I did pack a couple of peanut butter and jelly sandwiches. Maybe I'll eat those. Last week Mom brought home from the grocery store some of those windmill cookies you like. She got mad at Liz and me, saying "Why aren't you eating them – you asked for them?" Then she remembered we didn't. They were your favorites. She got really sad.

We used to play that game we called "building houses." And you said if you could build it any way you wanted, no expense spared, you'd have a big tower and a moat, with a big, heavy drawbridge that made a thunk when it landed. Sort of like a castle, but not cold and drafty, warmer, like a bungalow – you thought bungalow meant some kind of tree house built low in branches. Warmer, like with sun shining in lots of windows. You with your moat and me with a water fountain in the living room, something to dangle my fingers in on hot days.

In this house where I am right now, you can pick out any room you want, but we'll go see the one I picked for you a bit later. The builders will never finish this house, according to Dad. At least not this builder. Eventually, they'll sell, and someone will finish the row of houses, but for now, this house is yours. Scott's house. Until I get Mom, Dad, and Liz to make the other one better. I don't think you're Casper the Friendly Ghost or anything, Scott. I just don't want all the traces of you to be the sad, angry traces.

The cicadas are so loud, like some kid making clicking noises, almost unconsciously. I'm tired now, and I'm going to rest a bit before I start painting. I'm thinking about that last boy The Caretaker killed. Do you think he just got so tired that maybe he wasn't even afraid anymore, his head full of cotton, his eyes heavy, so that by the time it happened he was ready to drift off anyway, relaxed for the first time in hours? I like to think he was there, and then he was gone. The in-between part is too painful to think about it.

261

You were there, and then gone. There and then gone. I think that's what Dad mutters when he falls asleep in the chair with the paper: *There and then gone, There and then gone.* Like the pastor said at the memorial service: *With us for a short time and then gone.*

Remember that Halloween when Mom was Doris Day? She wore that blonde bob wig and those capri pants. The Mary-Tyler-Moore-when-she-was-Laura-in-The-Dick-Van-Dyke-Show pants. The close-fitting sweater that hugged mom's ribs. And every time the trick or treaters summoned her to the door, she would waltz through the house on tiptoe, singing "Que Sera, Sera," almost, but not quite at the top of her lungs, her voice sailing, mellow but throaty. We heard it for the half hour before we left for the trip around the block, and when we came back two hours later, she was still singing. The babysitter had arrived by then, and mom went to the bathroom to reapply her lipstick. "I should have been in pictures," she said to us, loud enough so that dad could hear in the other room.

"I always thought Doris Day had a big mouth," Dad called in.

Mom made a hurt face at us and then yelled back to him, "Big voice, not big mouth." And though we groaned and pretended to hate it, for months after Halloween, we asked for it as our lullaby. She toned it down and sang it from the hallway, making it float into our rooms. Come to think of it, you were only four or five. Liz and I thought it was the happiest song.

I saw the movie, though, a couple of years ago. And Doris Day does have a big voice. She sings that song after they kidnap her son, and when she finds out he's probably locked somewhere in the mansion she's in, she sings louder, while the listeners' faces

262

become transformed from pleasant, enjoying faces to those displaying surprise and discomfort. They wince at her volume, but she doesn't care; she just closes her eyes and keeps singing. And then you see the boy's face; he *is* locked in a room. When he hears his mother's voice, his face is the same face Odysseus wore when he told his shipmates to tie him to the mast and let him hear the song of the sirens. The boy leans against the door and wears that wounded look of longing. Or maybe it's her face – I can't remember. But it isn't happy; it's really not a happy song at all. How could we have been so wrong about that? How could Mom have fooled us with her lilt and her perky walk, notes sailing upward, only upward, when outside all those shadows gathered behind pumpkin faces, candles flickering and then out?

Well, now I am more than a little afraid. Earlier, when I knew there was a good chance that someone in a bathroom down the street was drawing water for a late bath after her second shift or that someone might be in his living room, turning the knob on the television, listening to it ratchet, ratchet, ratchet from channel to channel to find a movie, I didn't feel so alone. But now, as I look out the window, I see darkness throughout the neighborhood – maybe a few porch lights, but mostly darkness.

He could come here, The Caretaker. I bluffed when I said I had insurance. Your dying provides no insurance. Bad things can keep happening, can't they? There's no limit on disaster.

All the coverage of the The Caretaker on television and the newspapers leads us all to imagine and speculate and try to figure it out for ourselves, as if the figuring out would give us some sort of insulation or protection. I understand the energy behind that aim because I've spent the last year imaging the order of things that happened on the day you died, so that I could comprehend what happened and why it happened. I know it's a little different, because the detectives want to understand the killer's motives. I know your motives. Adventure! Or maybe you were practicing for some future world record in crossing the English Channel. You always set your sights on bigger risks than I could ever fathom.

I think the value of my imagining different possibilities for the things that happen in life, especially the things that happened last summer, is that it gives me an out. Takes me off the hook for the responsibility. I don't want to face that. I don't want to take that responsibility. And I understand better now that Mom and Dad must feel it, too. I felt like it was all on me, but mom sees it as her fault, too, for going to work. What else could she do if she wanted a better house? How else would we get there? And Dad didn't understand how much she wanted to be a part of moving forward, and I'm sure he hates himself for that.

So, let me just say this clearly, Scott. I know that it was mostly my fault, especially in those hours when we were at the beach. Whether I had reason to fall asleep doesn't matter. I was on the job. Instead of lying on the hill, I should have been with the mothers and babysitters, sitting upright on one of the benches, or playing in the sand, all of us fighting off our middle-of-the-day sleepiness. Had I been there, occupying that space, you wouldn't have attempted that swim. I know that in my heart.

I want you to know that I'm sorry. I'm asking for your forgiveness. If I'd stayed awake that day, I could have told you what a goofball idea you had. Swimming across the lake – you really just got the hang of swimming last summer; what made you think that you were tough enough to swim that far? If I'd stayed awake, when I saw you move past the buoys that mark the swimming area, I could have called out, "Hey, get back here, buster!" And you know that you would have come back, however much you griped; you would have come back and thrown yourself down on the bench next to me. That's the hard thing for me – knowing that if I could have stood up and yelled, just one yell, just SCOTT, your name, everything would be different.

I didn't tell anyone, Scott, but for all of those months during school, I tried to convince myself that you'd been stung by a bee. It would make sense, right? You start swimming, you get stung, and then that awful reaction happens. There are two problems with that theory. The biggest problem is that we could never know that for sure, not now. The second, which is hard for me to say out loud, is that I still fell asleep. And no matter what, I have to take responsibility for that. In a lot of ways, then, whether you got stung by a bee or not is irrelevant. I have accepted that fact.

At some point, you must have known you weren't going to make it, and more than anything else, I wish I could have been there for you. I don't want to imagine the details, but when your head went under water again and again, and you finally didn't have the energy to bring it up, I want to believe that some crazy end-of-life euphoria took over, and you experienced this spectacular fireworks show in your head, with warm vivid reds and blues, and you weren't angry, or afraid, or cold. I want to believe you were in a state of wonder.

Dawn will arrive around six o'clock tomorrow morning. If I start a little before that, I can use the flashlight. The pre-dawn glow will be just touching the windows, the pink seeping in. You will

265

like the room I picked for you. It's a corner room, right next to the bathroom, but it looks out over this crooked tree in the backyard. I wouldn't put it past you to climb out the window and onto one of the limbs like Hayley Mills in that old *Pollyanna* movie we used to watch. I can't believe I made you do that pretend play that one year, when I told you I would be the glad girl and you could be Jimmy the orphan, because like you, he always got into trouble.

I wanted to paint the car on the ceiling because that's where you wanted the poster to be, the one mom and dad said you couldn't tape to the ceiling. A few nights ago, I lay so long on your bed, trying to paint the strokes in my head, reaching my hand up, seeing how much I would fall short, wondering what kind of gymnastic moves Michelangelo learned when he cricked his neck day after day in the Sistine Chapel.

It was a fanciful idea, but I'm a realist at heart, right? No, not a realist, really, but I couldn't carry a ladder over here on my bike – that much I know. So, I'll have to paint it on the wall. But I've been practicing, in the sketch pad Sheldon gave me. I've studied shapes and how to show depth. But I'm painting the car on the wall right next to the window, so if you use your imagination, you can leap into the car and sail out into the sky like Chitty Chitty Bang Bang. Except this car is a Camaro, the red one. I know I won't get the corners and angles right, but when you look at it, you can pretend I'm Monet, or Seurat, and all the slashes of color and points of light will add up to something bigger than each small stroke. At least that's what I'm hoping.

I filched the poster paints Liz had down in the basement for her student council campaign last year; there was still a whole container of red there. I'm not as talented as you. I looked through that sketch book in your bedroom. I never knew you had that talent. I will make mistakes with the painting, and you'll have to forgive my crude art.

The first stroke is the hardest, Mrs. Ciaralli used to say. Be bold. Don't hold your breath in a timid way. Slap it on. Sheldon says it's about feeling free, not so much confidant but sort of unrestricted. I guess if I'm unrestricted enough to trespass into this house, I'm unrestricted enough to paint on the wall.

So here goes. I really wish I could have done this at home. But they keep the house so empty that I know you'll never come. And when it's not empty, it's loud. I want to tell them that they're just driving you out; they don't seem to understand that. Here is better. It's so quiet, and even though it's empty, the solitude is full, in a peaceful sort of way.

But you don't have to stay here forever. When you turn sixteen and get your driver's license, you can drive right out of here, off the wall and out the window, into the sky. You can touch down wherever you like. I wish you could take me with you.

The sunrise glow is expanding now. That last time we made a donut run early in the morning with dad, he made such a big deal about our getting up at the crack of dawn, and then there we were, knees next to knees on the front porch while he was still inside. You talked about how with indoor light, we flipped switches and the light came on above us. But on the porch, the crickets so close in the grass that we might have nudged them with a toe, the birds starting to make a few stray chirping sounds, you talked about how outside the light came from the bottom up. It didn't start from the sky; it started from the ground. The color moved up, touching the grass, the houses, the horizon, and finally the sky, like a magic wand escaping from the underworld, fleeing brightly to God, leaving everything infused with merciful light. It feels like that in this room, like heat is rising from the register, though I know the duct work isn't done and there's no furnace in the cellar.

I won't ask you what you think; I'll tell you. It's not bad. Better than a smudge. A few good lines, some texture, even. And you can even see the steering wheel behind the chrome-like plate glass that makes up the windshield – it glimmers through.

I will sleep now. I was kind of afraid of spiders before, but there's enough light now that I'll open the sleeping bag and shake, and shake, and shake. And soon, as I'm drifting into sleep, I'll hear the people go by, walking their dogs, maybe just getting a little exercise in before their day starts. Part of me wishes I could invite them in, tell them about your room, your car, how happy you are to be here in this neighborhood. They would have loved you as their paper boy. You would roll your papers, wrap them in plastic on rainy days, tuck them inside the screen door, always making sure to latch the door so the wind didn't catch it. All the nice touches you told me you'd do this fall, when you moved from the world of play into the world of work, as you began that first paper route. I know I must let go of the things I imagined for your future.

I'm tired, so I can't talk about it now. If I wake up and I feel better, we can talk about it then. You know I won't go back home if it means leaving you here. You'd have to come with me. And with your car here – well, I don't know. We'll see.

Epilogue

Iris's parents separated not long after that night she stayed in the New Subdivision House. Her dad found an apartment, and he and her mom were almost joyful about taking a break from their marriage. They said they didn't want Iris to think she pushed them to the separation with her overnight disappearance, but she made them see the need. Ironically, the whole family still ate a meal together once a week, at a restaurant Iris or Liz picked out, and Iris was touched by how kind and loving her parents seemed to be as they talked to one another. Iris and Liz grimaced at the liver and onions their dad ordered at whatever restaurant each week, but their mom argued that it was a good thing. If he moved back in, she said, he might figure out by then that liver and onions wasn't going to be on the regular family menu. The rest of them were happy with chicken or pork chops or salad.

They talked about the fishing trip they might take some time, all four of them, or maybe a canoe trip down the Au Sable River. Their dad brought brochures to the restaurant once, the names and phone numbers of a few cabins they could rent. Iris watched him eat his strawberry rhubarb pie, and as he held his fork up in the air, almost like an artist, resting after a brushstroke, he looked boyish, happy to be planning something. But he knew, somehow, to put the brochures away after a few minutes. Iris's mom said, "Let's give it some time. Sounds like a fun trip, but it's water, after all. Who knows, though?" They all tried to stay open with each other instead of shutting down on topics of conversation or possibilities. Iris thought they were all learning new ways of coping from their support groups or psychologists or friends.

Liz graduated from high school and attended the local community college. Richland Dairy moved her away from the ice cream cases and into the back office – actually, the main office. She helped the bookkeeper, and the closest she came to the ice cream occurred when she bought some herself, on a hot day, before leaving work to come home to Iris and her mother. Sometimes, on the hot nights, she came to Iris's room, Scott's old room, at nine o'clock or so, and Iris knew it was their escape time. Liz drove and Iris commented on the scenery, sometimes narrating made-up stories about the people they saw out the windows. They often stopped for soft serve – at Dairy Queen or Cate's Corner, though more often than not it was Richland Dairy they went to, for hot fudge sundaes with pecans. They sat in the parking lot and watched the teenagers gather, the girls tan, their belly buttons resting above the line of their bell bottoms. As they saw young girls look up slyly into the boys' faces, they would glance at each other and then look down at their pecans, floating in a sludge of ice cream and chocolate. Liz talked more now than she used to, not about anything in particular. She told Iris that she saw Michael's dad with a blonde woman, her hair cut wispily around her face, face dark from the sun, eyes wrinkled. He nodded to Liz, and she nodded back. She'd heard earlier in the summer that Michael was at some college with a baseball scholarship, but since she didn't really talk to his dad, she didn't know for sure.

On one of their summer evening drives, Liz told Iris about the argument between their parents late on that summer night they'd found Iris missing from her bed. Liz had been convinced at that moment that their parents hated each other, though she knew that they all probably hated each other that morning or maybe even that whole year. And Liz told Iris that when she thought her sister was dead, the only good thing was that for the first time since Scott died, she forgot to hate herself, forgot to hate Iris. She just wanted Iris alive.

Iris had been at the New Subdivision House, asleep after painting her car mural, when she heard a noise from the basement. With the bright light streaming in so many windows, Iris hadn't been afraid, but she'd never expected to see her sister framed in the doorway of the room in which she'd chosen to sleep.

Liz told her later that she'd known about the house, had followed Iris there one day on the way home from work when she'd seen Iris crossing Williams Lake Road into the New Subdivision. But she'd held off on saying anything to their parents, wanting to determine first what the house meant to Iris.

That was when Iris told her the Rosemary and Karl story, and Liz stayed silent the whole time, two wrinkles in her forehead deepening in concentration and concern. She told Iris that she needed to let it go – that she and their mom would handle it. And when Iris protested and said she didn't want to violate Rosemary's trust, Liz said that sometimes the hardest thing about being a teenager was

271

figuring out when you could manage things on your own and when you were in over your head.

Since they didn't go to the beach anymore, they went to a lot of movies. Liz saw a flyer at the community college about a film series at the Detroit Institute of Arts, so they went to a couple movies on Friday nights. The last one was *A Star is Born*, the old version with James Mason and Judy Garland. They'd seen Judy Garland a dozen or more times over the years, heard her voice singing "Somewhere Over the Rainbow." As Iris watched her, not the little girl with braids anymore but the ingénue, the songstress, she thought of her mother singing over a pot of spaghetti on the stove, first Doris Day, then Judy Garland, never really herself, but whoever sang the song. And Iris wondered if after Scott died, her mother created a place to travel to in her head, so she could be somebody else, wearing someone else's stockings of pain.

Scott had told Iris back when they were younger that unlike most kids, he didn't love Scarecrow best. He wanted to be Tin Man or Lion. Then he wouldn't have to work so hard or be so good. The Scarecrow wasn't allowed to screw up, he told her. If he did just one wrong thing, he would let Dorothy down.

When they got to the point in the movie where James Mason lies in bed, his face panicked, trapped, wearing anguish, Liz reached over and put a cool hand on Iris's arm. Iris wanted to whisper in her ear *Whose face do you see?* It could belong to any one of them, that face. In James Mason's eyes you could see how many mistakes a person could make, how you had to walk so carefully through life to make sure that you didn't screw anything up for anybody else. But no matter how carefully you walked, no matter how

272

many cracks you avoided so you didn't break your mother's back, there were all those chasms out there anyway.

And even if you were perfect, the world could screw things up for you. You could make the mistake of sending a boy out of the driveway alone on his bike, and he might never come home again. But if you went with him, if you put the bike away and made him walk, if you held his hand at your side, fingers laced, there could still be a force, human or otherwise, to wrench the arm away from you, and no matter how tightly you held on, how much you fought, you could still lose the arm, feel it pulled away, the energy in those fingers the last good thing you would ever know. And it wouldn't be your fault. But you would never believe that.

Their mother gave up smoking and took up yoga just before their father moved back into the house. Liz and Iris agreed that the yoga buoyed her spirits. Much of the time she walked around the house with a faint smile on her face, not too much removed from the old mother they knew. Iris couldn't help but think that in a delicate lotus position, in the early hours of the morning, her mother watched the soles of her feet, and in that neat hollow there, between her bare feet, she saw Scott's face – the flashy, charming one, the one belonging to the demolisher of a thousand ice cream cones. The one that sauntered into a summer world with no apprehension, just the wondrous anticipation of things to come.

They didn't talk much about The Caretaker, who was never apprehended. Years later, after Iris had moved away, after their house was sold, their parents gone to Florida, Iris was driving in the area briefly and heard the retiring prosecuting attorney interviewed on the radio. When the radio interviewer asked him about his biggest disappointment during his years in office, he said, "Oh, without a doubt, it would have to be that we never caught The Caretaker. It was a nasty series of tragedies, and I felt bad for the families that I was never able to bring anyone to justice."

The killer stopped right in the middle of that summer of 1974. It turned out that the final murder they heard about was the last one the authorities thought he committed. But since he didn't seem to be able to stop himself, something must have stopped him. The police speculated that maybe he was incarcerated for some other crime, or maybe he was the victim of other violence, perpetrated against him. After so many years, although the case was never closed, the trail went cold. But the prosecutor was right; those families would have benefited from having closure. The kind of closure you got when you finally figured out some of the causes.

For months after Iris returned home that morning, after she'd painted the car on the wall of that vacant house, she wanted to tell Rosemary how sorry she was that she'd failed her. The irony was that Iris desperately wanted to talk to Rosemary, to seek and to offer help in making sense of the issues they faced, but Iris, too, was a failed communicator, a failed listener. The shirts Rosemary wore to school that year after Scott died fell cleanly over her middle, no bulges, no gaps. Her face stayed thin, never went puffy. Sometimes, when Iris's mind wandered farther than she wanted that very next year, before she learned how to turn it off or turn it to another channel, she would think of Rosemary and see a flash of a white table, Rosemary's feet in stirrups, her knees spread wide, her face turned to the side, eyes clenched tight. And Iris couldn't imagine who would be in the waiting room beyond, who would hold her purse or her jacket. Liz told Iris a few weeks after she painted Scott's Camaro that their mother had talked to Rosemary's mother. And Rosemary never called again. But Karl's car disappeared from his sister's driveway.

Every summer, Sheldon and Iris had a fish fry in his backyard. Sheldon stopped painting houses once he'd paid the hospital off. Now he painted for pleasure and carved these little wooden magnets he sold at craft shows, as well as a huge wall-sized watercolor of the blackfin cisco. They laughed about the fact that his miniature cisco magnets were such a hit at the shows. Sometimes Iris went into his studio and walked along his table full of freshly shellacked wood miniatures gleaming under the lights.

And Iris always stood for a few minutes in front of the big cisco. The underlighting made certain scales glisten silver-red and black. The eye was a luminescent orb from which all the tears in the lake could release themselves at any moment. Sheldon told her he'd given it one of her eyes, apologized that it was only one, but after all, it was a profile. When Iris looked at it, she saw one of those old Irises. One of the extinct ones.

After their mom and dad got back together, Iris sat out in the back yard on some summer evenings, usually with a book. She read intently, but then, after she'd immersed herself for a good hour, she emerged from the book and sat in the same back yard she sat in before everything happened. Once the neighbor cut the motor on his lawn mower, Iris could hear the lake sounds. The power boat hums rose from the water, filling Destan Drive behind their house because that's where the summer sounds reverberated the loudest, in that last street before the lake. Light voices drifted up from the sand, or the water, it was hard to tell which. Shouts of encouragement went out from a boat somewhere, and then, and though it was close to dusk, an engine revved, and it seemed clear that someone else was going out to ski.

She could break her leg, the skier, but she could just as easily fall gracefully into the water like a debutante falls into a potential suitor's arms, like Judy Garland falls into James Mason's arms. Or like Rosemary fell into Karl's arms. Not so gracefully. For some eight-year old girl on the shore, her feet buried in the sand, her arms propping up a thin-ribbed body, there was the anticipation of meeting the lake in that way, sometime off in the future. Past the docks, the buoys, out in the middle where there were no boundaries, where a person sank or swam.

Iris closed her book then and went inside to the room she shared with Scott when she visited her parents. She sat on their bed, looking at the small shelf in the corner that held a few of his old model cars and model airplanes. The photo of a crudely painted red Camaro sat propped against the bowl with swirls of blue and green that Iris had made at the end of that second summer, at the workshop for kids who'd lost something.

Iris could retreat into this room for the rest of her life but still never know enough about the past, never see enough of her brother's face. But she knew, too, that there would be some days when he still called to her from outside the window, his nose and purple-red lips smooshed against the mesh, the screen bouncing with the weight of his face. *They've all gone in, Iris, but it's still light. Come out and play.*

Author's Note

This book is a work of fiction and therefore contains a series of events that are not based in fact or reality. Yet I would be remiss if I failed to mention that the novel was largely inspired by my family and my childhood summer environment in a working-class beach community on Williams Lake in Oakland County, Michigan.

In addition, I feel compelled to note that several readers might recognize a few similarities between the serial killings referred to in the novel and those occurring in Oakland County during the 1970's. The Oakland County Child Killings took place when I was in high school and were never officially solved, although the case is still under investigation. While the killings referred to in these pages do not match the original murders, I wanted to honor the victims and their families and note that I consider these murders to be a formative part of my coming-of-age reconciliation with evil in the world. I had only a tangential involvement in this incredibly sad story, through the delivery of facts by my local newspaper and the black-and-white news coverage on our family television screen, yet the imprint has remained. I offer my condolences to the families of Mark Stebbins, Jill Robinson, Kristine Mihelich, and Timothy

King, and all other families that still may be waiting for answers related to that series of crimes.

Likewise, the only other element of the book that I want to highlight as being based in reality is the inclusion of the MIA mentioned in the text. Colonel Patrick T. Fallon was an actual MIA officer, and before the age of the Internet, I learned a bit about him one Fourth of July, when a network news station focused on his story. I have also since learned that Colonel Fallon's wife, Jean Fallon, and their two daughters honored the Colonel with a grave site at Arlington National Cemetery and a memorial service. My thoughts go out to this family and all others who have not been granted closure with respect to their loved ones lost in service to this country.

I would like to thank early readers of this novel, including my sisters, Linda and Lori Newton, and friends Jerry Bower, Marie Griffin, Barbara Hranilovich, Landis Lain, David Orrin, and Adrienne Sharp. In addition, many thanks to Valerie Laken, Anne-Marie Oomen, and Katey Schultz for edits, prompts, and publishing suggestions that helped me climb over the last bit of barbed wire to a final revision.

Thanks also to my husband, Tim Dalton, for reading innumerable versions of this book over the years and helping me sort out what to keep and what to relinquish; in addition, he produced an early version of the hybrid map (part truth and part fiction) of my old beach neighborhood. My son Connor Dalton read the penultimate draft and served as a diplomatic cheerleader through my last major revision. Thanks for your loving and gentle approach, Connor. My daughter, Rachel Dalton, read various portions over the years and sought out some last-minute editors among friends for mini-parcels of the text. Much gratitude to Rachel, Manette, Mike, Mary, Laura, and my sister Lori for their help with this task. My son Nathaniel Dalton read pages also and lived in a house with his Zoom-addled father, his revision-addled mother, and a heart-breaking but essential revolution related to racial inequality that swept through our nation for huge chunks of the 2020 pandemic. Thanks for your wisdom and companionship, Nate.

Cousin Fred Newton helped to procure last-minute details about the place known as "Kandahar" which appears in these pages.

My artist friend Barbara Hranilovich has enriched my life with color and imagination for many years, and I'm so pleased to have her inspired marks on the cover of this book. Buckets of love for this fig, Barb!

In my acknowledgements forr *Winded: A Memoir in Four Stages* I thanked the many childcare providers who cared for my children while I wrote. This was the novel I was writing back then, so thanks again!

To Kevin Atticks, my publisher, and Kelley, Mackenzie, and Samantha, Loyola University Maryland students, I send wheelbarrows of good will and gratitude; thanks for nurturing this manuscript during the pandemic and learning hands-on processes in virtual environments. I send appreciation to my new publicity team at MindBuck Media - Jessie Glenn, Emily Keough, Deborah Jayne, Rachel Taube, and Bryn Kristi. I look forward to working with you in the months ahead!

As always, I am buttressed by my health care team - my psychologist, oncologist, psychiatric nurse, internist, and the many pharmacists and techs who keep me alive and in good humor. Thanks to health care workers everywhere for their incredible service to us all.

To the friends who've supported me throughout my cancer journey and the even more gnarled route to book publication over these many years, I remain charmed by and eternally grateful for your generous acts of kindness.

And so we flutter, into the cosmos.

Author's Note

This book is a work of fiction and therefore contains a series of events that are not based in fact or reality. Yet I would be remiss if I failed to mention that the novel was largely inspired by my family and my childhood summer environment in a working-class beach community on Williams Lake in Oakland County, Michigan.

In addition, I feel compelled to note that several readers might recognize a few similarities between the serial killings referred to in the novel and those occurring in Oakland County during the 1970's. The Oakland County Child Killings took place when I was in high school and were never officially solved, although the case is still under investigation. While the killings referred to in these pages do not match the original murders, I wanted to honor the victims and their families and note that I consider these murders to be a formative part of my coming-of-age reconciliation with evil in the world. I had only a tangential involvement in this incredibly sad story, through the delivery of facts by my local newspaper and the black-and-white news coverage on our family television screen, yet the imprint has remained. I offer my condolences to the families of Mark Stebbins, Jill Robinson, Kristine Mihelich, and Timothy

King, and all other families that still may be waiting for answers related to that series of crimes.

Likewise, the only other element of the book that I want to highlight as being based in reality is the inclusion of the MIA mentioned in the text. Colonel Patrick T. Fallon was an actual MIA officer, and before the age of the Internet, I learned a bit about him one Fourth of July, when a network news station focused on his story. I have also since learned that Colonel Fallon's wife, Jean Fallon, and their two daughters honored the Colonel with a grave site at Arlington National Cemetery and a memorial service. My thoughts go out to this family and all others who have not been granted closure with respect to their loved ones lost in service to this country.

I would like to thank early readers of this novel, including my sisters, Linda and Lori Newton, and friends Jerry Bower, Marie Griffin, Barbara Hranilovich, Landis Lain, David Orrin, and Adrienne Sharp. In addition, many thanks to Valerie Laken, Anne-Marie Oomen, and Katey Schultz for edits, prompts, and publishing suggestions that helped me climb over the last bit of barbed wire to a final revision.

Thanks also to my husband, Tim Dalton, for reading innumerable versions of this book over the years and helping me sort out what to keep and what to relinquish; in addition, he produced an early version of the hybrid map (part truth and part fiction) of my old beach neighborhood. My son Connor Dalton read the penultimate draft and served as a diplomatic cheerleader through my last major revision. Thanks for your loving and gentle approach, Connor. My daughter, Rachel Dalton, read various portions over the years and sought out some last-minute editors among friends

About the Author

DAWN NEWTON is the author of *Winded: A Memoir in Four Stages,* which details her journey with stage IV lung cancer. She was trained as a fiction writer and received scholarships to attend Michigan State University and Johns Hopkins University. Dawn has taught composition and creative writing at several colleges and in K-12 classrooms in Virginia and Michigan. Her essays, poems, and short stories have been published in various literary magazines. She has three grown children – Rachel, Connor, and Nathaniel – and lives with her husband, Tim Dalton, and their dog, Clover, in East Lansing, Michigan.

Apprentice House Press

Loyola University Maryland

Apprentice House is the country's only campus-based, student-staffed book publishing company. Directed by professors and industry professionals, it is a nonprofit activity of the Communication Department at Loyola University Maryland.

Using state-of-the-art technology and an experiential learning model of education, Apprentice House publishes books in untraditional ways. This dual responsibility as publishers and educators creates an unprecedented collaborative environment among faculty and students, while teaching tomorrow's editors, designers, and marketers.

Outside of class, progress on book projects is carried forth by the AH Book Publishing Club, a co-curricular campus organization supported by Loyola University Maryland's Office of Student Activities.

Eclectic and provocative, Apprentice House titles intend to entertain as well as spark dialogue on a variety of topics. Financial contributions to sustain the press's work are welcomed. Contributions are tax deductible to the fullest extent allowed by the IRS.

To learn more about Apprentice House books or to obtain submission guidelines, please visit www.apprenticehouse.com.

Apprentice House
Communication Department
Loyola University Maryland
4501 N. Charles Street
Baltimore, MD 21210
Ph: 410-617-5265
info@apprenticehouse.com
www.apprenticehouse.com

CPSIA information can be obtained
at www.ICGtesting.com
Printed in the USA
FSHW021720060521
81134FS

9 781627 203395